William Sharp, John Parker Anderson

Life of Heinrich Heine

William Sharp, John Parker Anderson

Life of Heinrich Heine

ISBN/EAN: 9783337415518

Printed in Europe, USA, Canada, Australia, Japan

Cover: Foto ©Raphael Reischuk / pixelio.de

More available books at **www.hansebooks.com**

LIFE

OF

HEINRICH HEINE

BY

WILLIAM SHARP

———

LONDON

WALTER SCOTT, 24 WARWICK LANE

NEW YORK : THOMAS WHITTAKER

TORONTO : W. J. GAGE & CO.

1888

CONTENTS.

CHAPTER VII.

CHAPTER VIII.

INTRODUCTORY NOTE.

THE comparatively recent publication of Heine's fragmentary Memoirs—not those which he himself tells us he destroyed, but the biographical record which, rather more than a year before his death, he commenced at the instigation of a friend—has thrown a flood of light not only upon the childhood of the poet, but upon the influences which moulded him and the sources to which we may trace certain idiosyncrasies of his genius. In 1867 his enthusiastic biographer, Adolf Strodtmann,[1] brought together all the then available material relative to the boyhood of Heine, and it was taken for granted that nothing had escaped the industry of his research. Moreover, Heine has himself through out his writings been so prolific of hints and statements concerning his early life that even without the new light of the Memoirs there was no poverty of detail. But in these late " Confessions " we learn for the first time what were the most immediate and most potent factors in the

[1] From whose "Heine's Leben und Werke" Mr. Stigand's and other briefer accounts in English derive their *data*.

mental and, to some extent, spiritual development of the poet whose extraordinarily complex genius has been to many the source of as much confusion as of intellectual stimulus, of as much bewilderment as charm.

Heine was born on the eve of the nineteenth century, and if we glance no further back than the decade preceding his birth, it will easily be seen at what a crucial period in European history he first saw the light. The long despotism which had held the greater part of the Continent in bondage was rapidly undergoing disintegration, not, as history has proved, to the triumph of democratic freedom, but more or less in that direction.

The nearer we are to history the more impressive are its superficial aspects, and, though the sensibility of childhood to purely extraneous influences must necessarily be very limited, they may be far from impotent in degree. Before his tenth year Heine was a practically imperceptive onlooker amid great events; indeed it may be said that the Spirit of Revolution breathed upon him from his very birth. The first French Empire had been founded, the famous Code Napoleon promulgated. 1806 saw the dissolution of the inchoate German Empire, and the founding of the Rhine Confederation. Battle after battle had quelled the most militant of the German States. The violation of national rights had become the order of the day. Finland was divorced from Sweden; the Tyrol was subdued; Spain had been overrun; and Holland was annexed. The one bright outlook for humanity amid all this bloodshed and bloodthirst, this insane violence and criminal debauchery of potentates, this scornful rape of the liberties of the people, was the abolition of the traffic in slaves. It was a slight thing to bleeding Europe, but it brought comfort to many brave souls, appearing, as it did, as a rainbow above the blood-red horizon of the immediate future. Patriots could not but dream that a greater abolition of even more igno-minious slavery would follow in time, and among these dreamers were none more ardent than the oppressed Jews of Central Europe. Heine was a little seven-year-old Jew when the slave-trade was proclaimed illegal, and even then, as we now know, he was aware that the stain of Israel was deeper than that which was the inheritance of the children of Esau.

Although at the time only in his twelfth year, Heine was not too young to be deeply impressed by the news of the disastrous ending of the French Invasion of Russia. The flames of burning Moscow cast so fierce a gleam across all Europe, from the Volga to the sea-quays of the Loire, that even in the humble town of Düsseldorf there was a little Jewish schoolboy who trembled when he heard of the thousands dying daily amidst the snows, and whose heart was filled with awe at the thought of the silent brooding emperor riding solitarily on his white horse, a more vivid and terrible reality than that other Rider upon a white steed drawn by good Master Albrecht Dürer nigh upon three centuries gone by, which often the little Heinrich had looked at fearfully in his uncle's print collection. One of the most touching passages in the " Reisebilder " is that describing the return march through Düsseldorf of a miserable remnant of one of Napoleon's crack regiments of Grenadiers, and how among them young Heine recognized the French *tambour,* Le Grand, who had been the idol of his earliest childish romance.

Still a child was he, as I have said, when he first learned that "Jew" and "Pariah" were in the Germany of his day very nearly synonymous terms; and ere he had outgrown his boyhood he had come to suffer that bitter heart-complaint of his race, that *Juden-Schmerz,* that Grief of Israel, which is the most pathetic and the most terrible of all national sorrows. In his own words, "The history of the Jews is tragical; and yet if one were to write about this tragedy he would be laughed at. This is the most tragic of all." Of him even more than of Moses Mendelssohn might Kayserling's words be quoted: "Every page of history reminded him of the suffering and the spoliation which his kindred had through centuries patiently borne, and of his own homelessness."

Heine has often been blamed by the more ignorant or more prejudiced of his countrymen for his French proclivities, and for his unsparing satire of the Germans and most things Teutonic. But while it is advisable to remember that the French and not the Germans were dominant in the Rhine provinces at the time of the poet's boyhood, the only thing that is of moment now is that he was essentially one of the men of no nationality. The greatest of German lyric poets, he was otherwise a typical cosmopolitan. There was nothing parochial in his type any more than in his genius. As has been well-remarked of him, his nature embraced the remotest eras: in soul he was an early Hebrew; in spirit an ancient Greek; in mind a republican of the nineteenth century.

LIFE OF HEINE.

CHAPTER I.

"I WILL write of Heine; of the poet whose genius has torn up the treaties of Vienna, and carried the boundaries of France to the Rhine; of that tearful trifler, that sardonic sentimentalist, that strange, sad, significant fellow, who laughs at old legends over his wine, and shudders beneath the black Lürlei-rocks in the twilight. I will write of him, not only because he is strange, sad, and significant, nor because he tears up treaties, and quizzes Kaiser and Vaterland, and parodies the songs of Israel by the waters of the Seine—but because the music of his melodies 'beats time to nothing in my brain' to-day; because, in this sweet Rhenish weather, I have first learned how exquisite is his singing, how subtle and how true is the rhythm of his genius." Thus wrote, some thirty-five years ago, from Oberwesel-am-Rhein, an anonymous critic : and in this spirit should the biographer or student of Germany's foremost singer approach the subject of the poet's life and works. In Heine's many-sidedness there is somewhere fascination for every one ; in his songs there is music for all.

A well-known passage in the "Italien" book of the "Reisebilder" sets forth that the author first saw the light on the opening day of the present century. It is sufficiently clear that Heine had no intention to mislead his readers : he simply wished to make a good point. "I am eighteen ; how old are you?" asks the fair Francesca whom the susceptible poet encounters at Lucca ; and for answer she hears that her admirer was born on the morning of New Year's Day, 1800. "There," joins in Francesca's friend, the Marquis Christoforo, "have I not always told you that he was one of the first men of the century?"[1] As a matter of fact Heine was born in a small one-storied house in the Bolkerstrasse of Düsseldorf-am-Rhein, on the 13th of December, 1799. This house is still in existence, and, as No. 53, Bolkerstrasse, is occupied by a stationer ; but save as the birthplace of the poet it has little interest, for the romance of his childhood was not under the parental roof—moreover, the Heine family moved to a larger house across the street when Heinrich was in his eleventh or twelfth year.

The Heines were Jewish through both the male and

---

[1] Curiously enough neither Heine nor any of the biographers, commentators, or essayists who have quoted or alluded to this passage, seems to have realized that the remark is in fact a pointless one. The year 1800 was, of course, not the first year of the nineteenth century but the last year of the eighteenth. To have been one of the first men of the century Heine should have been born on the 1st of January, 1801.

female lines. About the middle of the eighteenth century the daughter of one Meyer Schamschen Popert married a small dealer or petty merchant called Heymann Heine, and bore her husband six sons, only the second and third of whom have any interest for the biographer of the poet.

Heymann's third child, Salomon, became one of the wealthiest men in Germany, and known far and wide as the Jew-prince of Hamburg. He married a Goldschmidt, and lived in ever-increasing prosperity until his death near the close of 1844. This Salomon had six children, of whom Amalie (Heine's first love) was the fourth; to the others it is not necessary to allude meanwhile, though the heirs of Salomon Heine were, as will be seen later on, responsible for much of the mental and physical misery which prostrated the poet in the last decade of his life. Samson, the second son of Heymann Heine, had little of the shrewdness and energy of his brothers, Isaac and Salomon; his tastes were æsthetic, and his sympathies neither Jewish nor German. He was an amiable and handsome young man, and by his personal attractions, and a passion for the flute, was able to gain as wife the daughter of a well-to-do physician of Jewish race, the courtly Dr. Simon von Geldern of Düsseldorf.

The easy-going, æsthetically-inclined Samson Heine and the energetic, exceptionally well-educated and intellectual Betty von Geldern set up housekeeping together in the Bolkerstrasse of the old Rhenish town. There, in due course, four children were born to them, of whom the eldest was Heinrich. Thereafter came Gustav, Charlotte, and Maximilian.

Gustav, like his elder brother, inherited the intellectual

bias, and in maturity found scope for his mental energies as founder and editor of what is still a foremost Viennese newspaper ; Maximilian followed the example of his uncle and became a physician, and ultimately achieved a good position in St. Petersburg, whither he had gone to court fortune ; while Charlotte married in early life a Hamburg merchant named Moritz Embden, and had a daughter who afterwards became the Princess Della-Rocca. The three persons who had most to do with Heine's mental development were his mother, his uncle, Simon von Geldern, and his father.

It is indubitable that the romance appertaining to the Geldern family (for the elder Simon's father had been a strange and picturesque figure, and deeply impressed the boyish imagination of his great grandson) materially affected the future poet. To his father's kith and kin, his *Sippen und Magen*, as he spoke of them, Heine rarely alluded. But, as he shrewdly remarks, his paternal grandfather must have been something more than "a little Jew with a big beard " to have been able to woo and win the daughter of the rich Hamburg banker Popert, " the extraordinarily beautiful woman " who died in the year of her famous grandson's birth.

It has been the habit of biographers of Heine to speak slightingly of his father—to regard him, as Mr. Stigand does, as a man of small mental endowments, or, like another critic, "as a weak, foolish, and vulgar 'emancipated' Jew." Vulgar, Samson Heine certainly was not. In appearance he was handsome, and in manners refined : he was, indeed, as his son says, the inheritor of his mother's great beauty. Though Madame

Heine was of a more energetic and intellectual nature than her husband, and Simon von Geldern indubitably in most respects the latter's superior, Heine loved neither so well as his father. In the "Memoirs" he expressly states that his father was of all human beings the one whom he had most loved; that even after the lapse of more than twenty-five years he could barely realize that he had actually lost him; and asserts that scarcely a single night had passed wherein he had had no thought of him who had so long before departed from life. It is absurd, therefore, in the face of these direct statements and the unmistakable kindly affection pervading the Reminiscences, to assert that Samson Heine was a mere nonentity, without recognizable influence upon his son. It was from his father, and not from his mother, that Heinrich inherited his love of music, of art, of æsthetic surroundings, of personal daintiness: indeed it would seem that it is the poet who owes most to his father and the intellectual gymnast who derives from his mother.

Heine is emphatic upon the dominant influence of his mother in his intellectual development. She had, he tells us, very high-flown ideas with regard to him, to which all her educational plans had reference. "She played the chief part in the history of my development; she made the programme of all my studies; and even before my birth began her plans for my education." Like many intellectual speculators, however, Madame Heine found that she had reckoned without idiosyncrasies stronger than theoretical arrangements; and one by one her aerial castles came toppling to the ground.

/ She was a woman of great energy of character, and of

exceptional mental culture; though curiously undeveloped
æsthetically for one who had had visions of romance in
her girlhood, and had allowed the siren-note of a handsome young Jew's flute to win her thoughts from pelf and
social position.   Her religious belief was a severe Deism,
which (so says Heine) was well adapted to the prevailing
drift of her reasoning.   She was a disciple of Voltaire and
Rousseau, and had for hobby the science of education
When yet a young girl she was obliged to read Latin
Dissertations and other learned publications aloud
to her father, and often, her son remarks, astonished
the old man by her questions.   She had a horror of
imagination, and for romantic legends and superstitious
folk-lore entertained a supreme contempt.[1]

On the other hand, she was of an unselfish nature.
Though in some things penurious, she was mainly
so only with regard to her own person, and she could
even be extravagant in her charity and liberality to
others.   Her eldest son never forgot the debt he owed to
her.   On that dreadful mattress-grave where his last few
years pitiably held death at bay, he expressed himself fer-
vently on the sacrifices she had made on his behalf: and
well he might, for when he was studying at Bonn and his

[1] " Her reason and her sentiment were thoroughly healthy, and
it was not from her that I inherited fanciful and romantic inclinations.
As I have mentioned already, she had a perfect dread of poetry,
took from me any romance that she might find in my hands, did not
permit me to visit the theatre, forbade me to take part in popular
amusements, watched over my acquaintances, scolded the maid-
servants when they told ghost stories in my presence—in short,
she did everything to guard me against superstition and poetical
fancies."—H. II.

father's fortune was almost swept away, Madame Heine sold her necklace, earrings, and other valuable and treasured jewelry in order to secure for her son a living during the unremunerative period of university study.

But valuable as was his mother's influence in his mental development, the strong literary bias which, as early as his twelfth year, began to manifest itself, was mainly due to his uncle, Simon von Geldern. This "Uncle Simon" was a man of marked individuality, strange in appearance as well as eccentric in his views. Chief among his hobbies was that of authorship. With an idea in his brain and a pen in his hand he was at the Gate of Paradise; when he could write *finis* to the neat formal manuscript, his rapture was of the peaceful joy of those who have entered in. But notwithstanding his "stiff court style," and frequent pedantry of subject, Simon von Geldern's example had direct effect upon his nephew. Still more important was his unrestricted loan of books of all kinds, and his permission to Heinrich to seclude himself in a certain wonderful garret, of which, and his day-dreams there, Heine gives in his "Memoirs" a most picturesque account.

Those familiar with the poet's autobiographical allusions will recollect how often he is "Harry" rather than "Heinrich" or "Henri." And the eldest-born of Samson and Elizabeth Heine was actually christened Harry —not, as he points out, in avoidance of the "almost scurrilous native diminutives of Heinrich," but in honour of one of his father's friends, an English gentleman who acted as his correspondent in Liverpool. But though the poet always liked to be called Harry, the name was in

his childhood the source of bitter annoyance, as he
amusingly narrates in the " Memoirs."

Heine's childhood was a mixture of romance, amusement, torment, and schoolboy *ennui.* When not in
school he would be in the haunted garret at " Noah's
Ark," as his Uncle Simon's house was locally called;
when not playing with other children on the Schloss-
Platz, he would be fraternizing with the French soldiery;
when not in mischief he would be lying adream in the
castle gardens, or wandering about with a vague wonder
in his heart and a yearning for he knew not what. But
with all his love of mischief and his high spirits, he does
not seem to have cared much for the delights of ordinary
boyhood; no doubt the grandson of "a little Jew with a
big beard" was held in even greater contempt from the
fact that he was weak enough to occasionally expend his
pocket-money in the purchase, "from the hard-hearted
country-lads," of larks and linnets, thrushes and black-
birds, with the sole object of their liberation. Not that
his spare cash was never spent upon more mundane
objects. The various accounts in the "Reisebilder" and
the "Memoirs" of his school experiences are very entertaining and most wittily told. What tortures he suffered
from verbs ! The only distinction which Herr Samson's
first-born could discern between the *verba irregularia*
and the *verba regularia* was that the former were more
frightfully difficult, and in consequence involved far more
floggings. The school was in a Franciscan convent, and
in the dank cloisters adjoining the room wherein the lads
of Düsseldorf suffered such mental and physical pains
there used to hang a great crucifix of grey wood. Before

this image—the grim carving of which, with the bleeding eyes that stared with mournful persistency, long continued to haunt his dreams, Heine often prostrated himself in agonized prayer, imploring, "O thou poor Deity, once tortured like myself, if it be possible, grant that I may remember the *verba irregularia !*"

But even the irregular Latin verbs were not so terrible as Greek. "Of Greek I cannot trust myself to speak. The monks of the Middle Ages were not altogether wrong when they pronounced Greek to be an invention of the devil. God knows the woes it caused me. With Hebrew I fared better, for I always had a strong liking for the Jews, though to this very hour they crucify my good name. But even in Hebrew I could not get on so well as my watch, which was on intimate terms with the pawnbrokers, and thus picked up much of the manners. and customs of the Jews. . . . For some of my German. I was indebted to Professor Schramm, who wrote a work on everlasting peace, and in whose class we were always at fisticuffs." But it was in the French class that he made most progress. The teacher was an eccentric Abbé D'Aulnoi (or *Daunoi*, as Heine, probably forgetfully, alludes to him in his Memoirs) "with elastic features and a brown wig, who capered about when he was giving a lecture on his 'Art Poétique' and his 'Histoire Allemande.'" If the irregular verbs were more difficult, the French alexandrines were not less distressful. These metrical crimes Heine never could forgive. The French alexandrine was to him a metre that must surely have been invented by Procrustes—a perfect straight-jacket for thoughts which, considering their

tameness, stand in no need of such bondage ! Often,
even upon his mattress-bed, he thought with horror of
the time when he had to translate into French alexandrines
the address of Caiaphas to the Sanhedrin from the hexameters of Klopstock's "Messiah !"   "God pardon
me ! I cursed the world, and the foreign oppressors who
wanted to impose their versification upon us ! I might
have been willing to die for France, but to make French
verses—never !" Even in the ordinary French lesson,
where he felt more at ease, there were pitfalls into
which he fell. In the third book of the "Reisebilder"
he relates one now famous episode. "I remember, as if
it were yesterday, the trouble I got into over *Religion*.
Six times, at least, I was asked, ' Henri, what is the
French for *der Glaube* (Faith)?' and six times I answered,
each time with a greater burst of tears, '*le crédit*,' and
the seventh time my questioner, turning purple with rage,
shouted ' It is *la religion*,' and a rain of blows followed ;
and all my schoolfellows burst out laughing." But once
away from the school in the Franciscans' convent, what
delight it was to join the French *tambour* who was quar-
tered upon the Heine household—the small, nervous,
fiercely-mustachioed, fiery-eyed drummer of Grenadiers,
"who looked like a very devil, and yet was such an
angelic character." How gladly Master Harry polished
the veteran's buttons and pipe-clayed his waistcoat ; how
eagerly he listened to the instruction his idol occasionally
chose to impart ! For though Monsieur Le Grand knew
only a little broken German, he could convey much
essential information by means of his drumming. Thus
when his young questioner would ask the meaning of

"Liberté," he would beat the "Marseillaise," and would be understood; to explain "Égalité" he would play, "Ça ira, ça ira . . . les aristos à la lanterne!" whereupon his meaning became clear. Once Le Grand wanted to explain the word Germany, and so he beat a primitive simple measure which is often played at fairs for dogs to dance to, the tune of "Dumm, Dumm, Dumm" (stupid); whereat Heinrich was angry, but— understood him.

Day by day his martial ardour and enthusiasm for Napoleon increased. He would lie on the grass in the palace gardens listening to Le Grand's drumming, and seeing in vision the Emperor crossing the Simplon, with the eagles screaming above the glaciers—the Emperor clasping the standard on the Bridge of Lodi—the Emperor in his grey cloak at Marengo—the Emperor on horseback at the Battle of the Pyramids amid smoke and barbaric Mamelukes — the Emperor at Austerlitz, at Jena, at Eylau, at Wagram!

"But what were my feelings," he exclaims in the "Book of Ideas," "when I saw him at last with my own eyes—O beatific vision!—himself, the Emperor." It was indeed an eventful day for all Düsseldorf when the great captain rode into the town in his simple majesty. How the green *allées* became glorified with the splendid uniforms of the staff, how the air seemed to palpitate with the fanfares of a hundred silver trumpets! But as for Napoleon himself, "he wore his plain green uniform and his world-famous cap, and rode carelessly, with a loose seat, his beautiful white palfrey, whose neck he often patted goodnaturedly with his right hand. His face was of the same hue that we see in marble busts of Greek and Roman : the features wore the same expression of calm dignity that the ancients' have, and on them was written, ' Thou shalt have none other God but me.' "

The Napoleon glamour never quite left Heine, though in after years he found himself a leader in an army who knew not the autocrat of old, who indeed loathed his name as that of a renegade and traitor. But to him he was ever the great captain, the man of might, the child of Destiny : the greatest of all men who had been born in latter days—a sinner beyond reckoning, yet hero beyond praise. Yet to him the man always was the man. "I never praise the dead," he remarks in the "Italien" section of the "Reisebilder," "but the soul of a man of which the deed is only a garment ; history, in fact, is nothing more than the old wardrobe of the soul of humanity."

This imperial fervour, nourished as it was by his companionship with Le Grand and by endless rumour of great and mighty deeds, influenced the budding poet as well as the enthusiastic boy. He began to write odes and lyrics, which, though probably worthless, helped to clear his mind and exercise his metrical dexterity, remarkable from the outset. It was when still a boy, indeed, that he wrote a lyric which, when published, was soon everywhere caught up—"The Grenadiers." Though so simple and pathetic a poem, I have encountered no metrical translation of it which at all conveys the beauty of the original—indeed it seems to me to have been one of the least fortunate of Heine's lyrical poems in respect of translation.

Once again he saw Napoleon, on the occasion of the Imperial review of the Grenadiers ere they set forth on their march to Russia : once again he was fascinated by that marble face, and that calm, inscrutable gaze. But now he had to bid farewell to Monsieur Le Grand, who marched away proudly drumming, for was not the Emperor about to put the seal upon his greatness ?

The tenth chapter of the third book of the "Reisebilder" is devoted to the account of how Heine saw Le Grand again. He was no longer a child, but a youth—though more in thoughts and perhaps in manner than in years : and his heart was sad with the dire tale that had come of the perishing of *La Grande Armée* amid the steppes of Russia and the frozen waters of the Beresina.[1]

It is to this episode that we owe "The Two Grenadiers," in connection wherewith it should be borne in mind that the author did not write from the imitative impulse excited by the French Napoleonic poets, as has been asserted, but entirely spontaneously. "Die Grenadiere" was composed in 1815, at which time Béranger had not written his analogous poems "Le Vieux Drapeau," "Le Vieux Sergent," &c.

The books which most affected Heine's boyish imagination were "Don Quixote," Sterne's "Sentimental Journey," and "Gulliver's Travels." Upon these, and upon the Rhine legends, the writings of a few of the romantic poets of his time, and the folk-songs of Sefchen

[1] Readers unfamiliar with German should consult pages 150–155 of Mr. Storr's admirable version of the "Travel-Pictures" (the "Reisebilder") in Bohn's Series : better still, they should obtain the volume.

(about whom I shall have something to say presently),
his swift and robust fancy fed and mightily developed.
In his thirty-seventh year he wrote an introduction to an
édition de luxe of the great work of Cervantes, wherein he
gives a charming picture of his boyhood and of his secret
reading haunt in the Avenue of Sighs in the old Schlossgarten of Düsseldorf. But the biographer who dwells overlong upon childish records, however interesting they may
be to him and even to his readers, almost inevitably comes
to lay too great stress upon what is more or less general
to all childhood. Rare indeed are the instances where
any really exceptional deeds and sayings distinguish the
childhood of men or women of genius from the infancy
of other people: what is advisable is to commemorate
only what is genuinely characteristic. Therefore I need
not enlarge upon the childhood of Heine. One or two
important episodes, however, yet remain to be chronicled.

The poetic descriptions of boyhood-remembrances to
be found in the first part of " The Florentine Nights "
must not be taken as autobiographical; but the narrative
is not wholly fictitious, and we may accept as genuine
the account of the strange feeling of oppression, awkward
bashfulness, and vague fear that waylaid the boy-poet
when, in an old garden, he came upon the supine statue
of a Greek goddess, and stared upon the white, finely-
chiselled bosom, shining forth from the high grasses which
environed it: and of how he visited the carven yet life-
like loveliness again by moonlight, and, while a sweet,
shuddering sensation flowed through him, pressed his
lips against the cold lips of marble with wild and passionate tenderness.

The most romantic episode in Heine's boyhood and early youth was the outcome of a disagreeable incident. The boy whom he most hated was forced one day to kiss his hand, while this Jupp Flader's grandmother (overcome by Herr Heine's munificence) praised little Harry's beauty to the skies. To avert the disasters invited by such exaggerated adulation, "Nurse Tippel" superstitiously insisted upon Harry's going with her to a woman who had the reputation of a sorceress—a disreputable creature known as "Die Göchin," as having come from Goch and having been the wife of the public executioner who had dwelt there. Heinrich went, and was duly anointed against malfortune. At first he was simply disgusted and perhaps a little awed, but still he returned occasionally, and by the time he was sixteen he paid frequent visits to the abode of "Die Göchin," attracted thither not by the mysteries of sorcery, but by "a magic stronger than that of all the bombastic Latin philtraria." This attraction was a niece of "Die Meisterin"—as the executioner's widow was also called—a beautiful girl of sixteen, but so developed physically as to appear four or five years older: tall and slender in figure, small waisted as one of the quadroons of the West Indies, and in her tightly clinging dress "like a statue in a wet garment." Even when describing this lovely Jewess after long years of *sturm und drang*, Heine waxed eloquent. "No marble statue, however, could compete with her in beauty," he writes in his Memoirs, "and every one of her movements revealed the rhythm of her body, I might even say, the music of her soul. None of the daughters of Niobe had a more finely-cut face. Its colour, just as that of her skin in general, was of a changing white. Her great, deep-dark eyes looked as if they had just pronounced a riddle and were waiting quietly' for an answer, while the mouth with its strongly-curved bow and oblong teeth, white as ivory, seemed to say: You are stupid, and never will be able to guess it." Her hair was of an extraordinary red; perfectly blood-red Heine calls it, and mentions how when it was tied in long locks under her chin it was as though blood were welling forth from her throat in red streams. Moreover, the voice of Josepha, or, as she was generally called, Sefchen (or "Red Sefchen "), had in *timbre* a strange resemblance to that of her young lover. Often when she spoke under any excitement he was startled, thinking that he heard his own voice; while her song was wont to recall dreams in which he heard himself singing in the same manner and in tones identical.

Sefchen knew many fugitive old songs, and to these young Heine listened eagerly. Once when she was singing a weird *märchen* her emotion overcame her, and in quick response the tears rose to her listener's eyes: in another moment they had fallen sobbing into each other's arms, where they remained for almost an hour, speaking not a word but looking at each other passionately and sympathetically, as it were through a veil of tears. Afterwards, Sefchen copied for her friend the stanzas that had broken down the last barrier between them—not in ink, but in her own blood. One is inevitably reminded of the most dramatic episode in the "Divina Commedia," though Sefchen was more fortunate than Francesca in that no knife-thrust abruptly climaxed the ecstasy of her passion. All the girl's relations on the male side were or had been executioners, and the ignominy of her kindred left a stain upon her of which she was keenly conscious. She knew that she was shunned by most reputable folk, and she in turn avoided company. There was, too, a certain wildness about her that, along with the vague and terrible shadow of the sword which seemed to haunt her life and thought and very presence, had a sombre fascination for Heine. She was hardly human at times, it seemed to him, with her dreamy and mysterious thoughts, and an occasional obstinacy and unreasoning perversity. Even in her dreams, as she once told him, she did not commune with human beings, for she dreamed only of animals. Surely lovers never knew the rapture of the first kiss in stranger circumstances than those wherein Heine for the first time laid his lips against " the haughty mouth " of " Red Sefchen." She had been telling him some weird experiences of her girlhood, with particular allusion to a sword which her grandfather had buried with fantastic nocturnal ceremonies. This weapon had been used in a hundred executions, and thereafter had to be put away : for is it not known that a sword which has drunk blood five-score times acquires a horrible personality, that a lust for slaying possesses it, a thirst and torment that can only be appeased in like manner as are the lusts and passions of humanity—by the oblivion of the grave? It was not until after the death of Josepha's grandfather that " Die Göchin " heard from her niece of this buried sword, whereupon she had at once hastened to the spot and disinterred it. One day, importunate in the absence of

" Die Meisterin," Heine urged Sefchen to let him see the weapon. She assented without a word, and speedily stepped back from an adjoining room with the gigantic sword, which, notwithstanding her thin arms, she swung powerfully, while she chanted half-threateningly, half-roguishly, some words from the song already alluded to—

> " Say, wish you to hang on the lofty tree ?
> Or wish you to swim in the dark blue sea ?
> Or would you kiss the naked sword
> Given to us by our Lord ? "

Her companion answered in the same melody : " I will kiss the naked sword "—adding immediately, " And I will kiss little Red Sefchen." Sefchen did not dare to resist lest she might harm him with the fatal steel (athirst as the hundred-deaths blade would be for blood), and so she had to permit her lover's arms " around her fine form, and his kiss upon her haughty mouth."

I have spoken of Heine as Sefchen's lover, but as a matter of fact he was ignorant of aught of passion till this kiss unloosed the bonds that held in leash his unconscious desire. The kiss itself, he asserts, was not from any tender feeling so much as out of defiance to society and all its obscure prejudices, mockery at the blood-stained weapon of the law, and at the infamy commonly attached to any one who voluntarily came in contact with the odious executioner-brood. But here it is the Heine of forty years later who speaks, the Heine who never forgot his *métier* of defiance and ridicule of the conventionalities, not the sixteen-year-old budding poet fired with imagination and the electric ardour of adolescence.- It was not the latter, we may be sure, who thought of society and its prejudices when the sight of Sefchen's beauty suddenly sent his hot blood leaping through his veins ; no kiss of protest was it that Sefchen's "haughty mouth" knew—nothing less than the first impulsive embrace of newly-awakened desire. That it opened the gates of passion Heine admits. Having kissed, he was at the same moment aware of the fiery breath of love.

We hear no more of Josepha after this. With discreet silence her lover simply acknowledges his first passion as only a prelude to the tragedies of his later life. It was but a case of Romeo in love with Rosalind ere he had met his Juliet. In love, he remarks, there is—as in the Catholic religion—a preliminary purgatory in which one may become accustomed to being roasted ere one enters the real, everlasting hell !

It is not difficult to realize how potent the influence of Sefchen must have been upon such a youth. The romance and mystery of the strange girl's life must necessarily have fascinated him, while there can be no doubt that her lore of *Volkslieder* and *Märchen* first awakened in him a love for that kind of poetry ; that this was so, indeed, he expressly states. In the Memoirs he alludes to his earliest published poems, the "Traumbilder" ("Dream Pictures"), as having a kind of gloomy colouring and even cruelty, "just like that attachment to Sefchen, which threw its blood-red shadows over my young life and thoughts." These early poems of Heine's are very remarkable, not only for their imaginative quality and technical excellence, but for

their individual note and their subtlety of metrical
music.

Among the "Dream Pictures" the most imaginative
are those written in the author's sixteenth and seventeenth
years, either for Sefchen or under her direct influence ;
particularly should mention be made of "Ein Traum,
gar seltsam schauerlich" ("A Dream of Fearful Mystery"),
"Im süssen Traum, bei stiller Nacht" ("In happy sleep,
in stilly night"), "Nun hast du das Kaufgeld" ("Thou
now hast the money"), "Was treibt und tobt mein tolles
Blut" ("Headlong madness stirs my blood"), "Ich kam
von meiner Herrin Haus" ("I came from the house of
my mistress"), "Ich lag und schlief, und schlief recht
mild" ("I was asleep, and calmly slept"), and "Da hab
ich viel blasse Leichen," &c. ("Oft have I conjured pale
spectres").

I would fain give an English rendering of "Ein Traum,
gar seltsam schauerlich," but the poem is overlong for
present quotation.   It contains some remarkably beautiful writing.   It was no mere versifier who saw in vision
the fair garden with its sunlit spaces, waving greenery,
rapture of birds, and "thousand-tinted flowers" with their
"balsamic odours," in whose midst—by a marble fountain
—a beautiful maiden stooped and laved a garment of
white cloth, while in a sweet but strange voice she sang

> "Flow, flow, water flow,
> Wash the linen white as snow"—

till she gave answer to his question, "who that robe of
white shall wear?"—

" ' Be ready soon ' she sang aloud
 ' I wash for thee thy dying shroud ! '—
 And scarcely had the words been said,
 Like wreaths of mist the vision fled."

Nor could any other than an imaginative poet have
delineated that weirder scene in the wild and gloomy
wood where, amid the interlacing arm-like boughs of
huge and ancient trees, the dreamer imagines himself
standing and listening intently ; suddenly the intermittent heavy stroke of a woodcutter is heard far-off, and
through brake and thicket the visionary forces his way
till he gains an open space :—

" There, in the middle of the wood,
 A mighty oak-tree towering stood ;
 And there the wondrous maid I see,—
 She hews the knotted old oak-tree.

Stroke follows stroke, as, swift and strong,
 She swings her axe, and sings her song :
 ' *Blade, blade, broad and bright,*
 Hew the oaken plank aright "—

nor knows he till he has questioned the maiden, that she
hews the planks of his coffin. Once, again, he sees the
maid upon a lonely and barren waste, singing a wild
song with the refrain,

" Spade, spade, sharp and strong,
 Dig the grave deep and long "—

and knows that he shall not see her any more, for his
weird is nigh fulfilment.

Again, I should have liked to quote the uncanny
" Bride and Bridegroom " poem (" Was treibt und tobt

3

mein tolles Blut?") where the dreamer sees a marriage feast, but in the bride recognizes his own beloved ; how the bridegroom gives her a cup of wine, but "Woe! my crimson blood she drank ; " and how the apple which she takes and in return gives to her lord, who with his knife severs it in twain, is nought else than his heart.

Thus before Heine left his native place, and the dearly-loved haunts by the Düssel and the Rhine, to begin the battle of life, he knew that he had "the bird in the heart," and that no ordinary song was his, or that which he knew would come in the fulness of time.

CHAPTER II.

WHEN Madame Heine realized, after the down-fall of Napoleon, that there was no longer an opening in the military profession for her eldest son, she was sorely exercised as to how to help the hand of Providence. The Rector Schallmeyer, who presided at the Lycée, and was a friend of the Heines, urged that his clever pupil should be educated as an ecclesiastic with a view to his ultimately becoming an abbé. But though Heinrich in later life relished the idea—for he thought that as an unattached abbé he could comfortably have served both God and Mammon—neither he nor his shrewd mother considered the rector's project favourably.

As for the profession of medicine, Heine would have none of it. His *métier*, as time was to prove, was not to wound people with lances but with verbal poniards—much more agonizing instruments than those kept in leathern cases. In the administration of black draught he would probably have proved an empirical fraud: in the application of biting satire he was without a rival.

Finally, after some tears and remonstrances, Herr Heine's first-born was convinced that he had no option

but to yield to his parents' wish that he should enter
upon commerce as a banker's clerk at Frankfürt-am-
Rhein.   ,

And now the time came for the sixteen-year-old boy to
learn the humiliation and misery of being a Jew. The
taunts and jeers of his schoolmates had been but gnat-
bites after all; he had then been a child, and had
thought only of his own insulted dignity—now he was to
realize that his people were still Pariahs in some parts of
Christendom, and that there was bitter cause for the
hatred of the Israelites against the Gentiles. As if lepers,
the Jews of Frankfürt were compelled to live within the
gloomy and dirty precincts of the Ghetto, where, upon
Sundays, they were confined from dawn till midnight;
and if any Jew ventured upon one of the public pro-
menades he would be hurried from the thoroughfare
like some unclean creature or rabid dog. A hundred
insults awaited the son of Israel at every corner ; he was
robbed, wronged, and grossly illtreated whether he was
in the wrong or in the right. No wonder, then, that young
Heine, proud by nature and resentful against even the
shadow of tyranny in any guise, hated Frankfürt, felt
all the latent Jewish enthusiasm stir within him, and
became determined at any cost to escape from the
degradation which enveloped or threatened so many of
his race. When we remember "Jehuda Ben Halévy,"
and the "Rabbi von Bacharach," we cannot consider
that this Frankfürt experience was a mere worthless
episode of wretchedness for the young poet, though
none can wonder that to him it always so appeared.

After some seven or eight weeks of residence in the

Ghetto he left Frankfürt behind him with the heartfelt wish that he might never set foot again within its gates.

Some months went idly by at Düsseldorf, wherein Heine read omnivorously, though mainly in the domain of romance. Sterne and Scott were his favourite foreign authors, though in poetry he mostly imitated Arndt and Brentano. It was most likely at this time that he came to regard Sefchen in other than the aspect of a child ; but we have no definite record as to this, and can only indulge in surmise based upon natural probabilities.

At last, in the early autumn of 1816, the question of his vocation was solved by a suggestion on the part of his Hamburg uncle. Salomon Heine was by common consent the "genius" of the Heine connection—that is, he was lucky far beyond the average in business, so much so that if he but washed his hands in a jet of water it immediately became an outflow from the Pactolian fount. A cross-grained, boorish, but not ungenerous or unkindly man, he did a great deal of good in an autocratic way ; and though scrupulously hard in money-bargains, was wont to open his purse to quite a crowd of related and connected beneficiaries. Ultimately he became the richest banker in Germany, and even in the second decade of the century was known as the wealthiest Jew in Hamburg. It was thought a great thing, therefore, in the Heine household in the Bolkerstrasse of Düsseldorf, when Harry was despatched to the German Liverpool to begin life in earnest as an employé in the "house" of Uncle Salomon.

For nearly three years he remained in the gloomy commercial city, which, though infinitely preferable to

Frankfürt, seemed to him a town of automata, machinery,
and grim facts, with nothing of what makes life beautiful.
As for himself, he was soon to find something that made
life show brightly enough in perspective, though this did
not affect his feelings towards Hamburg and its citizens.
Sorely he missed the Rhineland ; resentfully he endured
the northern chill and gloom.   Had Heine been a
Neapolitan he might have made an excellent *lazarone;*
but as he was a commercial clerk in Hamburg he was
forced to take refuge in the land whereto the lamp
of his genius led him, and wherefrom he returned daily
with a new thought in his mind or a new song upon his
lips.

At this time he began to develope that love of dainty
refinement in dress (his enemies of course called it
foppishness) which characterized him through most of his
life ; and altogether he seems to have been a comely
youngster.   Fine linen and lace ruffles he specially
affected, and he was the better able to indulge himself in
this respect from the fact that he abhorred smoking, and
was so moderate a drinker that it is recorded of him he
never tasted beer until he went to Paris.   He was slight
in figure, about five feet eight in height, delicately featured
with straight finely shaped nose, good but sensuous lips,
an expression at once of reserve and of good-humoured
cynicism, blue eyes that could look dreamy or fiery by
rapid transitions, and hands and feet more like those of a
woman than of a man.   His quickness of sympathy, intellectual alertness, and incandescent wit made him a
charming companion when he was in a genial mood ;
while his cynical smile, his satire, his stiletto speech

made him dreaded by more mentally cumbrous individuals who consciously or unwittingly gave him offence.

It is not to be wondered at, therefore, that Heinrich Heine, though only a clerk (and anything but an industrious apprentice !), made an impression upon his lovely cousin Amalie. As for himself, love seems to have come to him like the dusk in "The Ancient Mariner"—in one stride. Sefchen was forgotten, and all other visions became phantasmal. The fair golden-haired girl, who was only a year younger than himself, but whose beauty was so developed, involuntarily bound him at once to hopeless thraldom ; though if he had prophetically perceived the misery and life-long heartache which lay in the train of his passion he would have fled *verdammtes Hamburg*, as mariners the rock of the Death Siren.

Heine himself has made so few direct allusions to this passionate dream of his youth and scarcely less passionate regret of his manhood, and the whole matter is so veiled in obscurity, that the biographer would be unwise who dogmatized upon the main point at issue—whether Amalie Heine ever really loved and practically betrothed herself to her cousin, or whether she played with his affection for lack of more amusing entertainment ; whether, if love *did* exist between both, Heine was sufficiently scrupulous of the obligations of such love ; or whether, if Amalie never realized the ardour and depth of his feelings, he was not in great measure to blame therefor.

Although he met with considerable kindness at his uncle's hands, he was always more or less of a black goat among the very white and fleecy sheep of the Salomon Heine *entourage*. Probably he was aware that any

definite engagement of himself and Amalie would not
be entertained for a moment, or not until his business
prospects were so promising as to satisfy every one concerned—an epoch which he knew would commence with
the occurrence of the Greek Kalends. It was probably
with a desperate desire to prove himself a "possible"
suitor that, when he found he was making no headway in
his uncle's business, he set up for himself under the title
of "H. Heine and Co." As was to be expected, the
experiment was absolutely unsuccessful. But ere this he
seems to have committed himself to Amalie, and by
some too prompt and eager declaration to have alarmed
or perhaps repelled her. There is an interesting letter,
which bears the date of 27th of October, 1816, but is not
included among his collected writings and correspondence, addressed to a friend in Düsseldorf named Christian
Sethe. This lengthy epistle—a very remarkable letter
from so youthful a correspondent—is mostly taken up
with wailing and gnashing of teeth in the Byronic fashion,
and with sentimental emotion after the manner of that
most wearisome of young men, the love-lorn Werther; but
in it there are some direct and genuine utterances. We
may gather from it that he by no means saw Amalie
regularly, or at any rate frequently, for, after a Wertherian
passage about long years of feverish yearning, the torture
of hell, and the wailing of the damned, he exclaims,
"But to be near her, and yet often for long long weeks to
pine in vain for a sight of her, one's sole happiness on
earth," &c., &c. Again, we gather that Amalie was un-
sympathetic to his poetry, for he remarks : "It wounds me
deeply, too, that *she* for whom alone I sung, that she

should have snubbed my songs in so cruel and cold-blooded a fashion, and have played me such a shrewd turn in this respect." Finally, there is the distinct assertion of the repulsion of his suit; for " I have the clearest, the most irrefragable grounds for believing that I am wholly indifferent to her." That this important letter is not misleading as to date—which in the absence of corroborative facts it would almost certainly be—is assured from its endorsement by Christian Sethe—*"accepi den* 23 *Nov.,* 1816."

It would appear, however, that the fair maiden who caused him such sufferings was not uniformly unkind : for if she never read, nor even listened patiently to his poems, she allowed him to dream that his heart's desire might possibly be some day accomplished. It was this dream, this vision, that made Hamburg bearable to him ; this, and the growing conviction that he was slowly qualifying himself for that literary life which was his hope.

As was inevitable, Uncle Salomon at last realized that his nephew from Düsseldorf was unfit for a mercantile career—that he was, in a word, as the old merchant curtly but pityingly described him, the fool of the family. So the "fool" was informed one day that his prospects of success in business were as unlikely as his marriage to the King's daughter ; and that the sooner he made some effort in another direction the better it would be for him and all concerned. It was nigh upon midsummer, and Heine was in his nineteenth year : so he probably received his uncle's admonitions with secret joy, even before he guessed their real import. Nothing could well be worse than continued residence in *verdammtes*

Hamburg, and gladly would he become a sailor on the
Baltic, or emigrate, or enlist, or do anything that would
remove him from the hated town, ⌐wherefrom, but for
Amalie, he would long since have fled.   It was, therefore, with pleasure that he heard from Herr Salomon
of the parental and avuncular plans for his welfare.
He was to go to Bonn, and there become a student
of law, to the end that he might become *Doctor Juris;*
but with the stipulation that he was to return to Hamburg, as soon as he had taken his degree, and there
court fame and fortune as an advocate.   This plan
involved his conversion to Christianity, or its profession ;
for no Jew might presume to administer Teutonic
wisdom, or plead for or against a Christian in the liberal
courts of Germany.   To this, however, neither Uncle
Salomon nor Samson Heine and his wife saw any objec-
tions ; for their faith was of that adjustable order that
could, like the beggar's cloak, be worn with either side
outward as might be convenient.   The point was not
unduly emphasized ; as a business man, Herr Salomon
would not have condescended to enlarge upon so trifling
an incidental matter as a change of religion, when
material interests were at stake.

   So one summer's day in 1819 the merchant-banker
said good-bye to " the scapegrace," and in so doing
handed him the first instalment of the annual "assistance " of five hundred thalers, which he had promised to
allow his nephew in addition to the amount the latter's
parents had agreed to disburse for the same purpose;
and " the fool of a boy " replied politely, and protested
with all the usual arrogant complacency of youth ; and

then, with a last look at the house where Amalie dwelt,
and with his box more full of books and manuscripts
than of worldly vanities, set gladly forth for the golden
Rhineland. Notwithstanding many "snubbings," and a
frequent coldness and tantalizing reticence, on the part of
Amalie, he seems to have departed in perfect confidence
that she would hearken to no other suitor, and that when
he next appeared at his uncle's house with all his legal
honours it would be as the betrothed husband of his
cousin.

The next two or three months at Düsseldorf were
among the pleasantest in Heine's youth. His love for
the Rhineland intensified, and in the intervals of his
Latin and other studies preliminary to his college-career
he had many opportunities of enjoyment. Moreover he
was already, in a small way, of some repute. In the early
decades of the century there was not, in Germany at any
rate, such a multiplicity of bardlings as now covers the
civilized world; and a youngster who had his lucubrations
accepted in the *Sentinel*, or the *Gazette*, or the *Post*, was
immediately looked upon by his relatives with anxiety—
for would not the gods be jealous, and take the youth
unto themselves ere the bloom of his adolescence had
faded? Genius, fortunately, is as deceptive as heart-
complaint : were it more prevalent it would doubtless
prove as virulent among the young as consumption.
However, like measles, it is harmless enough when in a
mild form, and when the patient is in his or her teens.
Thus it was that Heine found himself spoken of as a
poet on the strength of rumour, and to a certain extent on
account of the Arndt and Uhland-like contributions to the

Hamburg Watchman and other prints. Many a dream
he dreamt in those green alleys in the Schloss gardens,
or when wandering with his friend 'and fellow-student,
Joseph Neunzig, along the banks of the Düssel; and
when the time came for him to leave for Bonn he was
far more occupied with attempted rivalry of his favourite
poets than eager for the mysteries of the Pandects.

Heine arrived in Bonn just in time to participate in
the last of the Student-Guild demonstrations which the
Prussian Government—the pettiest and least liberal that
ever held sway in Europe—had determined to suppress.
Among a crowd of enthusiastic youths, he ascended the
Drachenfels by torchlight, and by the side of the huge
bonfire lit upon the summit drank confusion to the foes
of Germany. A sonnet among his "Early Poems"
("The Night-Watch on the Drachenfels") commemo-
rates this event; but after a vivid depicture of the scene
he very characteristically concludes that the consumma-
tion of his patriotic fervour was an exceedingly bad cold.
At that time Bonn was the Oxford of the Germanic
States. Not only were many famous men—including
Augustus von Schlegel, the critic, philosopher, philologist,
poet, and dramatist—professors of its faculties, but there
were also among the students an earnestness and zeal
which ultimately bore worthy results.

The Romantic spirit was then flowing through all that
was best in the collective genius of Germany, and foremost among the intellectual stimulators of his time was
the chief of the romanticists, Schlegel. His wide culture
unlocked the doors of many treasures, and not only
Shakespeare and Calderon, but the stirring epic poetry

of young Europe, and even something of the riches of
the East, were by him made available to all who would.
When Heine went to Bonn, "the immaculate Augustus"
was at the height of his fame, and the young poet worshipped the Herr Professor with an ardour only inferior
to that of his Napoleonic passion. There is no doubt as
to Schlegel's strong influence upon Heine ; and from one
of the disciple's sonnets to his master—as well as from
other sources—it is clear that the famous Romanticist
took an interest in and directly encouraged his youthful
admirer.

But Heine had other acquaintances at Bonn who
exercised a more or less important influence upon his
mental development. Chief among these were two
fellow students named Simrock and Hundeshagen, the
latter of whom was also his private tutor. Even as a
youth Simrock had made an enthusiastic study of Old
German literature, and as Hundeshagen was equally
versed in mediæval æsthetic history, Heine could not
have had better guides and comrades in his poetic pilgrimage. The " Nibelungen-Lied " was at that time the
absorbing topic. Schlegel lectured upon its manifold
beauties ; students annotated and wrote upon it ; poets
imitated or derived from it. With the " Nibelungen-
Lied," the "Chanson de Roland," and other relics of the
Carlovingian Cycle, and "Ossian," all attracting the attention, admiration, and argument of literary Europe, it
would have been strange if the intellectual and eager
band of young men at Bonn had not responded to the
Romantic war cry. As for Heine, he for a time identified
himself heart and soul with the Romantic Renascence,

although at no period did he lose aught of individuality.
Even in his criticisms of so universally criticized works
as the " Nibelungen-Lied " he was entirely original. The
language of which it is composed, he wrote long after he
had left Bonn, "is of stone, and the verses are little
rhymed blocks of granite : here and there out of the
crevices red flowers peep forth like the oozings of blood,
or the long ivy trickles over it like green tears."

Nearly all his comrades were " poets," and in such a
hotbed of simmering talents anything quintessential
speedily found its way to the surface. To the delight
and admiration of his friends, Heine's " Junge Leiden "
came swift upon each other, and a few intimates spread
the rumour of the fine quality of a play in progress which
in due time would astonish the world under the title of
" Almansor."

Having (notwithstanding an exercise of satirical by-play
which might have caused trouble had not the fates been
propitious) early in December adequately passed his
examination, he duly matriculated as a student in law and
general science. From the very outset, however, he took
little or no interest in legal study, and treated it very much
as the Irish peasant takes care of his pig—by leaving it
to take care of itself.

When the ensuing summer arrived at last, and the time
came for professors and students to disperse whitherso-
ever they would, Heine bade good-bye to his comrades,
and with his small amount of luggage, and a large accumulation of manuscript, migrated to the pretty little village
of Beul on the opposite side of the Rhine. Here he
continued to study, not the " Institutes " and the

"Pandects," but all sorts and conditions of poets, ancient and modern; and here, instead of annotations, notes, and college exercises, he devoted his leisure to verse-writing and further scenes of "Almansor."

Just as the swallows were wheeling and shooting round the old church spire of Beul and over the blue waters of the Rhine ere their southward migration, the young student-poet suddenly determined to act upon advice which seems to have been given him from Düsseldorf or Hamburg, and to change his quarters from literary and fascinating Bonn to erudite and sedate Göttingen. It cannot have been altogether voluntarily that, knapsack on back, he tramped north-westward through Westphalia to "respectable Hanover," though doubtless the prospect of change and intellectual variety had its fascination.

At Göttingen he greatly missed the literary atmosphere to which he had been accustomed at Bonn, but in the friendly interest of the justly famous Sartorius he found some compensation. He had not been a week in the decayed old town ere he perceived the parochialism and absurdity of the general routine of life, and as Heine could never refrain from satire when anything was disagreeable to him, his keen eyes took note of all the susceptibilities and shortcomings of the place and its inhabitants. Readers of the "Harzreise" will know to what amusing use he put those experiences. But if the literary and social fascinations of Bonn were adverse to legal studies, scarcely less so were the rigid pedantry and stupidity of the educational methods at Göttingen. Heine laboured through his duties very perfunctorily, and devoted much more time to "Almansor" than to Gaius or Justinian.

In any case the young poet-student would probably have left " Georgia Augusta," as the university was called after its founder, George II. of England, at the end of the winter term ; but his departure was settled for him by an official decree of rustication.   Indifferent as he was to the purse-proud and family-proud noodles of the student clubs, and careful as he was to avoid disputes with strangers, he one day found a quarrel forced upon him by an arrogant *Junker*.   The latter had dogmatized offensively upon the Student's Code of Honour, which Heine had in turn scornfully alluded to as *leges barbarorum :* and the upshot was that, after a gross insult which he could not overlook, Heine challenged his adversary to a duel with pistols.   The affair was nipped in the bud by the rumour of it having reached the authorities.   The *Junker* and his seconds were sentenced to a brief term of imprisonment, and the more innocent, though as challenger more officially reprehensible, party received *consilium abeundi.*

Here, then, was a golden opportunity to betake himself to Berlin, and one that he determined not to let slip. Berlin, dull, pedantic, a baby city swathed in red tape, as it was, was yet at that time the centre of the keenest intellectual life of Germany.   True, Goethe, emperor in the world of letters, held his court elsewhere and abominated the Prussian capital, yet Hegel, Fouqué, Varnhagen von Ense, Chamisso, Willibald Alexis, Edward Gans, Grabbe, Franz Bopp, and many others famous in philosophy, science, and *belles lettres* rendered Berlin the German London of the day.   For this intellectual life Heine was athirst, and moreover he was anxious to come to some arrangement about the publication of his poetical writings. Again, he felt certain that in Berlin he would make much swifter progress with his law studies; and, finally, he was eager to make use of the introductions which had been promised him by Schlegel and others, particularly those to the Varnhagens, whose *salon* was then the foremost place of literary meeting in Germany.

Almost from the first day of his arrival in the Prussian capital things began to go well with him. At the houses of the Varnhagens and of Elisa von Hohenhausen he met every one of intellectual repute, and formed friendships which were of immediate as well as ultimate value.

One of the most valuable of his introductions, however, was, curiously enough, from his Hamburg uncle. This was to a Jewish merchant named Moses Moser, who, although deeply engaged in business, was a man of exceptional culture and intellectual attainments. A disciple of Hegel, he was yet as familiar with *belles lettres* as with philosophy; and, though a metaphysician, was also a shrewd man of the world. What mattered much to Heine was that Moser moved in the best literary circles of Berlin, and that from the outset he did his best to serve his young acquaintance. The two remained lifelong friends; and much of our knowledge of the mental experiences of the poet is derived from the long and frequent letters which in youth and manhood he addressed to his friend. Moser soon gauged Heine's nature, and his advice and help were often to the point. So well aware was he of his comrade's whimsicality, that he received in all good humour letters which assured him that his correspondent did not like him because he was a

4

magazine of virtue, or because he knew "Spanish and Syriac and Hegelian, English, Arabic, and Hindostani," or because he had lent the writer his money and even his overcoat, or because of his anxiety and interests for " my welfare," and so forth, but simply on account of "a silly trick of manner I have noticed in you, and an absurd expression that escapes you."

No longer, as at Göttingen, bored by professorial pedantry, Heine now attended the various classes at the Berlin University. Even the law lectures were no longer provocative of deadly *ennui*—but then the professor was no other than Edward Gans, the brilliant Jewish convert whom Hegel considered his most promising disciple. Under the influence of Gans, Heine rapidly acquired a keen philosophical interest in jurispudence, and he even projected, and to some extent proceeded with, a legal treatise upon the historical public law of the Middle Ages. Like many another ambitious scheme from the same fertile but inconsequent brain, this treatise came to naught. He also attended the lectures of Niebuhr upon Roman history, of Bock upon classical antiquities, and of Neander upon theology. These eminent professors were by no means all the famous men whom Berlin University could then boast. Bopp, the great philologist, lectured upon comparative philology; Von der Hagen upon early German literature; and Wolff upon the ancient literature of Greece. None, however, had greater influence upon Heine than Hegel. It was not until many years after he had left Germany that he admitted the extent and depth of this influence. The personality of the great philosopher, however, did not attract him. Hegel's conversation, he says in his "Confessions," was chiefly a kind of monologue sighed forth spasmodically and with a monotonous voice. Alluding to his impressions after the first lecture he heard the philosopher deliver, he writes : " I saw how Hegel with his comico-serious face sat as a brood hen on the fatal eggs (atheism) and I heard his cackling ; to speak fairly I seldom understood him, and only at last by subsequent recollections did I arrive at an understanding of his words. I believe he did not desire to be understood, and hence his involved fashion of exposition." From the "Confessions" also I may quote, in connection with Hegel, another and more famous passage. "One beautiful starlit night, Hegel stood with me at an open window. I, being a young man of twenty-two, and having just eaten well and drunk my coffee, spoke with enthusiasm of the stars, and called them the abodes of the blest. But the master muttered to himself, 'The stars ! Hm ! hm ! The stars are only a brilliant eruption on the firmament.' 'What !' cried I, ' then is there no blissful spot above, where virtue is rewarded after death?' But he, glaring at me with his pale eyes, remarked, sneeringly, 'So you want a bonus because you have supported your sick mother and re-frained from poisoning your brother ?'"

There was one house in Berlin where all that was worthiest in the society of the capital at that time fre-quently met. At this hospitable *salon* no political or religious differences were allowed to interfere with intel-lectual and social intercourse, and here it was that Heine spent many of his happiest hours. The hosts were Varnhagen von Ense and his wife Rahel. The latter was the most cultured woman in Germany, and was a person of infinite charm. Heine, like almost every one who came in contact with her, was fascinated by her sympathetic insight, her grace of demeanour and diction, her geniality and nobility of nature. All his life he never ceased to look upon Rahel Varnhagen as the noblest woman of her period. Varnhagen himself exercised much the same potent attraction upon those who were admitted to his intimacy. While a thorough man of the world, he was an ardent liberal, and an enthusiast in the cause of the people. As a writer upon military history he was the friend of the Court party, and so was able to exert considerable influence in many directions. He and his wife were from first to last staunch friends of the young poet, and did him good service in divers ways. Through the Varnhagens he came to know and be intimate with Rahel's only rival as the Madame Réca-mier of Berlin, the Baroness Elisa von Hohenhausen. At this lady's house, where he met nearly all the poets and writers of the day, he was always welcome. The Baroness believed in him as the German Byron, and was never happier than when he would consent to read aloud some of his poems, or passages from his MS. tragedies, " Almansor " and " Ratcliff."

Ere Heine had left Göttingen he had endeavoured to arrange with Brockhaus of Leipzig for the publication of a small volume of poems—an invitation which that gentleman had declined with the customary polite thanks. Through Varnhagen, however, an offer reached him from the editor of the chief literary paper, the "Gesellschafter," and very thankfully the young poet agreed that a series

of his verses should appear in Herr Gubitz's columns.
It was in May that they first saw the light, and although
the circulation of the "Gesellschafter" was comparatively
very limited, the poems attracted immediate attention
from the literary world on account of their simplicity and
genuine lyric lilt. So pleased was the proprietor of the
paper that he offered to publish Heine's verses in book
form, and in the course of the summer the little volume
appeared. The appreciation it encountered was emphatic, and the name of Heine was spread abroad : one
editor of a poetical record even included him among the
leading younger poets. It did not bring any cash to the
author, but it procured him—what was then of great
importance—a definite position. From many authors,
moreover, he received welcome and encouragement.
Perhaps nothing in this way pleased him more than a
letter from Baron de la Motte Fouqué, the author of
"Undine," which, along with the most cordial expressions, warned the young poet against undue dalliance
with grotesque or exaggeratedly gloomy subjects. Heine
replied in a letter breathing admiration and gratitude in
every line, nor did he ever forget the warm words which
were voluntarily sent to him by the veteran writer.

Notwithstanding the pleasant society in which he
mixed, his many literary projects, and his improving
prospects, Heine would seem to have been by no means
so happy at this period as his biographers have made
out. In an inscription to Rahel Varnhagen in a copy of
his maiden volume, he alludes to her patient sympathy
with "the poor, sick, bitter, morose, poetic, and unendurable man," and elsewhere he mentions his prevalent

despondency.   He had, however, the genuine poetic
temperament of swift respondence to the mood of whatever companion he might be with, and of intense
susceptibility to all extraneous influences.   Thus to
some he appeared a gay, careless, and somewhat dissi-
pated youth; to others a sombre enthusiast; to others,
again, as a student "sicklied o'er with a pale cast of
thought;" and to many as a brilliant conversationalist
and charming companion.   His cousin, Hermann Schiff,
has recorded of him that he was at this time somewhat
taciturn in general demeanour, though animated in the
presence of ladies; that he spoke with a light voice and
in a deliberate and rather monotonous tone; and that in
appearance he was slender and youthful, with face pale
and smooth as an olive, though with a prevalent look of
fatigue.   Among other than distinctly literary acquaintances with whom Heine became intimate in Berlin was
his loyal friend of after days, Count Eugen von Breza.
It was in the country residence in Posen of this companion that he spent some pleasant weeks in the summer
of 1822.

At this period the dominant literary influence in
Berlin was that of Sir Walter Scott.   That of Byron had
waned somewhat : that of Goethe had become more and
more exclusive.   The songs and poems of Schiller,
Uhland, Chamisso, and other poets had lost something
of their stimulus through familiarity, and the Romantic
epoch was in its decadence.   The Neo-Romantic movement was at hand, but till Heine's voice became a power
it had few results.   Great as was Heine's admiration for
Scott, he could not but regret that a true outflow of

appreciation should have ended in a mere fashionable
and unreflecting craze. That Lessing and Goethe, two
of the greatest literary factors of the modern world,
should be neglected for a foreign romancist, however
eminent, seemed to him a dismal prognostication for German literature. Nevertheless it was undoubtedly under
the more or less direct influence of Scott, of the foreign
wave of Romantic sentiment led by the great Scottish
poet-novelist, that he wrote his tragedies " Almansor "
and " Ratcliff."

Even the repute, however, which Heine gained by the
first part of the " Book of Songs" did not suffice to help
his tragedies over the quicksands of stage-representation.
To these two plays I shall return presently : meanwhile
a few words must be devoted to the poems.

The title of the first cycle of "The Book of Songs"
(*Buch der Lieder*) is "Youthful Sorrows " (*Junge Leiden*).
It consists of the Dream-Pictures (*Traumbilder*); nine
Songs (*Lieder*); twenty Romances (*Romanzen*); and
thirteen sonnets—one addressed to Schlegel, two to the
poet's mother, and the other ten, under the title " Fresco
Sonnets," to Christian Sethe.

In the eleventh poem of the third section, " The
Minnesingers " (*Die Minnesänger*), there occurs a
quatrain which may be taken as indicative of Heine's
early poetic bias : " Phantasy is the Minnesinger's eager
steed ; Art is his shield ; and Song is his sword." Phantasy
is the spirit which animates most of his early poems ; a
fancy now grotesque and weird, now delicate and gracious,
anon cynical and bizarre, or exquisitely pathetic. His
actual song-motive is the heart-wound without which,

as he says in this Minnesinger-poem, the true poet cannot sing sweetliest. The Dream-Pictures, the Sefchen poems as they might be called by a biographer, have been already alluded to. They are powerful and imaginative exercises, but in form are imitative and, indeed, are essentially to some extent derivative. Yet they are none the less original and idiosyncratic; from the bent of mind of which they are indices Heine, moreover, never wholly diverged. There is nothing among the writings of the Romantic poets superior to that weird dream-poem wherein the narrator sees the maiden washing his shroud, again swinging her axe as she hews his coffin, and yet again singing—

> " Spade, spade, sharp and strong,
>   Dig the grave deep and long,"

as out upon the lonely moor she delves the sods that are soon to rest above his body. In the third of these "Traumbilder" there is an allusion to his cousin Amalie's treatment of him. Probably this poem was written in the summer of 1821, just before the publication of the book; it would be about this time that Heine must have heard of the prospective marriage of his cousin, an event which occurred in August.[1]

In this brief poem the "Todeswund," the mortal heart-hurt of the Minnesinger, is only too evident. The few *Lieder* are sweet and graceful, but are not specially distinctive. Among the Romances the longest and most

---

[1] Under the title "Der Glückwunsch" (Congratulations) it appeared in the Hamburg *Abendzeitung*, signed "H. Heine, Berlin."

impressive is the legend of "Don Rodrigo." The sombre
"Mountain Echo," through its fine musical setting, is
well known in this country, as well as by Mr. Bowring's
admirable translation.

After "Don Rodrigo" ("Donna Clara, Donna Clara"),
and the gloomy and impressive "Belshazzar," the
"Romances" conclude with two pleasant pieces, "On
Hearing a Lady Sing an Old Ballad," and the cynically
humorous "When the Spring comes with the Sunshine."
The sonnets, though they lack the exquisite form of those
of Heine's one-time enemy Platen, are strong and vigorous
exercises in a metrical mould alien to the poet's essentially lyrical genius. The two addressed to his mother are
full of genuine affection, but there is more of Heine in
the Fresco Series. One of these might serve as a modified "apologia pro vitâ suâ."

> "I laugh, too, at the apes that *look* so wise,
>   And swell themselves to arbiters of thought;
>   I laugh, too, at the craven good-for-nought,
> Who with his poisoned steel in ambush lies.
> For when Good Fortune's wreath of Life's best flowers
>   Is smitten by the hand of adverse Fate,
>   And shattered at our feet lies all forlorn;
> And when the heart within the breast is torn,
>   Torn, broken, cleft in twain, and desolate—
> Why, shrill, ironic laughter still is ours!"
>
> (*Trs. by J. Ackerlos*).

Neither of Heine's tragedies had any success: upon
the stage they had none at all. "Ratcliff" was never
even put upon the boards, and "Almansor" (partly, it
must be admitted, owing to a miscarriage of local prejudice which arose from a similarity of surnames) was hissed

unmercifully at Brunswick Theatre on the one and only
night of its production. Neither is without merit;
" Almansor," indeed, seems to me at any rate a very
much finer production than it does to Mr. Stigand and
other English commentators. The only adequate essay
upon this play is that by Saint-René Taillandier, to
which I would recommend all who wish to know more
about "Almansor" and " Ratcliff."

Fatalistic dramas (*Schicksals Dramen*) were the vogue
about 1820, and no doubt Heine was biassed by the
prevalent taste. But the real germinal influence which
resulted in "Ratcliff" was that of Sir Walter Scott: in
form this earliest drama took after Schiller's " Robbers."
It is strange to us to read in a German play of a young
Scottish nobleman called Ratcliff: of MacGregor, and
Duncan, and Macdonald, and Douglas, of Edward and
Betty, and of William and Maria. The hero, consumed
with a hopeless passion for the fair Maria, goes to
London, and with an expedition that would have delighted a Carolinian rake, gets quit of his substance,
takes to highway robbery, and generally misbehaves
himself. He kills his rivals in love in an ingenious
if bloody fashion, ultimately elopes with the repentant
Maria, but, on interception, stabs that sentimental
damsel, performs the same deed upon his last remaining rival, and finally commits the happy despatch by
means of a handy pistol. With all its crudities and in-
congruities, however, it is not devoid of some striking
passages. Notwithstanding Heine's self-asserted possession of " that wonderful intuition which renders an
objective reality quite unessential to the poet," his

knowledge of British life and of the proprieties of
nomenclature are very, very vague.

"Almansor " is in every way a superior composition.
The scene is laid in Spain in the fifteenth century, some
years after the fall of Granada. Almansor is the last
remaining scion of a noble Moorish family, and his affections are centred upon a beautiful girl named Zuleinia.
Death and madness, murder and passion, are the factors
here as in "Ratcliff," but the movement is more dignified, the action more dramatic, the background more
picturesque in itself and much more deftly wrought.
Heine knew the æsthetic and dramatic value of incidental strains of wild or pathetic music, and as in "Ratcliff" he introduced with effect the refrain of a weird
Scottish ballad, so in " Almansor " the harp-player strikes
an ominous note at a crucial moment. Ignorant of
imminent doom at the hands of the infuriated moun-
taineers—for Pedrillo has not yet startled the company
with his shrill scream of terror, "Allah, have pity upon
us! Jesus, Mary, Joseph! We are lost! They come!
They come!"—Ali calls upon the attendants to afford
amusement to the guests. The harp-player thereupon
sings the following song, of which I only attempt a prose
translation :—

*"In the court of the Alhambra stand erect twelve great marble
lions : and near by is a mighty basin of purest alabaster.*
*Low within this basin float roses in full bloom, wondrous of hue:
red, red are they with the blood of the many knights who have made
merry at Granada."*

These plays are poems in dramatic form rather than

tragedies in the stage acceptation of the term.   Heine
called them tragedies just as Goethe so designated the
first and second parts of "Faust"; but they are rather
symphonies where divers tunes blend and interfuse.
There is a prefatory dedicatory note to "Almansor,"
wherein the author writes: "Do not consider that this
poem which I inscribe to you is absolutely fantastic.   I
would have you note that it is by turns calmly epical or
violently dramatic.   Here and there, betwixt the episodes, blooms many a lyric flower with fragrant heart.
The whole is written, as the saying is, from my heart."
The psychical interest of these two plays is that they indicate the precise moment when Heine quitted the poetic
fraternity of the Romanticists without having yet rejected
the garb of the brethren, in order to follow the pioneer
and revolutionary army of the age.   Henceforth the iron
is in the soul of the singer.

Between the publication of "Ratcliff" and "Almansor" Heine had written a number of lyrics: and in
allusion to this circumstance he gave them the collective
title "Lyrisches Intermezzo."   This "Lyrical Interlude"
might be called the "Wood of Love": the dawn, the
noon, the decline of love's day amid the songs of birds
and the erst joyous and then sad and ominous voices of
the winds among the trees—all are here.   The poems
and snatches of song—fragmentary, and yet each as
exquisitely complete as a nocturne by Chopin or a
Swedish folkstrain by Grieg—are sixty-five in number.

It is quite impracticable to attempt to do justice to
this fascinating "Interlude" by mere expressions of
admiration.   One can but say that none could read these

brief lyrics without recognizing that no such singer had
ever before so charmed the German ear, and that not even
Burns lilted a sweeter and more irresponsible note.
Many of the pieces are known wherever Germans con-
gregate, for they have been set to music perhaps equally
imperishable : such, to mention a few, are " Im wunderschönen Monat Mai," "Wenn ich in deine Augen seh',"
"Lehn deine Wang' an meine Wang'," "Auf Flügeln
des Gesanges," " Ein Fichtenbaum steht einsam." [1]

The briefer and more irresponsible these lyrics, the
more untranslatable are they. That of the Pine and
Palm has been oftener translated into English than any
other of Heine's poems. I have selected Miss Bessie
Craigmyle's version as the one that seemed to me best.

> " A Pine-tree standeth lonely
> On a far Norland height,
> It slumbereth, while around it
> The snow falls thick and white.
>
> And of a Palm it dreameth,
> That, in a southern land,
> Lonely and silent standeth
> Amid the scorching sand."

It would be impossible for any poet to more exquisitely
express the vague informulate yearning of the soul than
Heine has done in this flawless lyric. Only Shelley,
among all the plaintive choir who have sung with their
" breast up-till a thorne," could so have given voice to his
secret pain.

[1] 1. In the wondrously-lovely month of May. 2. When I look
into thine eyes. 3. Lean thy cheek against my cheek. 4. On the
wings of song. 5. A Pine-tree standeth lonely.

CHAPTER III.

BUT for the great sorrow of the marriage of his *Geliebte*—that deep wound which never wholly healed—Heine's two years in Berlin were among the pleasantest of his life. Intellectually as well as physically he lived every moment. Had he, indeed, been more chary of *abandon* to the manifold excitements and pleasures which lay in wait for him, he would probably have saved himself much after-bitterness and pain.

But at last the nervous headaches which had commenced in childhood became more frequent and more intolerable. He realized that a change was necessary; nor did he disguise from himself the fact that he was doing nothing towards adoption of a definite profession. By this time, moreover, his family was in straitened circumstances. His parents had had to leave Düsseldorf, and had ultimately settled in the dull little town of Lüneburg, where they lived partly on their own small capital, and partly on the assistance given by Salomon Heine. Here Heinrich determined to go for awhile, to recoup his strength and to think over his prospects.

When he left Berlin about the beginning of May, 1823

it was with anything but a lightsome heart. Departure signified the renunciation for a time of the society which had meant so much to him, of the friends in whom he had so delighted, of the literary stimulus which had been so invaluable. Moreover, he was now no longer a no-body—merely a clever Jewish youth with creditable introductions. He had made his mark, not less surely though limitedly. As the author of the promising and in many ways remarkable "Young Sorrows," and of the in every sense noteworthy "Lyrical Interlude," of "Rat-cliff," and of "Almansor," he had gained a foremost place among the youngest writers of Germany. His repute had not spread throughout the country, though in the Rhineland he was known not only as a poet, but as a Berlin correspondent and as an able and fearless reviewer. It did not render the home-going more enticing in prospect that his writings met with little or no appreciation from his relatives; even his mother lamented that her Harry was not in some reputable trade or honourable profession.

At Lüneburg a deep depression settled upon him. He could not then see his way to making a living by litera-ture; he had the utmost aversion from business; and for the profession of medicine he was not capable; while for that of the law, for which he cared little, it would be necessary to discard the Jewish faith and embrace Chris-tianity. From the outset Heine disliked the idea of apostasy, yet he could not but be influenced by the urgent parental and avuncular advice which almost daily admonished him to look to "the main chance," particu-larly as in Berlin he had seen examples of conversion

among the most able of the Jews who there fought their
hard fight against Prussian prejudice and bigotry.
More and more fascinating became the idea of a migration to Paris, but, alas, the wherewithal necessary to begin
life in an alien land was not forthcoming.   It was
economy that kept Heine so long in Lüneburg.   Even
the correspondence with the Varnhagens and other valued
Berlin friends, and the inexhaustible kindness of his
friend Moser in sending him books, periodicals, newspapers, and all the literary gossip of the day, proved
insufficient to dispel the despondency which came upon
him in the City of Ennui, as he called the stagnant capital
of the old Duchy.

Even physically the change from Berlin wrought little
good.   It became evident to every one that he was
ailing, and he met with no opposition from his father
when he declared that get to the bracing sea-air he must,
as otherwise he should soon be unfit for legal or any
other studies.   When this determination was backed up
by medical advice, it was agreed that he should go to
Cuxhaven for a few weeks.   But how to get the needful
funds?   Heine had not saved a farthing, had, indeed,
left a few small debts in Berlin : so he determined to
make another application to his uncle, and in person.

It was with feelings of poignant regret and remembrance that the young poet found himself once more in
hated Hamburg, the city of his first passion, the place
where Amalie had won his love, played with it, and discarded it as an outworn toy.   Greatly to his chagrin he
encountered his uncle Salomon just as the latter was
about to leave Hamburg on some business journey.   The

old banker was impatient, and would not listen to explanations or give advice; however, he briefly promised that the allowance of four hundred thalers (£60) should be continued quarterly, and in addition handed "the scapegrace" the sum of ten *louis d'or* wherewith to betake himself to Cuxhaven.

Heine lingered in Hamburg for a day or two, all the time tantalized and fascinated by, though wretched in, the renascence of his old emotions. Through the daylight hours he wandered listlessly about, thinking of Amalie, now with tears, now with bitter upbraidings. Sometimes he would meet one of the family-connection who would sneer at the "stupid one of the family" and at his prospects, his "poetry stuff" and his literary aims, but who went away with an unpleasant smarting of the moral hide, for Heinrich's wit had now become as keen as a razor and his satire as bitter as gall, and he never lost an opportunity of stinging comment or scathing sarcasm.

The poetical outcome of this visit was the series of passionately sad songs forming part of that section of the "Buch der Lieder" known as the "Heimkehr" (the Home-Coming, the Return)—the genuine outflow of a heart filled with sorrow and bitterness. From his letters to Moser and other friends it can be seen that he suffered even more than is manifest in his verse; and it is quite certain that the love-poems of the "Heimkehr" were not mere "literary agonies," as one of the poet's enemies publicly urged. The most pathetic of these snatches of song, for they are seldom more than three or four verses, and sometimes consist merely of a quatrain, are Nos. 23

5

("Ich stand in dunkeln Traümen "—" In a sad reverie I stood"), 26 (" Mir träumte,"&c.—"I dreamt; and mournfully shone the moon"), 31 ("Deine weissen Lilienfinger"—"O thy snow-white lily-fingers "), 46 ("Herz, mein Herz, sei nicht beklommen "—" O heart, my heart, be not o'ercome "), and 49 ("Wenn ich auf dem Lager liege "—"When on my couch I'm lying"). Frequently, however, there is a note of cynical bravado or of mockery, as in No. 6 (" Als ich auf der Reise zufällig "). In this lyric—little better than doggerel, poetically considered—he records how he came upon his sweetheart's family, and how they welcomed him, and complimented him upon his looks although he had grown dead-white with sudden pain ; how he asked after their aunts and cousins and many a tiresome friend, and even for the little puppy that he had been wont to caress ; and how then, as if he had just called her existence to mind, he inquired after his married sweetheart, and learned that she had just become a mother—whereupon he begged them to convey to her his congratulations and heart's-greetings. The lyric suddenly becomes poetry. The last two quatrains describe how " the little sister " tells the fate of the puppy when grown to doghood, and how, as she speaks, the poet suddenly sees in her smile and in her dark eyes the vision of his lost love. No translation can adequately convey, to the reader ignorant of German, the pathos, the haunting melancholy of those hopeless little love-songs.

The fresh salt breezes of the North Sea wrought a temporary cure, and Heine took long walks along the Cuxhaven sand-dunes, bathed, sailed, and generally enjoyed himself without having to pay the penalty of insufferable headaches. It would have been a period of unalloyed content but for the love-memory which gnawed at his heart, which forced again and again to his lips songs sad and hauntingly sweet, or cynically bitter and reckless : but for this, and one other serious worry of a pecuniary nature. The latter was a quarrel with his uncle on a breach of agreement, but after much resentment on both sides Herr Salomon was at last convinced that he was in the wrong. To make amends for his assertions to the contrary, the old man finally wrote and agreed to pay his nephew one hundred *louis d'or* (£80) for another year, that is, for the year 1824.

The outcome of this unpleasant affair was a determination on Heine's part to free himself as soon as possible from the state of dependency upon his uncle which was so distasteful to him ; he would even voluntarily agree to apostasy, or to anything in reason, in order to gain a livelihood. In this strain he wrote to his friend Moser, who gave him in return wise counsel against precipitancy and petulance, and particularly urged him to be more heedful in the exercise of his biting wit.

But otherwise how delightful it was at Cuxhaven ! What a revelation the sea was to the young poet ! From the very first day when he saw it in solitary majesty (for the salt water he had seen from Hamburg was "a mere mercantile fluid") his heart responded to its music, its significance, its mystery. Eye, nor ear, nor mind ever tired by those sandy dunes, that pebbled strand, those weed-haunted shallows, those ceaseless waves, that rhythmic unending utterance so full of meaning and yet so inexplicable; that broad expanse of moving waters whereon great ships passed with every wind, and wherefrom at sunrise and sundown the brown-sailed fishing smacks made for the havens along the shore; where at night the moon laid her Jacob's-ladder to dreamland and the stars trailed serpentine scintillations from deep to deep; where there was peace, and rest, and inspiration, forgetfulness or calm amelioration of past sorrows, phantasmal visions, exhilarating desires, hopes, determinations.

From that time onward the passion for the sea entered into Heine's being, and became a part of, a motive force in, his genius. He loved it as no German poet had ever done before him, as not even any English poet, with the exceptions of Shelley and Byron, had loved it. He was not to write his finest sea poems till he went to Norderney, but even this first visit to the North Coast was eventful in song. It is the sea music that makes " Die Heimkehr " so fascinating a volume, this and the sad songs to which it forms so rich an under-melody: the sea music of " Wir sassen am Fischerhause " ("We sat in the fisherman's cottage, and gazed upon the sea"), " Du schönes Fischer-mädchen " (" Thou lovely fisher-maiden "), " Der Mond ist aufgegangen " ("The moon is risen"), "Der Sturm spielt auf zum Tanze" ("The storm strikes up its dance song "), " Der Abend kommt gezogen " (" The twilight falls : mists veil the sea "), and "Das Meer erglänzte weit hinaus " (" The sea yet shone with sunset gleams "). Sometimes the passion of his love rises irresistibly, as where, in one of the sea poems, he suddenly breaks out into and concludes with—

" To your bosom take my head,
    Soul and body I surrender !
    Sing me dead, caress me dead,
    Drain my life with kisses tender."

Of all the songs in the " Heimkehr " the most
familiar are, " Du schönes Fischermädchen " and " Die
Lorelei," the Water Fay of the Rhine.   The latter,
indeed, is probably the most widely known of all
Heine's poems.   It has been translated into every
European and several Asiatic languages, and has been
set to music scores of times by German, English, French,
and Russian composers.   As a poem it is as typical of
its author's genius as any short single example could be :
the touch of pathos, the poetic atmosphere, the romantic
feeling, and, as much as anything else, the sudden note
of mockery—as if the poet were laughing sardonically
at having so deeply enlisted the reader's sympathies—
all reveal the real Heine.   This lyric could hardly have
been written by any poet of Heine's time save Goethe
or Uhland.   But Goethe would have shuddered at the
closing discord as something entirely alien to the calm
of true art; while the most charming of sentimentalists
could never have sung of so pretty a romance with such
a disillusioning "aside."

"Du schönes Fischermädchen " is a lyric sung all the
world over.   It is, moreover, so typical of a kind of poetry
wherein its author has never been equalled, much less
surpassed, that room must be found for an English
version of it.   On the whole the best translation which
I have encountered is that by Mr. Stigand, though it may
very properly be objected that " And many pretty pearls,

my love," is not quite the same thing as "Und manche
schöne Perle "—*schöne* having a much finer significance
than is conveyed by "pretty."

> " Come, fairest fisher-maiden, here,
>   Put, put thy skiff to land ;
> Come close to me and sit thee down,
>   And prattle hand in hand.
>
> Oh, lay thy head upon my heart,
>   Have not such fear of me ;
> Thou trustest day by day thyself
>   Unto the wild, wild sea.
>
> My heart is like the sea, it hath
>   Its storm, and ebb, and flow ;
> And many pretty pearls, my love,
>   Rest in its depths below."

Some of the contents of the "Heimkehr" volume
were printed in the spring of the following year (1825)
in the "Gesellschafter," and the whole cycle was included later on in "The Book of Songs." The collection includes the blank verse "Götterdämmerung"
("The Twilight of the Gods "), a fragment that seems
to me to have been overrated by some critics, as it
is derivative and might have been written by almost
any of the poets of the German Romantic school ;
"Ratcliff" and " Almansor," respectively in blank verse
and in unrhymed octosyllabic quatrains (not to be confused with the poetic dramas bearing the same titles) ;
and " Die Wallfahrt nach Kevlaar " (" The Pilgrimage to
Kevlaar"). For heroic blank verse Heine had little
original faculty, and, to judge from the sparsity of his

poems in this metre, but slight inclination. The lyrical impulse was at all times dominant with him. Even such excellent exercises—characteristic, moreover, as they are to a considerable degree—as "Götterdämmerung" and "Ratcliff," not only show that in this measure he is hardly at his ease, but that it does not suit his swift and wayward, his impulsive and fantastically irregular genius. On the other hand, there is convincing proof, even in the "Buch der Lieder," that he was in no wise dependent upon rhyme. Some of his finest as well as longest poetical productions are in blank verse cast in octosyllabic trochaic quatrains, or in the irregular measures of the North Sea Cycle. In the fine poem entitled "Donna Clara"—where, I think, it is hypercritical to discover Heine's passion for Amalie—the poet has given vent to that bitter irony which was so often with him an overmastering impulse. "The Pilgrimage to Kevlaar" is a pathetic poem, of a beauty so spiritual as scarcely to be characteristic of the genius of its author.

When the six weeks at Cuxhaven had come to an end, Heine found himself in Hamburg again *en route* for Lüneburg. His original idea of mooting to his uncle his project of a migration to Paris was, he realized, now impracticable : had he even hinted at such a thing the wrath of the old banker would have been extreme. So there was nothing for it but to return to Göttingen in due course, and there endeavour to obtain the degree of a doctor of law. For the legal profession Heine felt his unfitness ; still, anything would be better than continued dependence upon his uncle's charity. Moreover, there was always the chance of an official appointment (through influence, after his formal conversion) or even of a professorate. As for the return to the University of Göttingen, he knew that he would probably make more way with his studies in that dreary resort than at Berlin, or even than at Bonn.

The three ensuing months were spent with his family at Lüneburg, not voluntarily, but for lack of funds, as the new allowance from his uncle was not to take effect till after the New Year.

It was near the close of the third week in January, 1824, that Heine left Lüneburg for Göttingen, where he arrived on the 22nd, and by the end of the month was again a student in the famous Hanoverian university. The spring of 1824 was passed mainly in close study, varied with exercises in imaginative prose and poetry, the most important of which was the (uncompleted) romance, "Rabbi von Bacharach," that powerful and picturesque fragment which was one of the most conscious outcomes of its author's " Juden-Schmerz."

In March he paid a flying visit to Berlin, where he enjoyed himself mightily for a brief space, and sniffed the entrancing fragrance of literary fame. On his way thither he halted at Magdeburg, in order to make the personal acquaintance of Immermann, whom at that time he considered to be the most poetic of all German poets, and with whom he had entered into a kind of literary league. In the Berlin *salon* of Elisa von Hohenhausen he was greeted as the German Byron; and though he had the good sense and discrimination to laugh at an obviously absurd comparison—absurd if for nothing else than the marked distinction between the

.mpu'sive but inartistic poetry of the great Englishman and his own essentially artistic, though incomparably simple music, was not insusceptible to the implied flattery, particularly as Byron was the one foreign poet with whom he found himself in entire sympathy. He had read all his writings with avidity, and had even translated into German certain favourite pieces. It was with no ordinary regret, therefore, that —shortly after his return to Göttingen—he heard of the death of the great poet at Missolonghi. It came upon him as a personal shock. "Byron was the only man to whom I felt myself related," he wrote, "and we may well have had a good deal of resemblance in many things."

Once back in Göttingen he worked steadily at the Pandects and literature of a like uninspiring kind, combined with ardent study of Jewish history and rabbinical lore, in particular relation to his Jewish romance which by this time had taken great hold upon his imagination. Among the innumerable schemes which were born of his fertile brain was another Faust poem, but, fortunately, he finally discarded the idea—the fulfilment of which would as certainly have been as maleficent for him in his lifetime as it would probably have been to his hurt in that hereafter of which he dreamed.

When the summer heats arrived Heine slipped a knapsack upon his back, and set off upon a pedestrian excursion —a memorable trip to him for the pleasure and ultimate profit and fame it brought him, and to all his admirers because the outcome of it was the immediately popular " Harzreise " (" The Hartz Tour ").

In this, the most generally appreciated of all Heine's prose writings, we have a series of brilliant scenes depicted in matchless fashion, with a shrewdness of observation, an exuberance of animal spirits, and a subtlety and keenness of wit, which even now appeal to readers as something uniquely charming, and fifty years ago came as a revelation to the German world ignorant of the blithe grace and flexibility wherewith its literary prose could become animated under the touch of a master.

It has often been a subject for curious comment that Heine did not tell any of his friends, not even his good angel Moser, about his meeting with Goethe, when he passed through Weimar. But this encounter (which Heine afterwards described at the end of the first book of "The Romantic School,") was so disappointing to the younger poet that he plainly preferred to hide his chagrin in discreet silence. It was, moreover, rather agreeable to him to be able to pique Moser's curiosity. To have nothing more to say about Weimar, then the chosen home of Teutonic "sweetness and light," or of its high-priest, than " the beer at Weimar is really first rate," was a refined form of torment for his Goethe-worshipping friend. That it was evasive, Moser must have been well aware, for he knew that his friend was so un-German-like as to relish neither beer nor tobacco. Later on he alluded to the letter just quoted, and in the answer thereto Heine wrote as follows :

1st July, 1825.

" By my silence about Goethe—my conversation with him at Weimar, and all the friendly and condescending words he addressed to me—you have, I assure you, lost nothing. It was only as the tenement that once held so much glorious life, only for the past, that he interested me. He excited in me a melancholy feeling, and I have grown to like him better since I have felt for him. But at bottom Goethe and I are opposite natures, and mutually repellent. He is essentially a man on whom life sits easily, who looks on enjoyment of life as the highest good, and though at times he has glimpses and vague feelings of the ideal life, and expresses them in his poems, yet he has never comprehended, much less lived it. I, on the contrary, am essentially an enthusiast, that is, so inspired by the ideal as to be ready to offer myself up for it, and even prompted to let myself be absorbed by it. But, as a fact, I have caught at the enjoyments of life and found pleasure in them; whence the fierce struggle that goes on in me between my clear reason, which approves the enjoyments of life and rejects the devotion of self-sacrifice as a folly, and my enthusiasm, which is always rising up and laying violent hands on me, and trying to drag me down again to her ancient solitary realm ; *up* I ought perhaps rather to say, for it is still a grave question whether the enthusiast who gives up his life for the idea does not, in a single moment, live more and feel more happiness than Herr von Goethe in his six-and-seventieth year of egotistic tranquillity."

As a matter of fact, Heine had looked forward to the interview with keen anticipations of pleasure. He would meet the king of German Song not as a subject, but as a prince of a native though unallied dynasty, with whom, moreover, lay the chances of inheritance to supreme honours when the throne should become vacant. His songs were already known and sung throughout the land: great things were expected of him ; and there were even critics of repute who did not hesitate to pronounce him the second of living German poets. Nevertheless he had no wish to rely solely on his reputation. Before he left Göttingen, he had, time after time, rehearsed appropriate speeches and telling points wherewith to charm the serene old man who was so accustomed to clevernesses that he would all the more readily appreciate anything really brilliant. Alas, for the vanity of human hopes—and particularly for the vanity of young poets! When the long anticipated hour arrived, and the prince stood before the king, all the clever speeches, telling points, and brilliant allusions vanished and left the mind a hopeless blank. A prolonged pause—a curious smile on the marble-like face of Goethe—and then at last the most brilliant and promising of the younger men of genius spoke:

"The plums on the road between Jena and Weimar are perhaps the most excellent that I have ever tasted!"

Heine has not recorded how long it took after this humiliating anti-climax ere the ice was broken: but it is certain that Goethe was kindly and appreciative, if not sympathetic. It is indubitable that, as Heine remarks in the letter to Moser quoted above, the natures of the two poets were opposite, and in some respects mutually repellent. It is equally clear from the same letter that the younger did not, at the time at any rate, fully understand the elder writer: and there is certainly something amusing in the most sensuous of German poets pourtraying himself as the renunciative idealist, the man whose enthusiasm impels him to sacrifice his life for the idea—though, as Mr. Storr aptly remarks, "We must bear in mind that he is pouring out his confidences to his most intimate friend, whom he is telling, not what he is, but what he would be." This letter has, however, great idiosyncratic value, and, with all its *schwärmerei*, may be regarded as a genuine index to the real nature of the poet who all his life delighted to cast dust in the eyes of

friends and foes alike—so profusely as sometimes to
obscure his own self-vision. If there were aspects of
Goethe's genius which his younger rival did not duly
appreciate or even understand, it is not less obvious that
the serenest of modern poets failed to comprehend the
author of the "Buch der Lieder." "He has all gifts except
love," was Goethe's sententious comment to Eckermann
shortly after that German Boswell had settled at Weimar
as his secretary : "he loves his readers and his fellow
poets as little as himself, and thus one is tempted to
apply to him the saying of the apostle, 'Though I speak
with the tongues of men and angels, and have not charity,
I am become as sounding brass or a tinkling cymbal.'"
There is indubitable reason for Goethe's criticism, but
he never became sufficiently acquainted with Heine to
perceive that the cynicism and mockery were as the
bitter rind to the fruit whose deep-set core was fresh and
sweet. At heart, the sweetest singer of Germany was as
manly as Burns, as blithe as Béranger : but life meant
for him Protest, and the deafness of the world to protest
invited cynical recklessness ; and burning pain and lightsome emotions, passionate hopes and wayward impulses,
wrought havoc of the fair dreams and purest aspirations
of early youth.

In Heine's bitterness, however, there was often something of common poverty of spirit. Oftenest he swung
his sharp-edged sword of satire not as an assassin or as a
swashbuckler, but as an enthusiastic and reckless icono-
clast : occasionally, however, he snatched up a club, and
flourished it with all the clumsy violence of the typical
Junker. There is nothing but personal resentment in his

expressed opinion of Goethe's remarks about himself, although the shaft was by no means devoid of at least a feather of truth.

Some of the poems and odd portions of "The Hartz Tour" were written during the excursion, but it was not tentatively concluded until November, when the author sent it to his friends in Hamburg as "an amusement for the women-folk." Later on he sent it to the "Gesellschafter."

Interesting and amusing to the readers of the "Gesellschafter" as it was, however, "The Hartz Tour" was by no means the brilliant production it was when published in book form as part of the first volume of the "Reisebilder" (the "Travel-Pictures"). Besides having been thoroughly revised, the later version had the advantage of the famous Brocken phantasy and the inimitable introductory caricature of Göttingen and its university. It is suggestive, however, of the difficulties of a literary career —when the reputation that has been gained is for high-class work, and particularly if for poetry—that Heine received only fifty louis d'or for the copyright of a book that for fifty years proved a source of considerable income to Herr Campe and his firm.

I need not long delay over this fascinating section of Heine's work : the "Travel-Pictures" are so well known, and a version scarcely less delightful in most respects than the original is procurable for a small sum.[1]

The "Harzreise" is more or less illumined by the

<hr />

[1] Mr. Francis Storr's " Travel-Pictures : and the Romantic School."

radiance of poetry—by, at least, the happy sunshine of youth, which is not so very far from being the same thing. Not only are the "Berg-idyllen," the hill songs, scattered through the record very delightful: the prose is often like that fabled bird born of the embrace of Sea and Sky, that bright creature of azure plumes, who, whenever its heart swelled with rapture, became for a brief while as a living sapphire. Appropriately enough, a lyric opens the blithe chronicle. "Away with the false atmosphere of 'society' and the *ennui* of civilization: hurrah for the liberal mountain air, the cloud-shadowed hill-sides, the torrents and cool streams, the voices of the winds and the songs of birds"—this is what the lyrical opening of the "Harzreise" amounts to. Here are the first lines of prose—which, with those that follow in the original, caused a hearty laugh throughout solemn Germany, unaccustomed to have its ears tickled with lightsome wit; a hearty laugh everywhere save in Göttingen, where amazement and indignation alternately prevailed, till they merged in profound disgust at the blasphemer.

"The town of Göttingen, so celebrated for its sausages and university, belongs to the King of Hanover, and contains 999 inhabited houses, various churches, a lying-in hospital, an observatory, a university prison, a library, and a Town Hall Tavern, where the beer is excellent. The stream that flows past the town is the Leine, and serves in the summer for bathing. The water is very cold, and in some places it is so broad that Ponto had to take a really good run to clear it. The town itself is pretty, and presents the most agreeable aspect—when we have turned our backs upon it! . . . The inhabitants of Göttingen may be roughly classified under the heads of student, professor, philistine, and brute; but between these four

estates there is no clearly marked distinction. The moʃt important
class are the brutes. . . . The Göttingen philistines must be
numerous as the sand, or rather as the flakes of scum on the seashore ; indeed, when I see them in the morning, with their white
bills and dirty faces, I can hardly conceive how God can ever have
created such a pack of rascals. . . . It is my painful duty to take
my friend, the author of the Topography of Göttingen, to task for
not expressly and emphatically contradicting the current scandal
about the big feet of Göttingen women. Indeed, I have been
occupied for some time past with a serious refutation of this heresy,
and with this express object have joined a class of comparative
anatomy, made extracts from the rarest volumes of the library, stood
in the Weenderstrasse for hours at a spell studying the feet of the
ladies as they walked by ; and in the exhaustive treatise which embodies the result of these studies, I treat of (1) feet in general, (2)
feet in the Old World, (3) elephants' feet, (4) the feet of Göttingen
women, and (5) if I can obtain paper of sufficient size, I will add
some copperplate facsimiles of the Göttingen female foot."

At Osterode, as he narrates further on, he had a dream
so apposite that we may be sure it was not all a dream :
therein, as in Paris many a bitter year later, he flung
himself at the feet of the carven Goddess of Beauty and
with enraptured eyes drank in the symmetry and immortal loveliness of her blessed body: "Hellenic calm
possessed my senses, and over my head, as in benedic-
tion, Apollo poured his sweetest strains." He awoke
with music still ringing in his ears, to find that it was the
bells of the cows being driven to pasture. Having
quaffed his coffee he started afresh by the Klausthal road,
and from one of the first heights looked back once again
at sunlit Osterode, with its red roofs peeping from the
green fir-forest like a moss-rose. Near Lerrbach the
hills grew steeper. "Beneath, the fir-forests waved like
a green ocean, and, above, the white clouds sailed along

the blue sky. The wildness of the landscape was toned down and tamed, as it were, by its uniformity and simplicity. Nature, like a good poet, will have no violent transitions. And, like a great poet, Nature produces the greatest effects with the fewest materials—sun, trees, flowers, water, and love: that is all. If, indeed, the last is wanting in the heart of the beholder, the whole is a poor enough picture, and the sun is only so many miles in diameter, and the trees are good for fire-wood, and the flowers are classified by the number of their stamens, and the water is—wet." In this brief passage Heine, more or less unconsciously, refutes a false accusation and utters a self-condemnation. His emphasis upon love in its broad sense—whether or not it be a new thought stimulated by some germane remark from Goethe—shows how well aware he was of the secret of the poet's heart, and how extreme was the verdict of the author of "Faust" upon his younger comrade. On the other hand, "Nature, like a good poet, will have no violent transitions," comes strangely from the poet who more than any other indulges in what Nature is asserted to avoid. At Klausthal the pedestrian rested awhile in order to visit the smelting works and the silver mines, of which he gives a picturesque description which is all the more effective from the fine note of human pathos wherewith it concludes.

Heine, however, is no guide-book chronicler. Those who expected a record of facts and industrial statistics must have been wofully disappointed. Of Osterode all he has to say is that it has x houses, y inhabitants, including z souls; and the only information anent the

6

route to Goslar is that "I got there somehow, but I can't
say how."

Goslar, with its pavements as rough as the hexameters
of the Berlin poetasters, proved to be a dull place,
though a romantic love episode made the evening pass
as though it had been spent in the Golden Isles.

Till late into the night thereafter he sat looking out
upon the moonlit Rammelsberg. Love and moonlight!
Thoughts of happy havens for the soul, of long vistas in
immortality, naturally thronged upon the young man.
But in his record thereof there is something of the bitter
humour of the already-quoted episode of his conversation with Hegel concerning the stars. "Immortality!
beautiful thought! Who first imagined thee? Was it
some Nuremberg shopkeeper, who, with white nightcap
on head and white porcelain pipe in jaw, sat some warm
summer's evening before his shop-door, and comfortably
mused how pleasant it would be if this would only last
for ever—pipe and breath never going out, to vegetate
on for all eternity? . . . . Love! Immortality! My
bosom grew suddenly so hot that I fancied that the
geographers must have misplaced the equator, and that
it ran straight through my heart!"

A charming description of the mines will be remembered by all who have read the "Harzreise." For one
evening Heine lodged with the friend of the Klausthal
miner with whom he foregathered; and to his short stay
in the pleasant miner-household we owe the lovely series
of lyrics which he wrote about the father and his zither,
the mother at her spinning-wheel, and the blue-eyed
mädchen with her shy whispered confidences. Outside

the hillside-shieling the moonbeams fall upon the fells
and the craggy heights, and the night-wind comes and
goes with its vagrant melodies; but within all is still and
dreamful notwithstanding zither and spinning-wheel.

> " 'Tis the right hour, 'tis the right spot !
>   Would you marvel greatly, dear,
> If I now the right word uttered,
>   At this instant, standing here?
>
> If I speak that word, the midnight
>   With the throes of dayspring quakes ;
> Stream and forest echo louder,
>   And the haunted mountain wakes.
>
> Zither's twang and elfin carols
>   From the mountain fissures ring,
> And the forest burgeons, maddened
>   With untimely birth of spring ;
>
> Burgeons into magic blossoms,
>   Fan-like foliage, flowers bright ;
> Breathes in myriad scents its passion,
>   Quickened by the season's might.
>
> Roses like red flames upstarting
>   Shoot from out the wild turmoil,
> Lilies rear their crystal pillars
>   Heavenward from th' enchanted soil." [1]

I would fain quote the beautiful description of the
Brocken, but that is impracticable. At the summit the
traveller came upon the Brocken Inn (*Brockenhaus*),
and was surprised to find it full. However, he managed

---

[1] These quatrains are from Mr. Francis Storr's charming rendering of the " Berg-Idyllen."

to obtain "a room the size of a closet, where a young merchant, who looked like an emetic powder in a long brown wrapper, had already established himself."

The wild account of the student's carouse would also have to be given in full to do it justice, as also, again, the much-admired description of the fount of the rippling, splashing, hill-stream, the Ilse, and of the beech and birch-clad Ilsenthal. The well-known lyric commencing

> "I am the Princess Ilse
> And I dwell in Ilsenstein,"—

embodies something of the music of "the laughing spirit of Ilsenthal."

Then follow some practical hints about the Upper and Lower Hartz, and a further expatiation upon the dancing Ilse and green Ilsenthal: and then the "Harzreise" concludes with the sudden passionate outcry of a wounded love. I can print but a condensation of it.

"To-day is the first of May. Like an ocean of life Spring over-floods the earth ; the white blossom-foam hangs on the trees ; all is bathed in a hazy glow. . . . It is the first of May, and I think of thee, fair Ilse—or shall I call thee A—— (Amalie), my favourite name? . . . . Green everywhere, the colour of hope. Everywhere miracles are working, flowers bursting into blossom, and my heart, too, will blossom again. My heart, too, is a flower—a strange, rare flower—no modest violet, no laughing rose, no pure lily, no simple flower that fades to-day to bloom again to-morrow. No, this heart is, rather, like one of those monstrous outlandish flowers from the forests of Brazil, which are said to blossom only once in a century. I remember as a boy seeing such a flower. We heard in the night a crack like a pistol-shot—it was the aloe blossoming. Next morning I saw to my astonishment that the low horny plant with its funny broad jagged leaves had now shot up, and bore on its head a glorious flower like a crown. We children were too small to look down on it, but from a wooden stand we peered down on the open calyx, and gazed at the spikes of gold, and inhaled the strange odours that issued from it.

" Yes, A——, not often and not lightly does this heart blossom—to the best of my recollection it has blossomed but once. . . . And however splendid the promise of its opening blossom, I fancy that from want of sunlight and warmth it must have shrivelled miserably, if it was not actually shattered by a dark wintry blast. But now it stirs again, and shoots in my breast, and if you suddenly hear a report—fear not, silly girl, I have not shot myself—but my love is bursting the bud, and is shooting up in lyric flashes, in immortal dithyrambs, in ebullience of song.

" But if this lofty love is too high for thee, girl, set thyself at ease and mount the wooden stand, and look down on the blossoming of my heart."

This brief account of, and the few excerpts from, the "Harzreise," will afford some idea of the freshness and beauty of the original : in order to understand, however, the full extent of this charm it is necessary to know German, not only for the sake of the clear-cut, nervous style of the narrative itself, but also so as to comprehend what a new direction was thereby given to the national literary prose. The whole of the " Reisebilder " is brilliantly written, but the " Harzreise " must, in many respects, be held the most important section, for it was at once pioneer and leader in a new realm.

CHAPTER IV.

THE winter and spring of 1824-5 were spent by Heine at Göttingen, mainly in university studies. In his leisure hours he revised the " Harzreise," and wrote freely though fragmentarily both in prose and verse.

As midsummer drew nigh, a deep oppression settled upon him. This was not due, or at any rate not mainly due, to any manner of poetic nostalgia, or even to the headaches which rendered so many hours of the spring days abhorrent to him; but to the imminence of that act upon which he had often brooded—his conversion to Christianity.

Even if I had the inclination, or this were the place, to discuss this matter of apostasy in all its complex detail, it would be impracticable to give here anything like an adequate summary of all the " pros and cons." A small volume upon the subject might easily be made from Heine's own writings—from his voluminous correspondence, his essays and prose compositions, and even from his poems. But it is easy to realize that far too much foolish disputation has already been expended upon an act which, at its worst, was involuntary so far as personal choice was concerned, and had several potent arguments in its favour.

Heine was proud of the splendid past of his race; proud of its vigour and intensity; its indomitable patience; its reticence in dark days, its exuberance in happier seasons; proud of its highest achievements and of its loftiest aspirations. In his heart brooded ever the *Juden-Schmerz*, the "great sorrow of Israel." The accumulated bitterness of centuries was often with him: and a deep resentment against the long tyranny of the ages wrought havoc with his "emancipated" sympathies. On the other hand, the narrow-mindedness, the bigotry, the gross aspirations, the impotent mental indolence, of the lower Jewish classes in Germany, filled him with angry impatience, when not actually with disgust. The Jew-German, the hybrid who clung to all that was worthless in Israelitism and imitated or adopted what was mean and vulgar among the Teuton Gentiles, was his abhorrence. Like the Mr. McTavish who preferred his whiskey neat and the water any time that might be convenient, he liked the genuine Jew but did not relish the amalgam. From his boyhood he had learned that to be a Jew probably meant social degradation and many hardships; that to be a Gentile signified such lordship over circumstances as might be in the power of the individual to attain. Father, mother, uncle, relatives, and friends both Christian and Hebraic, had persistently pointed out to him that not only worldly advantage, but duty (that poor, insulted, daily-tortured word), should impel him to a decision in conformity with their. advice. Heine was much too intelligent not to

perceive the cynical materialism which lay behind all the
delicately-veiled hypocrisy of the "duty" plea, but he
was forced to recognize the justice of two points : that,
in accordance with German law, he could not as a Jew
follow any of the liberal professions (except that of
medicine, for which he had no capacity) ; and that he
had availed himself of his uncle's generosity to the
express end that he should, when the time came, take
his degree of doctor of law—which could not be done
without a prior separation from the Israelitish persuasion.
Moreover, it must be borne in mind that Heine had had
no religious training worth the name. His father had
been indifferent to all save the letter of Judaism ; his
mother had never disguised the fact that she was a
philosophical Deist of the Voltairean school. Early left
to understand that Reason was the sole arbiter amid the
turbulence of creeds, the young poet very naturally came
to believe that the religious profession of the individual
was a matter of no importance, since Jew and Christian,
Deist and Atheist, Agnostic and Mystic lived much the
same lives, had much the same virtues and vices, enjoyed
or suffered from much the same woes or pleasures, and
lived comfortably or uncomfortably with much the same
ideals. It was a case of *sauve qui peut*—but the salva-
tion to be sought was immunity from the ills of life, and
not enfranchisement from the wrath of any gods that be.
It is to Heine's credit that, in these circumstances, he
was, both before and after his "conversion," torn this
way and that by conflicting emotions; that he despised
the law, but even more those who yielded to its demands;
that he scorned, even while he fulfilled, his own act.

Two years ere he nominally became a "Protestant and a Lutheran to boot," he wrote as follows to his friend Moser : "As you may imagine, the question of baptism is much discussed here. No one of the family is against it except myself : and this self is a very obstinate person. You know enough of my ways of thinking to be able to infer that baptism to me is an act of indifference, that I set no great store by it as a symbol, and that the power to defend the rights of my unhappy brethren is likely to weigh more with me. Notwithstanding, I consider it a degradation and a stain upon my honour to submit to baptism in order to qualify myself for State employment in Prussia. I really don't know how I shall get out of this fatal dilemma. I shall end by turning Catholic in desperation, and hanging myself. We are living in evil times ; rogues take the lead, and our leaders must turn rogues. I understand very well now the words of the Psalmist, ' Give me my daily bread that I may not blaspheme Thy name.' My principles are not in the least influenced by the thought of wealth or poverty, but my actions unfortunately are. Yes, Heinrich Heine is very small. In fact, little M—— is greater than I. This is no jest, but my soberest, grimmest earnest." Later on, in a letter of even greater bitterness, the following passage occurs : "Solon said that no man should be counted happy before his death, and one may add that no one before he dies should be reckoned an honest man. I am glad that old Friedländer and Bendavid are old and will soon die, so that they at least are safe, and our times will not be open to the reproach that they have not produced one blameless character. Forgive

me my ill-humour, most of it is directed against myself.
I often get up at night and stand before the looking-
glass and rail at myself."

It is indisputable that Heine would have had the sympathy of all high-minded persons if at any cost he had
refused to debase himself by a lie. Later on he had to go
to Paris; true, he might have gone earlier and trusted to
his intellectual powers—or have starved. But he did
not; and we have to look upon his action as impartially
as may be. In no country has his apostasy been so
condemned as in England. We are—of course—such a
deeply religious and spiritual people that the material
way of looking at life is abhorrent to us; *we* would never
let material interests clash with our noble principles. To
benighted foreigners it does sometimes seem as if the
upholders of the opium trade, the despoilers of the weak,
the land-grabbers *par excellence*, laid a little too much
stress on their immaculate motives in the conduct of
individual and national life—but of course that is Con-
tinental prejudice and envy. Still there are some among
us so un-British as to believe that nine-tenths of our
fellow countrymen would promptly have acted in the
same way as did Heine, had they been German Jews
early in the present century. The only distinction would
have been that the apostasy would have caused little
spiritual disturbance before, and none at all after, the
event.

It is quite certain that Heine did not discard Judaism
out of any spirit of mockery. He had little religious
belief—as things were, how could he have much, or any?
—and, on the whole, what disturbed him most was the

apparent severance from his race, the desertion from a *cause* rather than from a *creed.* When the irrevocable act had been performed, his eyes were opened to its worst aspects. He commenced to pay the penalty from the outset. To his enemies he was always the " Jew ": to loyal Israelites he was the apostate : to Christians— German Christians—he was a man and a brother, in the same way as a negro convert is a fellow-citizen of a Louisianian or South Carolinian. He endured his self-inflicted hurt with lifelong regret, and, to his credit, never sought to palliate his mistake.

It amounts to this: Heine's hand was forced; he yielded against his better judgment ; he fulfilled his duty to his relatives, as they and he conceived it ; and as he had not then a Deity to consult, he did not take Providence into account. That he acted reprehensibly may be admitted freely : that his action warrants abuse of him as a cynical mocker, as a sinner of sinners, is as absurd as it is hypocritical.

It was in later life, when the spirit of raillery had become the dominant impulse, that he treated the question with that mocking laugh with the sob below it which still sounds through literature distinct from every other voice. As co-religionists the Jews were, he declared, "an accursed generation (*ein Urübelvolk*), which came from Egypt, the land of crocodiles and priestcraft, and brought with them, besides skin diseases and the vessels of gold and silver that they stole, a so-called positive religion and a so-called church."

In a note to his "Latest Poems and Thoughts," he gives a different and a more whimsical account of his reasons

for apostasy : " That I became a Christian is the fault
of those Saxons who changed sides so suddenly at
Leipzig; or else of Napoleon who need never have gone
to Russia; or of the schoolmaster who taught him geo-
graphy at Brienne, and neglected to tell him that it was
very cold at Moscow in winter. If Montalembert
became minister and could drive me away from Paris, I
would turn Catholic; *Paris vaut bien une messe.*" But
between the Heine of Paris and the Heine of Göttingen
there is a very marked distinction.

It was on June 28, 1825, that Heine went to Heiligenstadt (a small Prussian town not far from Göttingen), and there, in the house of the clergyman of the
place, was baptised as a Lutheran Protestant. It was on
this occasion that he formally renounced his birth name
Harry for that of Heinrich—or, more exactly, for those
of Christian Johann Heinrich.

He had now nothing to keep him in Göttingen save
the matters of his doctorial degree. In the spring he
had, in accordance with custom, sent in his Latin Petition
along with a German letter addressed to the faculty. In
the latter he had set forth very frankly that though for
six years he had been nominally studying law he had
allowed his preference for literature to occupy much of
his time, although at Göttingen jurisprudence had carried
the day. He also alluded to " the persistent headache "
which had afflicted him for two years, and had so materially interfered with his duties. It was with a sinking
heart that he addressed his " Petition " to the Dean of
the Faculty, the crabbed old Professor Hugo : and while
he never expected to issue from the examination bril-

liantly, he much feared that his efforts would prove disastrously unsuccessful. Early in May the dreaded examination came off, and Heine just managed to avoid failure. Though he only took a third class, the Rubicon was crossed—and the main object of his university studies was achieved. It was between "Examinations" and degree-day that the formal conversion from Judaism took place at Heiligenstadt. When, on July 20th, the doctorial candidates had to display their Latinity to the best possible advantage, Heine came off but indifferently well—one mistake in the use of *caput*, indeed, caused much amusement to the audience and chagrin to himself. What, however, removed any sting was the kindly eulogium pronounced upon the young poet by Professor Hugo, an eulogium which included an allusion to Heine's poetic rank as only inferior to that of Goethe. After the ceremony the gruff old Dean said some pleasant things to the young doctor-of-law, and invited him to a ride and thereafter to supper. Formerly Heine had written of Hugo as an obtuse and grumpy old pedant : when he wrote to Moser after degree-day he remarked, "I find, therefore, that Gans is wrong when he speaks slightingly of Hugo. *Hugo is one of the greatest men of our country!*"

Although Salomon Heine was pleased that his *dummer* nephew had at last taken his degree and was now in a position to make his way in life, he refused to grant any further definite allowance. On the other hand, he recognized that Heinrich's health was not assured, and he agreed that the young "doctor" should have a thorough holiday by the sea-side ere attempting to settle down in Hamburg.

Heine yearned for the sea, not merely on account of its curative effect upon him, but because his passion for it was deep and permanent. He was now anxious to go to some more northern and more ocean-girdled place than Cuxhaven, and finally settled upon Norderney, an island off the coast of Holland. Although it was the resort of numerous Hanoverian families, there were many opportunities for any one who might desire solitude and simplicity of life.

The charming Book ii. of the " Reisebilder " (" Norderney ") describes Heine's way of living and what occupied him mentally at this time.[1] Lyrics are not interspersed in its pages as in the " Harzreise," probably because so many were then inspired by the sea that they would have crowded out the prose altogether. It was at Norderney that he wrote the first part of his beautiful and unique cycle of sea poems, twenty-two in number, collectively entitled " Die Nordsee " (" The North Sea ") —to which further allusion will be made later on.

The Norderney volume is as admirably written as it is interesting. There are two or three good translations of it (none better than Mr. Storr's), and all lovers of Heine's poetry, particularly of his sea poetry, should read what he has to say about the island and his stay there. But it is well worth perusal, apart from its descriptive interest, for the numerous poetic passages which render its pages so fascinating. Some of its sayings have passed into the currency of stock phrases: *e.g.*, " The human spirit has its rights, which are eternal, and will not be hemmed in by dogmas, or

[1] Although written in 1825-6, not published till 1828.

rocked to sleep by the lullaby of church bells : "—" Works of genius are immutable and immortal, while criticism shifts and changes. Criticism expresses the current views of the time being, and only appeals to that time ; and unless it is itself, in some measure, a work of art, it dies with its age : "—" No true genius will suffer any one to prescribe the paths it should follow, nor can any critic presume to indicate its probable course."

It is in " Norderney " that occur the fine sayings concerning Sir Walter Scott—particularly that of the more or less unconscious pathos, "the dominant note in his romances—the note that has sent a thrill of pain through the world." Scott's " History of Napoleon Buonaparte " he alludes to almost with more pity than scorn, as " a blasphemy in twelve volumes." Although Heine's admiration of Napoleon was excessive, and his hatred of England to some extent crude and incomprehensive, it must not be overlooked that everywhere save in England his views concerning the relative greatness of Wellington and Napoleon are more or less thoroughly endorsed.

Heine gave such free rein to his satire in " Norderney " that, especially in Hanover, he was heartily abused in turn. As in the instance of Autommarchi, Napoleon's physician, "a stiletto, rather than a style," would be the right word to use at times for his language. The Hanoverian and Prussian aristocrats did not relish freedom of speech, and for such licence of withering satire they would fain have repaid its author with an award similar to that granted to the unfortunate Bonnivard of Chillon.

He often looked back longingly to the time spent at

Norderney. For the most part it was occupied in long
rambles by the seashore; in sailing to and fro in a small
boat, at the will of the tides or light winds—-when his
chief enjoyment, as it was with Shelley, was to lie on his
back and look up at the drifting clouds—or in making
more ambitious marine excursions. In the evenings he
would wander along the moonlit sand-dunes, and live and
move for the time being in an enchanted world of nixies
and all manner of strange sea-creatures; or, when the
autumnal rains swept from the sea, he would sit in
some fisherman's hut and, while the fire gleamed and
flickered and the shadows sprang to and fro, would
listen to the weird or romantic legends he loved so well.
It was a happy season, and a fruitful one. He did not
wholly escape from the Hanoverian society which came to
Norderney for the bathing season, for a friend of the
Varnhagens, the Princess of Solms-Lich, insisted upon
showing off "her poet" to all her friends. However,
Heine—after recovery from a sudden, ardent, and very
brief "passion"—soon separated himself from his un-
congenial environment, and betook himself again to his
small boat, his lonely sand-dunes, and the rude cottages
of his fisher friends.

After a short stay with his parents in Lüneburg—a
visit memorable to him for the friendship he then formed
with a life-long intimate, Rudolf Christiani — he once
more took up residence in Hamburg, with the purpose
of making a living there in his legal capacity.

But his hatred of Hamburg increased rather than
diminished with familiarity. The life, the city, the customs and manners of the citizens, all were abhorrent to

him. As long as he lived he never ceased to anathema-
tise "that cursed Hamburg." His dire despondency
was increased by the dislike of some of his relatives, the
hostility of others, the gruff closefistedness of his uncle,
the taunts of apostasy levelled against him by Christians
who resented even a converted Jew, and by Jews who
hated a varnished Christian, and by such pettinesses of
animosity and uncharitableness as he never found elsewhere.

Uncle Salomon did not know what to make of his
nephew. Report spoke of him as a true and even as a
great lyric poet, as a possible rival to Goethe, Schiller,
and Uhland; but as the old merchant bitterly remarked,
if Heinrich had only shown ordinary cleverness he
would never have had to take to "making books" for
a living.

One outcome of this residence in Hamburg was acquaintance, and ultimately business-relations, with the
publisher, Julius Campe. The latter was in early middle
age, and the most pushing and independent of all German publishers: on the other hand, he was certainly
not of a liberal disposition so far as monetary outlay was
concerned. He was quick to perceive that Heine was a
man of exceptional mark, and it was under his auspices
that in May (1826) the first portion of the "Reisebilder"
saw the light. The "Reisebilder" ("Travel-Pictures") as
then published comprised the "Harzreise"—which had
already appeared in the "Gesellschafter"—the cycle of
poems called "The Return Home" ("Die Heimkehr"),
five legendary poems, and the first section of the "North
Sea Poems." Heine, or possibly Campe, considered

7

that it would be wiser to postpone publication of
" Norderney," with its Napoleonic acclaims and anti-
Hanoverian tirades, until the less " dangerous " first portion of the " Reisebilder " should create a demand for
future work by the author.

The book was an immediate success, and every week
its reputation grew. From the outset every one was
charmed with " The Hartz Tour," and with most of the
lyrics, although there was for long a protest against the
new and, as many thought, uncouth verse embodied in
the " North Sea " cycle. There were not wanting critics,
however, who recognized that at last Heine had fulfilled
to some extent the promise of his youth, and that in
power, beauty, and, above all, in distinction, the " Nordsee " was unrivalled in German poetry. These North
Sea poems must be read in the original, and even then
their perusal should be from the German standpoint.
Heine was aware of their inadequacy *as* sea poems ;
but, as he explained to his friend, Adolf Stahr, what good
would it have been to have written what no one would
have understood ? In 1825 the sea was as unfamiliar to
most Germans as were submarine wonders to schoolboys
ere the advent of Jules Verne. It was necessary that he
should be intelligible : and to be intelligible he had per-
force to dwell upon ordinary aspects and interpret only
the public music of the sea. Now it is different. Steam
has rendered solitude almost as scarce as a just man.
Every one knows the sea, and if Nereus still abide in its
depths he probably resents the vulgar familiarity wherewith his once inviolable realm is now daily insulted.
But in Heine's days such familiarity was rare ; and as for

assumed love, it was non-existent, because then conventionality had not demanded sentiment in speaking of "the uncomfortable water-way dignified by the name of Ocean."

The North Sea poems are written in irregular blank verse : they are, however, most resonant and musical—filled, as it were, with the robust harmonies which conveyed the unembodied song-breaths to the poet as he wandered by the wave-swept shores of Norderney.

Those who are unable to read the originals cannot do better, if they be familiar with French, than become acquainted with the "Nord-see" through the delightful version in rhythmic prose of Gérard de Nerval. There have been various renderings of a few or of all the North Sea poems by English and American translators, but while some of these have reproduced in no slight measure the beauty of thought and diction which characterizes the originals, hardly any adequately convey the simple and yet subtle music which makes Heine's own strains so enchanting. The following translation, however, is at once literal and poetic, and will convey to the English reader a good idea both of the manner and substance of the original.

FRIEDEN.

Hoch am Himmel stand die Sonne,
Von weissen wolken umwogt ;
Das Meer war still :

PEACE.

High in the heavens stood the sun
Cradled in snowy clouds ;

The sea was still:
And musing I lay at the helm of the ship,
Dreamily musing,—and half in waking
And half in slumber, I gazed upon Christ,
The Saviour of man.
In streaming and snowy garment
He wandered, giant-great,
Over land and sea ;
His head reached high to the heavens,
His hands he stretched out in blessing
Over land and sea ;
And as a heart in his bosom
Bore he the sun,
The sun all ruddy and flaming,
And the ruddy and flaming sunny-heart
Shed its beams of mercy
And its beauteous, bliss-giving light,
Lighting and warming
Over land and sea.

Sounds of bells were solemnly drawing
Here and there, like swans were drawing
By rosy bands the gliding ship,
And drew it sportively tow'rd the green shore,
Where men were dwelling, in high and turreted
O'erhanging town.
O blessing of peace ! How still the town !
Hush'd was the hollow sound
Of busy and sweltering trade,
And through the clean and echoing streets
Were passing men in white attire,
Palm-branches bearing,
And when two chanced to meet
They viewed each other with inward intelligence,
And trembling, in love and sweet denial,
Kissed on the forehead each other,
And gazed up on high
At the Saviour's sunny-heart,

The final impression made by "Die Nordsee," however, is not one of mockery or bitterness, but of pathetic
sadness and solemn beauty. We are ever reminded
of the poet's love for the windy dunes fringed by " the
deep-voiced neighbouring ocean," and are haunted by
his echoes of the sea's music. "I love it as my own
soul," he cries; "I often feel as if the sea must be my
soul. And as in the sea there are hidden water-plants,
which come to the surface only at the moment they
blossom, and sink again the moment that they fade, so at
times there float up from the depths of my soul wondrous
flowers of fancy which gleam and bloom and die."

Two months after the publication of the "Reisebilder," that is, about the end of July, Heine again
went to Norderney for his health's sake, and doubtless
also because he found the unbroken continuation of his
Hamburg life intolerable. Here, as in the previous
early autumn, he enjoyed and greatly benefited by his
stay in the island. Once again he spent the long August
days in lying idly in his drifting boat, for hours watching
the movement of the clouds overhead or gazing down
into the green depths below him, rapt in fanciful dreams
of buried cities, of strange sea creatures, of shy nereids
and perilous nixen : or, when the golden September
moon rose over the North Sea, wandered till long past
midnight along the wave-echoing sand-dunes. It was a
period of keen intellectual stimulus. Innumerable subjects for treatment in prose and verse haunted him from
waking till sleep—among other themes was his "Faust,"
which he had not yet determined to discard—and daily
the irresistible lyrical impulse rose like an intoxicant in

his heart and brain, and, as it were, burgeoned forth in blossom-snatches of song and flawless flowers of verse. Yet he was seldom free from the despondency which for many months past had caused life to be so full of *ennui* to him. A deep discontent, an irritation, a hesitant determination—these and other moods rendered him distraught and weary. Though he enjoyed himself less than on his previous visit, though "the pretty women were not so pretty as in 1825," nor was even the sea so romantic, he realized that the fault was with his own disposition. From the bathing he received marked good, and his headaches became more infrequent and much less violent. Nor, though disenchantment seemed the order of the day, was he altogether without those passionate illusions which come only to the enthusiasts of life. One moonlit night he walked by the sea along with a beautiful girl : no word was spoken, but hand in hand they wandered vaguely onward. "There was but one deep look, and the sea made music to it. The moon seemed to shine to show me that some glorious things existed yet for me in the world." This romantic "interlude," however, came to nothing—if we can so speak of an episode that left the bright glamour of romance over a day of youth, a light that died not from memory through all the weariness and suffering of the years that followed.

Towards the end of September, Heine returned to his parents' home in Lüneburg, this time by way of Bremen. What to do he knew not, though he had quite made up his mind not to attempt a legal or any other career in Hamburg. His wish to leave Germany grew stronger,

and moreover it coincided with advice from the Varnhagens, Moser, and other disinterested friends. As he
bitterly remarked, Germany was no place for a Jew—
even a converted Jew. His literary prospects were sufficiently good to enable him to feel assured of an actual
living, at any rate for a time; but he naturally feared
that if he exiled himself, especially if he took up permanent residence in Paris, he would give further cause of
offence to relatives, friends, and enemies, and render his
pen a very untrustworthy bread-winner.

The last quarter of the year was mainly occupied in
the writing and revision of the contents of the second
volume of the "Reisebilder." For some time past the
idea of a visit to England, or rather to London, had
taken possession of him, and he determined that if he
could come to a satisfactory arrangement with Campe he
would fulfil his desire while it was practicable. In
January (1827) he was, accordingly, again in Hamburg,
but it was not until April that he found himself able to
sail for the Thames—an event which occurred on the
very day when the second series of the "Reisebilder"
was published.

The volume consisted of the already described "Norderney," and of a third book called "Buch Le Grand,"
(after the Napoleonic drummer Le Grand, who made
such an impression upon the author as a lad in Düsseldorf at the time of the French occupation), besides the
second cycle of the North Sea poems, and some letters.

"The Book of Ideas" is the collective title of that portion of the "Reisebilder" which comprises the "Buch Le
Grand." It contains some very able, witty, and eloquent

writing, as well as much interesting autobiographical matter, but it is in point of construction inferior to the "Harzreise" or "Norderney." More than any other composition by Heine it shows the influence of Sterne, but even here, I think, his indebtedness is of a very vague kind. Upon much of the book I have already drawn when dealing with the poet's youth. In this "Book of Ideas" is the famous tirade against England for her "fell hospitality" to Napoleon, and the prophecy as to her humiliation in the fulness of time: an exaggerated and wayward impulse which the author himself laughed at in later life. The "motive" of the book would seem to be the cynical weariness and bitterness hinted at in the motto which is again and again quoted—"She was lovable, and he loved her; but he was not loveable, and she loved him not." In no other of his writings is Heine's love of abstract phantasy more remarkable than in some portions of "The Book of Ideas." Let the curious read, for instance, the fourth chapter, "The Flowers of the Brenta"; or the fifth, with its strange blending of Oriental and German sentimentalism; or the sixteenth, with its fantastic love episode; or that other episode in chapter eighteen of Laura and the knight. A fantastic dalliance with beautiful words, for often it is no more than this, is one characteristic of Heine's genius: the following is an example to the point—

"An enchanted nightingale is sitting on a branch of red coral in calm ocean, singing a song of the loves of my ancestors; pearls peep curiously from their shells, strange water flowers shiver with emotion, wise sea snails with iridescent china-towers on their backs crawl out to listen, sea-roses blush with confusion, yellow star-

fish and myriad-hued jellyfish stir and stretch themselves—all is
alive and agape " (chap. v.).

One of the wittiest things ever said by Heine concludes
the ninth chapter, that upon the death of Napoleon at
St. Helena. Here, as was the bitter humourist's wont,
he not only made a clever point, but paid off an old
score against a pedantic professor who had, moreover,
often given him deep offence by his sneers against
and hatred of the great Emperor.

"Strange," remarks Heine as he pulls himself up after
a burst of fiery eloquence, "strange, the three greatest
adversaries of the Emperor have already found an awful
fate. Londonderry cut his throat ; Louis XVIII. rotted
on his throne ; and Professor Saalfeld is still professor at
Göttingen."

The poet was in London when he heard from his
friend Varnhagen of the immense sensation his book
had caused. Almost immediately upon publication the
Government had issued an interdict against its sale in
Prussia, Hanover, or any of the North German States,
not only on account of its Napoleonic fervour, but from
its outspokenness and dangerous licence of wit. This
public prohibition, however, increased the demand, and
ere long it was privily circulated in every corner of Germany. The literary world was at once fascinated by its
power, and alarmed at what course the new comet would
take,—perhaps one that would prove so great as to
extinguish every lesser light ; while the general public
stood pleased, but agape.

Naturally the author was elated at the success of the
" Reisebilder." Admiration of the North Sea poems,

delight in " Norderney," doubt or abuse anent "The Book of Ideas"—all went to increase his reputation, and to make his voice a power in Germany. Already he had a considerable audience; now he could be sure that for whatever he might have to say there would thenceforth be no lack of audience. "If I preserve my health," he wrote to Moser, from London, "I can now do much. I have now a far-sounding voice. You shall hear it many a time thundering against the beadles of though and the oppressors of holiest rights." To use his own phrase, Heine now definitely enlisted himself as "a champion of the Holy Ghost."

CHAPTER V.

THERE has been among us, at different times, such an absurd outcry against that portion of Heine's "Reisebilder" known as the "English Fragments," that it is difficult to approach the subject without undue bias one way or another. One would think that Heine's satirical shafts against Frenchmen or Germans were mere unadorned truths, whereas anything spoken against England must of necessity be due to prejudice or envy! Or again, are we not nationally apt, to say the least of it, to be oblivious to the fact that we have ourselves long mercilessly ridiculed foreigners of all races? As some anonymous writer upon Heine once remarked, " His ridicule of English awkwardness is as merciless as— English ridicule of German awkwardness."

I do not intend to dwell upon these "English Fragments"—not merely because such dilation would be more or less controversial, but also because Heine visited England at a time with which *we* have nothing to do. Whether he found it as delectable as the city of Haroun al Raschid, or as foul as the native quarters of Calcutta, cannot matter to us, since the London of to-day and its present inhabitants have undergone such essential changes. These threescore years have wrought a vital improvement in the South-English ; they have made a great step—they have advanced from pigheadedness to mere insular obstinacy.

It will depend upon the knowledge and sympathies of the reader whether he be amused or offended by Heine's remarks upon England and the English. As one of his readers I may state that I see little or nothing to disagree from in his scathing criticisms : where I think he has gone astray is in his blindness to the better aspects of our social and national life, to our counterbalancing good qualities. It must be borne in mind, both by those who sympathize with and those who resent Heine's opinions, that he was not, at the time of his visit, well fitted to judge, so that his views, whether congratulatory or unfavourable, can have no real weight one way or the other. He arrived in anything but good health ; his prospects were the reverse of brilliant ; his pecuniary position was only temporarily assured ; he could not speak English, although he could read it ; trouble and suspense were then in the air, and all earnest folk were heavily preoccupied ; and the weather was wretched. If Heine had any thoughts of " Merry England "—and he had read Chaucer, Shakespeare, and Milton, at least in part—he might well have been disgusted ; a cold east wind swept the Strand from end to end, the roadways were thick with slush, and overhead the smut-stained snows drizzled and dripped. Could even a philosopher, much less a poet, be expected to be cheerful and to take sanguine views in these circumstances ? No wonder that

Heine exclaimed, "Send a philosopher to London, but no poet. . . . This downright earnestness of all things, this colossal uniformity, this machine-like movement, this moroseness even in pleasure, this exaggerated London, smothers the imagination and rends the heart." [1]

The best and wittiest remark in the "English Fragments" is that anent Liberty. "An Englishman loves Freedom as he loves his lawfully-wedded wife ; he regards her as a possession, and, if he does not treat her with special tenderness, yet if need be he knows how to defend her. A Frenchman loves Freedom as he does his chosen bride ; he will commit a thousand follies for her sake. A German loves Freedom as he does his old grandmother. And yet, after all, no one can ever tell how things may turn out. The grumpy Englishman, in an ill-temper with his wife, is capable of some day putting a rope round her neck. The inconstant Frenchman may become unfaithful to his adored mistress, and be seen fluttering about the Palais Royal after another. But the German will never quite abandon his old grandmother ; he will always keep for her a nook by the chimney-corner, where she can tell her fairy tales to the listening children."

About mid-June Heine went to Ramsgate. The sea wind and bracing Kentish air wrought great benefit to his nerves and general condition, and (as was the wont of this susceptible poet) he found time in the fortnight he was there to make love. The object of his inflammable affections was a blithe and beautiful *Irlandaise*,

---

[1] During his stay in London Heine lodged at No. 32, Craven Street, Strand.

she who afterwards figures so prominently in the fourth
(" Italien ") book of the " Reisebilder."

Among the poems he projected at this time was one to
be called " Ramsgate." The outline of it is interesting
as a model recipe in what Lord Lytton calls the *cuisine à
la Heine.*

" RAMSGATE.

" A great chalk cliff, like a woman's white bosom, upheaves
itself from out the sea, and the lovesick sea yearningly clings about
it, and sportively caresses it in the strong embrace of his wavy
arms. On that white cliff a high town stands, and there, on a high
balcony, is standing a beautiful woman, and she plays delightful
melodies on a Spanish guitar.

" Under the balcony stands a German poet ; and as the charming
melodies float down to him, his spirit involuntarily accompanies
them, and the words burst from him :

> " ' O were I now yon wild sea, thou
> Yon rock, round which his wild waves flow ! '

" Our German poet, however, did not sing these words, he only
thought them. In the first place, he had no voice ; in the second
place, he was timid. When that same evening he walked by the
side of the beautiful woman along the seashore, he was as silent as
the dumb.

" The waves wildly press against the white stone-bosom, and over
the water the moon throws her long beam, like a golden bridge to
the Land of Promise."

Lord Lytton is very severe upon Heine for having
in this and other instances, " committed emotions to
memory for future use." It is true that, as Goethe said,
emotions are like oysters and should be enjoyed fresh,
since they will not bear keeping ; also, so far, " that the
natural language of wit and passion is surely one of
spontaneous response to the challenge of the passing

moment." But surely remembered excitement may be as
keen—as it may even be more subtle, more rarefied
—as at the "psychical moment." Poetry, as one of our
own greatest poets has said, is "emotion remembered in
tranquillity;" and if Wordsworth had written "poetry is
emotion emotionally remembered," few, I presume, would
have disagreed from the dictum. What distinction is
there between noting down at the moment some scenic
effect or brilliant expression, some lovely or impressive
phase or transient aspect of human or external life, and
commemorating at some indefinite later date the emotion
wherewith such fortunate rainbow-glimpses were observed?
Many poets have taken heed of their emotions, as well as
of their observations, for "possible future use"; and it
might well be that the critical inquirer would find that more
poems of high quality—excepting short lyrics—have been
thus produced than as the immediate outcome of strong
feeling within the pristine duration of the latter. It is
possible, it is often inevitable, for the poet to experience the
poetic emotion without capacity for immediate adequate
expression; and in such an instance is it not well to con-
serve the impression till the emotion become rhythmic?
A few treasured words, a single word even, may be sufficient to call to mind a fair company of thoughts and
visions: without which record everything might have
passed into oblivion. Heine, though in a sense the most
impulsively lyrical of modern poets, did not disdain
"memoranda"—very wisely, I think, with all due defer-
ence to Lord Lytton. Here is one other example,[1] this
time commended by Lord Lytton for its beauty.

[1] Both are from the "Letzte Gedichte und Gedanken" ("Last
Poems and Thoughts"), 1869.

"BEFORE A CATHEDRAL.

"*Beim Anblick eines Domes.*

"Six hundred years wert thou a-building; and now, in a single moment, dost thou enjoy repose, after a labour of six centuries. As the waves of ocean, so around thee have flowed the generations of mankind, and yet no stone of thine has been shaken. This mausoleum of Catholicism, which it built for itself whilst yet alive, is the stony husk of an extinct sentiment. (The bells that strike the hours, above, ironically.) All within this stone house once flourished, a living word. But all within is the word now dead. It is only outside that it yet lives, in the stony rind."

The poet remained in London for a few weeks after his return from Ramsgate, and on the 8th of August, the day upon which Canning died, he brought to an end his only visit to this country. When he took his departure it was with a very slightly modified opinion of our many shortcomings. The nation might be a great one, and doubtless had many fine qualities, but he could not endure "the genuine British narrowness" (*echtbrittische Beschränktheit*), while, for purposes of speech, our very language was to him but *der Zischlaut des Egoismus*—the "hiss of egoism."

He did not, however, return straight to Hamburg, but, to the surprise of his German acquaintances, who thought he would shirk the company of those whom he had satirized so scathingly, suddenly made his reappearance at Norderney. The island, however, was too full, and, as he craved for rest and quiet, he betook himself to the neighbouring isle of Wangerode, for a fortnight's repose ere his return to Hamburg.

The first incident that occurred in the latter city was an angry interview between Salomon Heine and his "incorrigible fool of a nephew." When the latter set out for London his uncle, besides having paid his travelling expenses, gave him a letter of credit on Rothschild for £400 : this, however, he explained, was a mere matter of form ; it was not to be looked upon as a negotiable draft ; it was meant, in a word, to give weight to Herr Salomon's letter of introduction and its request for courteous assistance for Heinrich in the ways of pleasure and instruction. A few days after Master Heinrich had arrived in London, however, he had duly presented for payment this " formal " letter. With part of the money he had cleared off his German debts ; a goodly sum he had kept for " present and imminent expenses "; and the remainder he had sent to his friend Varnhagen von Ense in trust for him against the tolerably certain day of need. Heine really seems to have believed that his uncle intended the money for him ultimately, and that his warning only signified precautionary advice. Very wrothful was the old banker when he learned what had happened. When " the incorrigible " called at the office he was met with furious reproaches, to which he listened quietly with an aggravating, mocking air. To the culminating "empty-headed do-nothing, will you never be good for anything but to throw money out of the window ? " he replied, with an audacious insolence that staggered the great banker—" My dear uncle, did you really expect not to have to pay for the honour of bearing my name ? "

Heine had now definitely made up his mind that even if he did not migrate to Paris, he would not attempt to practise the legal profession in Hamburg. Yet he could give no satisfactory reply to his uncle as to what he would do, and so naturally wroth was Herr Salomon at what he considered reprehensible idleness, that he threatened all manner of repudiations.   Moreover a rumour came to the old man's ears that his nephew had fallen deeply in love with the beautiful actress Teresa Pache, and although he found that Heine was not really entangled, though certainly intimate, with the lovely "Star of Sevilla," he the more vehemently urged him to adopt whatever business or profession he liked, so long as he settled to "a reputable course of life."   It was while attending to the proofs of the " Buch der Lieder " that, through the good offices of Varnhagen von Ense, Heine received an offer from Baron Cotta, the famous Munich publisher.   This offer was that the poet should join the irregular staff of the " Morgenblatt," and assist in the editing of the " Allgemeinen Politischen Annalen ; " and, of course, it was gladly accepted.

Ere he left Hamburg he underwent a painful experience. One day he called at his uncle's house, and there met once more his cousin Amalie.   Although the wife of Herr Friedlander and the mother of two children, and in some respects a somewhat *passée* young woman of seven and twenty, she still had much of the old charm for her lover.   There were no reproaches, no " indiscretions "— they met, and they parted.   That is all we know.   Probably Frau Friedlander had a transient sentimental sensation, until her attention was attracted by her husband or one of her little girls ; as for Heine, he went forth from Hamburg feeling that the world " smelt of dried-up violets."

In the chill autumnal weather the poet travelled southward. At Lüneburg he stopped for a few days with his parents; nor when he bade them good-bye had he any foreboding of the fact that he would never again see his father. His mother was proud of his literary success; his prose she understood, his poetry she condoned. At the same time she shook her head in remonstrance at her eldest-born's waywardness—in three years he would be thirty, and yet he was without any assured income or even definite prospects. From Göttingen, which the author of the "Harzreise" must have entered with a curious sensation, but where he spent a pleasant flying visit to his friend Sartorius, he journeyed along bleak and muddy roads to Cassel. Here he met the brothers Grimm; but what makes his brief sojourn in Cassel so noteworthy is that it was on that occasion Ludwig Grimm the youngest of the three brothers, and an able engraver of portraits, made a likeness in profile of the poet—the only profile portrait of Heine that exists. But much more really memorable were the three days that he spent with Ludwig Börne at Frankfürt-am-Main.

Börne was a passionate enthusiast, of a type far too emphatic to suit the Hellenic temperament of the author of the "Buch der Lieder." The two men, indeed, were of radically opposite nature. Despite his Jewish blood, Heine to a great extent was, as he himself declared, a Hellene, a modern Pagan: Börne, on the other hand, was a typical Israelite. The poet was intensely sensuous and keenly realistic, alert for all emotions and experiences however perilous, exquisitely alive to the beautiful wheresoever and howsoever it might be manifested: whereas the patriot-politician and author was ascetic in his habits

and tastes, of a fiery and spiritual earnestness, mystical
in matters of religious belief, and inclined to despise all
men dominated by what is called the artistic temperament.   Each, however, enjoyed the other's company for
the three days of Heine's sojourn in Frankfürt, although
the poet realized ere he left that Börne's somewhat
sombre nature had resented his too markedly serene
indifference to what the older man considered vital
questions, and, even more, his delicate but too rapier-
like persiflage.   Had he foreseen the outcome of the
acquaintanceship, he would have avoided Frankfürt as a
place accursed.

Incompatibility of climate and constitution has played
almost as many sorry tricks upon sanguine folk as that
other incompatibility which is so familiar a plea in the
divorce courts.   From the outset, it is true, Heine feared
the effects of the harsh winter air of Munich upon his
far from robust state of health,—so much so that, notwithstanding Baron Cotta's liberal offers, he would not
undertake to remain longer than six months.   That his
fears were well founded is evident from the fact that not
long after his advent into the Bavarian capital he fell
seriously ill.   For Heine's sake it is much to be regretted
that Munich proved so absolutely unsuitable : had it been
otherwise, he would probably have settled in that city,
and prospered.   It was then, under the liberal *régime* of
King Ludwig, the Athens of Germany ; and, moreover,
the poet was favourably received not only by the Cottas
and their friends, and by acquaintances of the Varnhagens
and other Berlin intimates of old days, but also, on
account of his literary fame, by the aristocratic society

of the place. There was no lack of opportunity of work,
and Baron Cotta—a good and just as well as most able
man—was liberal in all his money dealings.

As soon as he recovered from his severe indisposition,
Heine set to work at his editorial and journalistic labours;
and in his spare hours spent much time in the picture
galleries, which even then made Munich so famous. A
keen sympathy with and insight into what was worthy in
art was one of his distinctive characteristics, and his letters
and articles from Paris show how discriminative and just
a critic he was. He also went out much in society,
and altogether enjoyed himself greatly. He was in the
temporary possession of ample means; and though "there
were only five and a half men in Munich who read," he
took pleasure in their company, and still more in that of
the light-hearted artist fraternity. As usual—" wonder-
fully pleasant relations with women, only they are neither
profitable to my health nor to my work."

When the summer came round, Heine would probably
have risked another winter in Bavaria and signed a new
agreement with Cotta ; but it unfortunately happened
that the " Political Annals " came to a sudden untimely
end, and that the editor-in-chief doubted if he could
collaborate again with his late comrade even if the proprietor set the journal on its legs once more. So the
poet-journalist determined to take advantage of the opportunity and make a trip to North Italy, and this he set
about doing with the less hesitation since he knew that
influential friends, both at King Ludwig's court and in
Berlin, were endeavouring to procure him a remunerative
professorship. It would, certainly, have been a strange

by-play of Fate if Heine had become a professor—a professor, above all, at Göttingen ! But no, it is impossible to think of " Professor Heine," the sedate colleague of the immortal Saalfeld !

Heine had another object in going to Italy besides recreation and instruction. He wished to obtain new effects for the third and concluding series of his " Travel Pictures." " This third series," he wrote to Moser, "shall be a man of war, far more fearfully equipped ; the cannons shall be of greater calibre, and I have discovered quite a new powder for them. Neither shall it carry so much ballast as its predecessor."

So one day in the middle of July, 1828, accompanied by his brother Maximilian (who had come to Munich to study medicine, and was glad of the opportunity of spending a brief holiday in the Tyrol with Heinrich), he set forth for that south for which he had so often yearned. In nothing was he more a Hellene than in his love for flooding sunshine and glowing colour, for his physical respondence to the combined fire and indolence of the Latin or Greek. The Orient and the South : the very words had magic for him. He discovered himself to be kin to Saadi and Firdusi, to Sappho and Anacreon, to Catullus and Theocritus.

At Innsbrück the brothers parted, and the elder was speedily on his way to Italy. At first the weather was wretched, but as he drove through the South Tyrol, the glory of July was upon the land. We can imagine the poet lying back in his post-chaise, looking ever eagerly southward, and perhaps humming the exquisite lyric of Goethe's, " The land where the citrons bloom." In his

"Italien" he has described how he entered Italy, the ancient town of Trent, as in a dream. From Trent he journeyed to Verona, of which he has given a charming record; and thence went by Brescia, Milan, and the battle-field of Marengo to Genoa. How his soul thrilled, he tells us, when the postillion suddenly informed him that they were travelling over the scene of Napoleon's great victory! The thought of war called to his mind the spiritual grandeur of that conflict of man with his mightiest hereditary enemy—Death : and from this he passes on to say that he would fain be remembered as a soldier for humanity rather than as a mere singer of sweet songs. "Poetry," he records, "has always been with me only a sacred plaything, a consecrated instrument as it were. I have ever placed but slight value upon poetic fame, and my future repute troubles me not at all. But if ye will do me honour, lay a sword upon my coffin, for I was an intrepid soldier in the war of the liberation of humanity."

From Genoa he proceeded by sea to Leghorn, and thence by *diligence* to the Baths of Lucca, among whose chestnut woods he remained for four gay and delightful weeks. Charming female companionship, including that of the "bright-eyed, wild-spirited" Irish lady whom he had met at Ramsgate, and a love affair — whether imaginary or partly true it is impossible to say—with the *ballerina* Francesca, made the hours when he was not riding in the forest or strolling by the torrent-courses pass speedily. At other times he kept himself to his room, and wrote some of his Italian sketches for trans-mission to Baron Cotta for insertion in the "Morgenblatt," prior to their publication in book form as the third series of " Reisebilder." We have no such fascinating record of Heine's stay at the Bagni di Lucca as of that of Shelley, who ten years before the advent of the German poet made these high Tuscan forests for ever dear to the lovers of our sweetest singer ; but readers of the last book of the " Reisebilder " will remember the amusing incidents therein set forth. One has but to think of Shelley and of Heine at Lucca in order to realize what an immense difference there is between mere sympathetic admiration and love : one may enjoy, sympathize with, take endless delight in Heine, but one cannot love him. He belongs to that elfin race of whom it is told that they are so charming they can love nothing or no one much save themselves, and who, when they are wooed by other denizens of Faerie, pretend to listen and then vanish and rouse the hill-slopes with their mocking echo-laughter.

From the Bagni di Lucca the poet went to Florence, with which he was delighted beyond measure. The literary outcome of this visit was the well-known fantastic but brilliant "Florentine Nights." In Florence he worked steadily at his "Italian Sketches," and ere long posted the several chapters to Cotta. Meanwhile he waited anxiously for news from Munich anent the expected professorship, but none came. The Minister Schenk had forgotten his promises, or possibly Court influences (including, it may be, that of an offended princess who had asked Heine to take coffee with her, but who had been somewhat arrogantly snubbed by the poet) had been brought to bear upon King Ludwig towards an adverse decision.

While filled with angry impatience, Heine was suddenly

seized with an intense longing to see his father. He could not account for what almost amounted to a foreboding, for during his six weeks' stay in Florence no ill news had come from Hamburg, whither his parents had moved in the summer; yet he could not restrain his apprehensive anxiety. Having hastily made the necessary arrangements, he suddenly set off northward. At Verona he was startled to find his presentiments well founded, for there a letter awaited him informing him that his father was dangerously ill, and adding that he would learn further news at Würzburg. At that town he heard of his father's death from paralysis on the 2nd of December, and of his burial in the Jewish cemetery at Altona.

Heine's grief was not only deep, but, as I have had occasion to remark earlier in this book, life-long. Below all his love-affairs, below his self-love, below his Hellenic lust of life and his Judaic passion for human rights, below every other sentiment lay, deep but unsullied, his love for the genial, kindly, vain, and unfortunate man who was his father. He admired and reverenced his mother, and his affection for her was strong and tender: but he loved his father.

It was a sad ending to what in a letter to Frederika Roberts he alludes as the most splendid year of his life: and the outlook was not the pleasanter from the fact that, as he had learned while hurriedly passing through Munich, the professorship he had looked for was definitely denied him.

After a short stay with his widowed mother in Hamburg he went to Berlin, and in April to Potsdam, where he seems to have lived a retired and melancholy life, though at work upon the "Italian Sketches" for book-form publication. He had temporarily lost heart, and was indifferent to what fate had in store for him : but what he felt most strongly was a growing resentment against the hardship, for one like himself, of life in Prussia. His health, moreover, became more and more uncertain, and the headaches from which he had so long inter- mittently suffered, grew more frequent and harassing : so that when August arrived he determined once more to seek the sea-cure. This time he went to Heligoland, where he remained two months, and then went to Ham- burg refreshed and strengthened by the sea-bathing and the bracing air.

It was January (1830) ere the last book of the " Reisebilder " made its appearance. These " Italian Sketches" were discussed throughout Germany, and even in France, Austria, and Russia : everywhere the scandal was considered too great, and yet everywhere every one sought the book. It was, of course, officially interdicted in Prussia, a matter which rather helped its sale than other- wise. It was pronounced the most brilliant, the wittiest, the most entertaining, the most immoral, the coarsest, the most dangerous, the most revolutionary, the most atheistical book that any German author had ever printed. In the main the first five epithets are unreservedly apt. There is no doubt but that the "Italian Sketches" did Heine more harm than good. It is true they added enormously to his reputation, and made him more than ever a power among the sons of men ; but portions of them raised up such anger and hatred, and even among his friends such indignation and sorrow, that in consequence he endured a life-long hurt. What saved and saves the book is its fine enthusiasm for humanity, its daring assertion of rights, its insight and prognostications,—this, and the wit and extreme beauty of much of the writing. But in parts it is vulgarly coarse and stupid, and occasionally even the style is slovenly. A gross error in taste and judgment was made in the savage attack upon Count Platen. Platen was a poet of considerable standing, though not much more than an accomplished verse-writer, and had un-justifiably attacked Heine : the latter was not a man to forget an enemy, and though he might not always draw the stiletto at the moment, it would simply be because the blade was not sufficiently poisoned. Still, even far greater aggravation would not have excused the attack at the end of the Lucca chapters, where the assailant, hyena-like, worries, drags through the mud and slime, and finally rends to pieces his helpless prey. The outcry against this abuse of critical warfare was as genuine as it was universal, and in after years Heine deeply regretted the misdeed. His own admission is that " Platen might have been a great poet, if he had only had a breath of poetry in him : that he possessed everything needful— pride, irritability, poverty, debts, knowledge—everything with the exception of poetry : in a word, he had thoroughly learned the art of poetic cookery—he wanted nothing but meat and fire to be able to cook. Still, that does not justify the attack I made upon him."

The weak point even in the finest portions of the " Italian Sketches " is that they are the words of a highly-wrought emotionalist, rather than of a thinker. It is true that poetic perception may perceive and foretell the undiscovered country before it is traversed by the intellectual pioneer: but such vision is apt to be accompanied with much delusive glamour. Had Heine known something of Italian, his residence in North Italy would doubtless have been more eventful for him and for us: but in the main he seems to have been susceptible only to the sensuous aspects of that unequalled background of history. It is when he alludes to Freedom that his sympathy is touched to the quick, that his insight is swift and penetrative, that his enthusiasm becomes passionate.

I have the less hesitation in passing by without detailed account the charming " Florentine Nights " from the fact that a tolerable English translation is procurable at a nominal price; but even upon the other chapters of the " Italian Sketches " though, so far as I am aware, no English rendering of them has yet been made, I cannot now dwell. I shall, however, have occasion in the concluding chapter of this volume to allude to some of the most memorable sayings of Heine, in connection with religion and politics, which are to be found in the last book of the " Reisebilder."

From Heligoland Heine went to Hamburg, for he had reason to fear that if he sojourned in Prussia he would ere long find himself in the official building at Spandau allotted, indiscriminately, to blood-stained criminals and political free-lances. Moreover, after his recent literary escapade, he did not relish the idea of the cold shoulder which would greet him even in the Varnhagen circle in Berlin.

There is a very ample and graphic record of him at this time by August Lewald, in the latter's " Aquarelle aus dem Leben." Lewald alludes to his delicacy, the marked tendency of blood to the head, the severe frontal pains, his sensitiveness to sounds (even a clock ticking by night rendered him sleepless and, next day, ill), and his indifference and despondency. Another acquaintance, Ludolf Wienbarg, has recorded the circumstance that Heine, during his Hamburg stay, always seemed like a delayed traveller: months after his arrival he had not wholly unpacked his portmanteau, and altogether was as one who had reached a halting-place for a night, and meant to resume his journey next day.

A miserable period it was he spent in Hamburg, and at last it became insupportable. In the early spring of 1830 he left the hated city for a Holstein village called Wandsbeck, where he could be sure of quiet and leisure, and where he hoped the beneficent influence of April would work him weal. By a curious coincidence—when it is recalled what happened in France a year and a quarter later—he became absorbed in the study of the literature of the French Revolution. To a friend he wrote that for the last ten days he had spoken to no one but Thiers and *dem lieben Gott*, and that he was deep in the perusal of the "History" of the one author, and in the Bible of the other.

In June he crossed from Holstein to the little isle of Heligoland, for the sake of the sea-bathing. One morning, after one of his sleepless nights from excess of vicarious suffering,[1] with his mind full of the passions

---

[1] We have Wienbarg's testimony to the fact that Heine was so overwrought by the story of the Gironde and the insatiable Guillotine, that his health materially suffered. Mignet's "History" sucked his strength away as though it had been a vampire.

and high hopes which accompanied the greatest event
in modern European history, he was thunderstruck by
the news of the Revolution of July. He hurled aside
the book he chanced to be reading, and in a moment
Mignet and Thiers and everything he had been studying
in his island solitude—the Bible, Homer, Treatises upon
Witchcraft, the "History of the Jews," Warnefrid's
"Lombards"—were swept from his mind. He seized
the newspapers, "seething hot intelligence from the Continent. They were sunbeams wrapped up in printer's
paper, and they inflamed my soul into the wildest con-
flagration. It was as though I would set on fire the
whole ocean up to the North Pole with the glow of
enthusiasm and the wild joy which blazed up in me. I
ran like a lunatic about the whole house, and kissed first
our stout hostess, and then her amiable sea-wolf." On
the 10th he again wrote exultantly : "Gone is my yearning for repose. I know now once more what I will, what
I shall, what I must do. I am the son of the Revolution. . . . I will crown my head for the fight of death.
. . . I am all joy and song, all sword and flame !" Here
speaks Heine, the passionate soldier in the War of
Liberation : and it is Heine the poet who writes, "Child
as I am, touching individual events occupy me more than
the whole story in all its significance. Oh could I but
see the dog Medor, . . . who sat till death by the grave
of his master in the court of the Louvre !"

A week or so later he was at Cuxhaven on the return
journey to Hamburg. His exultation is even more
effervescent than of yore; it bubbles up and seethes and
overflows, as though the fount of joy were inexhaustible.

Even in Hamburg, he hears, the people laugh and rejoice at the great event, the tricolour flaunts everywhere, from the mast-heads in the docks to the breasts of the rotund dames at the theatre, and in the streets the strains of the Marseillaise drown the cries even of the fishwives. Much of this imaginary jubilation did not exist, though no doubt Heine, in common with many other ardent liberals, believed in it. It betrays a sanguine nature indeed, that one who had known many disappointments, and whose knowledge of history was so considerable, could still, at the age of thirty, believe in the enfranchisement of the nations of Europe because of a revolution in Paris. The great deeds of July, he declares, will find an echo in the steppes of the Baschkirs as well as among the mountains of Andalusia; and " I see already how the Neapolitan holds his maccaroni and the Irishman his potatoes in his mouth, when the news reaches them : Punchinello is capable of seizing the sword, and Paddy, perhaps, of making a bull at which the Englishman will have no desire to laugh."

Hamburg had invariably acted upon the poet as an unwelcome *douche:* and, notwithstanding the Three Days of July, there was on the occasion of this visit to be no exception to the rule. He had been in the city about a fortnight, and had been effectively disenchanted, so far as the liberalism of the citizens was concerned, when suddenly the finishing touch to his hatred of Hamburg and its inhabitants was given by what the populace, and even the authorities, called the *Judenkrawall,* the Jew Riot, but which was nothing more nor less than a brutal and cowardly harrying of the unfortunate Israelitish

9

community. This shameful episode made Heine's heart sick with disgust and anger, that fanned the flame of what was a lifelong resentment. Now more than ever he thought of migration to Paris, that " new Jerusalem beyond the Rhine-Jordan, separating the sacred land of Freedom from the land of the Philistines." There, at least, "the arrogance of kings and the snarling of priests" would beat against deaf ears. He had at last reluctantly become assured that the fruits of the revolution had come to nought in Germany; that, at best, some seed had fallen which might in due time satisfy the sanguine. In France he would be able to see the advent of the tide that was bubbling and seething even in squire-ridden England and in priest-driven Italy.

For a long time past Heine had brooded upon expatriation. The thought was bitter to him, for, after all, he was a German. He was a dreamer of dreams, a singer of sweet songs, and he had no wish to eat the bread of exile or to scale the steps of alien patrons—much less to consort with all the political lions, jackals, and magpies, among whom he would inevitably find himself in Paris. To Italy? Alas, before every citron-tree would stand an Austrian sentinel. To Vienna? There the agents of Prussia and Russia were as ubiquitous and as potent as in Berlin. As for Munich, that was no longer feasible. To England, with " its hell of fogs," where he " would not even hang in effigy, much more live in person"? No, that would be worse than death; it would be to remain continually *in articulo mortis.*[1] To America?

[1] " When I was introduced to the Governor of Heligoland, the wooden Englishman stood motionless before me for a few minutes

Tha would be even worse, for it was further away—
"that frightful dungeon of freedom, where the invisible
chains gall still more painfully than the visible ones at
home, and where the most repulsive of all tyrants, the
mob, exercises its coarse dominion."

The many letters to Varnhagen von Ense written at
this period afford ample evidence of the perturbation of
spirit in which Heine spent day and night. But the
"pressure of the times," alluded to in the appendical
note written to his supplement to the "Reisebilder"
(Nov. 1830), was upon him, and Paris was as inevitably
his goal as is the vortex to the drifting boat in the neighbourhood of the whirlpool. The Spirit of Freedom
beckoned, and there was no resistance to that red-
capped Lorelei. In Germany this breath of freedom
had indeed blown out a few night-lamps here and there,
so that the red curtains of several thrones took fire, and
golden crowns grew hot under blazing night-caps; but
"already the old catch-poles are bringing out the fire-
buckets and smell around all the more suspiciously, and
forge all the more firmly their secret chains, and I mark
well that a still thicker prison vault is being invisibly
arched over the German people." Like Kunz von der
Rosen, the faithful fool of the Emperor Maximilian, the

without speaking a word, and involuntarily the idea came into my
head to look at him from behind, to see if somebody had forgotten
to wind him up. In fact, out of every Englishman there is engen-
dered a certain gas, the carbonic acid of *ennui;* and this I have
observed not only in England, where the air is heavy with it, but in
southern countries, where the travelling Englishman goes about in
isolation, and the grey aureole of *ennui* which surrounds his head is
sharply visible in the sunny blue air."

poet had shaken his head in such mad earnest over his country's distress that the fool's bells had fallen from his cap, and tears had usurped laughter.

It was time to take a decisive step, even if, despite all, the heart should receive its death-wound in expatriation.

When, twenty years later, Heine described his departure from Germany and advent into Paris, he did so with the cynical laugh which had long become so natural to him. About the time of the July Revolution he had grown quite tired of his existence, he relates in the "Confessions" (1853–4), and required some recreation. His native air struck him as unwholesome. Moreover, he had made the acquaintance of an old Berlin lawyer, · who had incidentally mentioned that the irons worn by political prisoners in the fortress of Spandau were very cold and heavy as ornaments, particularly in the un-warmed cells in winter time ; that no oysters were obtainable there, and that even meat was very rare, while there was no other kind of fowl but flies, which had a habit of making the soup more substantial by falling into it. So, as he had need of recreation, and as Spandau was too far from the sea for one to obtain oysters, and as he did not care for fly broth and disliked iron fetters, he thought he would take the advice of a genial commercial traveller from Paris, who assured him that there the populace did little else than drink champagne and sing the Marseillaise.

On May-Day he crossed the Rhine, and, as he could not obtain a glimpse of the puzzled old river-god, uncertain as the latter was whether his waters were French or

Prussian, the traveller dropped his visiting-card into the stream and trusted to its safe transmission.

It was on the 2nd of May, 1831, that Heinrich Heine entered the country of his adoption, and on the following day he beheld the city of his desire, his new Jerusalem. The first thing he noticed was that *Liberté, Egalité, Fraternité* had been erased from the street corners. Honeymoons, as he philosophically remarks, fly so quickly.

CHAPTER VI.

THE first business of a wearied poet is amusement;
so thought Heine. And what endless amusement
there was in the parade of the boulevards and the
thronged by-streets: how vivid the life, how animated
every citizen! How charming it was, moreover, to be
met everywhere with courtesy; to accidentally stumble
against a wayfarer, and not thereupon be greeted with a
curse *à la Berlin*, or a grumble *à la Londres*. If some one
jostled him, he says, without immediate apology, he felt
sure it must be a fellow-countryman; and if a pretty
woman looked a little sour, she had either eaten *sauer-
kraut* or could read Klopstock in the original. The
weather was magnificent, and Paris was in the plenitude
of her beauty; no wonder that the spirits of the sensitive
poet rose as swiftly as a child's laughter, and that his
heart beat the quicker. To improve his rusty fluency in
French diction he spent half an hour in the Passage de
l'Opéra with a pretty flower-girl. He found this method
of tuition so charming that he had frequent resort to it,
for even after he knew French as well as a countryman,
he had no doubt there were still Parisian *nuances* to be

acquired. He was thirty; he had hopes; he had money and he was in Paris; therefore he was happy. He saw everything in a golden glamour, and everything and every one seemed in a conspiracy to flatter his delight. For a time he inhaled with rapture the intoxicating aroma of life; like most men of his temperament and calling he inhaled too long and too deeply.

Many days were spent in sight-seeing, and a good many more in becoming naturalised to Parisian life. Ere long, however, Heine began to write for the " Allgemeine Zeitung," and other German papers, those charming Parisian letters which delighted his over-Rhine readers, and even now may be read with an enjoyment quite apart from their very distinct historical value. He was welcomed among his literary brethren, and, indeed, everywhere found hospitality; so that no better " Paris Correspondent " could have been obtained by any foreign journal. Moreover, for the first few months, his health was so markedly better that even his headaches became, as it were, reminiscent in their character. Altogether he was so well content that he wrote to a friend: " If any one asks how I am, say ' Like a fish in water,' or, rather, say that when a fish in the sea asks another how he is, the reply is, ' Like Heine in Paris.' " As there is not space here for even a condensed account of Heine's doings and dissipations during the first period of his Parisian residence, it must suffice to say that he speedily became a Parisian of the Parisians. Perhaps he knew that he was becoming a spendthrift of life's most valuable treasure, but, gambler-like, he expected that for him the " red " would always turn up.

Never did poet set foot in a new land with so many and such valuable introductions. So amply furnished was he, indeed, with these missives that he might well have exclaimed that he was more highly esteemed and recommended on his departure from his native country than ever he was while within its borders. He bore letters (fruitful of benefit, as it proved) not only to great financial celebrities like Rothschild—whom, as he wittily says, he came to know quite *famillionairement*—but to many eminent authors, artists, and musicians. Among the latter he frequently encountered Mendelssohn, and was intimate with Rossini and Meyerbeer; artists innumerable he met and associated with; and among the French and German authors and other celebrities whose acquaintanceship he enjoyed were Lafayette, Balzac, Victor Hugo, George Sand, Théophile Gautier, Michelet, Dumas, Sainte-Beuve, A. de Musset, Quinet, Victor Bohain, Gérard de Nerval, Ludwig Börne, Schlegel, Humboldt, and many others resident and migratory. It was not long before his Berlin and Munich æsthetic training stood him in good stead. Although it is impracticable to dwell here on the very large body of Heine's prose writings dealing with art criticism and music criticism, it may be stated that some of his most brilliant and able work is to be found therein—writing so brilliant and so able that it was welcomed by thousands of readers in both France and Germany.

To all intents Heine now became a Parisian—not a Frenchman, as his Teutonic enemies declared, but a Parisian. From this time forth he seldom left that *charmante Lutèce* he loved even more than the Angé-

liques, Dianes, and Hortenses, and other ladies of the
Passage des Panoramas chronicled in the "New Poems"
(*Neue Gedichte*), upon whom he expended so much time,
money, and, alas, health. Even a sojourn by the sea at
Boulogne did not invigorate the constitution which so
short a period as three months had definitely under-
mined.[1]

It was after his return from Boulogne-sur-Mer that
Heine was captivated by the extreme beauty and charm
of a young girl named Mathilde Crescence Mirat. The
attraction was mutual; but by agreement on either side
they waived formalities : in other words, to use the phrase
of the *Quartier Latin*, they married *au treizième arron-
dissement*. This beautiful, uneducated, unintellectual,
yet infinitely charming and loyal Parisienne was the good
angel of Heine's later years. She did not understand
him, but she loved him ; he was not the great poet, the
famous author to her—she could not even bring herself
to read his verses when she accidentally discovered that
he *was* a poet—but only the witty, perverse, and lovable
Henri. As for Heine himself—though he sometimes
laughed at her follies, he was ever loyal and loving.
Upon the eve of the famous duel arising out of the
Ludwig Börne episode, the young people walked one day
to St. Sulpice and were there made man and wife in the
ordinary fashion, an act, however, which was in no way

---

[1] Readers unfamiliar with German should not fail to make the
acquaintance of the volumes entitled "Lutèce," "Allemands et
Français," "De La France," "De L'Allemagne," and the "Correspondence," in the *Oeuvres Complètes* published by Calmann Lévy
(16 vols.).

due to any scruple entertained by either but to a natural desire on Heine's part that, in the event of his death, his life-partner should not be left unprovided for.

Although the Börne incident occupied a prolonged period of Heine's later life, and was the source of infinite annoyance to himself and others, it is unnecessary to dwell upon it here in full detail.   Briefly it may be summarized thus : Ludwig Börne had no sympathy with the poet's sensuous and purely artistic temperament, and his apparent lack of enthusiasm in many matters dear to the German refugees then congregated in Paris, while his sombre nature was roused by Heine's satirical shafts against his own countrymen.   With all his vigour he set himself to attack and damage his quondam friend, not merely from personal animosity, but from genuine conviction that patriotism demanded such a course of action. Both were right, and each was wrong. Börne was an enthusiast of fire, that cannot but consume, progress, and keep on consuming : Heine was an enthusiast of wind, that bloweth where it listeth. Börne saw the goal, and his life was spent in passionate endeavour to reach it : Heine also saw the goal, but in his heart of hearts was not quite sure if its gates were of gold or of tinsel, and in any case he was so much amused by the tragi-comedy of the race that he often preferred to sit by the wayside and laugh till the bitter tears came into his eyes—and then begin to laugh again.

From the time of the publication of Börne's " Letters from Paris " until three years after the patriot's death Heine maintained a dignified silence. He let injustice grow to calumny and calumny become grossest libel : his only answer to the accusations of his fellow-republicans and reformers on either side of the Rhine was to open his purse more unrestrainedly than ever to any German applicant, and to give the most disinterested assistance to any needy or distraught friend, acquaintance, or stranger. Nevertheless, the wound gangrened. Probably if the poet's health had not grown so much worse he would have had more control, but suddenly his restraint gave way, and he published his "Ludwig Börne : A Memoir." With much superficial impartiality his barbed remarks were too often tipped with mortal poison. What was worse was his stooping to shameful defamation of the private character of one whom he had called his friend, and of that of the lady to whom the latter's "Letters" had been addressed. It was the husband of this lady who, a year after the publication of the "Memoir," challenged the author to mortal duel. It is true that Heine ultimately offered a spontaneous apology to the lady whom he had so inexcusably assailed, and that he caused all the libellous passages to be expunged : unfortunately, if one throw a stone through a stranger's bed-room-windows it is not sufficient restitution to voluntarily pay the glazier's bill. There is no palliation for Heine's conduct, and the indignation which it caused, both in Germany and in France, was amply deserved. It was not only that his attack was the very quintessence of wormwood; his having stooped to gross personalities could not be condoned.

This episode belongs to 1841. In the preceding decade Heine's work was mainly journalistic, for the great part consisting of the artistic and musical criticism to which allusion has already been made. Ill health, ever growing worse, debts, enmities, and violent German attacks upon him by Wolfgang Menzel and other jackals of inferior aggressive power, but in effect almost equally harassing, had, latterly at least, more than counterbalanced the multiform pleasures of his Bohemian life.

With all his faculty of fascination he was constantly estranging friends. It was as though a million spirits of satire possessed him, and whenever he opened his mouth one leapt forth and became verbally tangible. As the generality of people prefer to read or hear about possessed individuals rather than to come in contact with them in the flesh, it is no wonder that when Heine gave greeting with his right hand and pinched agonizingly with his left, acquaintances fought shy of him. Even in matters of opinion many of his friends, particularly of the Börne type, could make nothing of him. They never knew where he stood. He repudiated Judaism, he repudiated Christianity, he repudiated St. Simonism, he repudiated Deism, he repudiated Atheism; a republican, he repudiated monarchism, and thereupon repudiated most republicans, apparently on the ground that they were indifferent as to change of linen and smelt of garlic; a soldier in the liberation of humanity, he preferred to do his marching by deputy, and allowed himself frequent and unrestricted furloughs. In a word, he was, as they say across the border, "no canny."

So far as means went, the poet and his wife would have been fairly comfortable if the coin which came to the household had not been of the kind that burns holes in pockets. Since Heine had taken up residence in Paris, his Uncle Salomon, convinced that his nephew was an irretrievable black sheep so far as his following any reputable business was concerned, had agreed to make him an annual allowance of 4,000 francs (£160). The annual income made by the poet-journalist himself averaged about 3,000 francs. Unfortunately, a yearly income of from £250 to £300 is not a superabundant one for two young people without an idea of thrift, and still less so when the purse-strings are constantly being tugged by impecunious and importunate acquaintances. Debts accumulated, and the outlook became black when a considerable amount of money which had been deposited with a friend went to look for the shadow of the wind.[1] In his extremity Heine appealed to his uncle, but was met with a decisive refusal. Heedlessly, but recklessly, and, as it proved, unfortunately, he then had recourse to the secret fund expended, for political though unformulated purposes, by the French Government upon refugees of all nationalities. Of course this circumstance ultimately became known, and involved much savage abuse and malicious misrepresentation ; but, though Heine's action was not an altogether defensible one, it is quite clear that he never undertook any obligation in consideration of the small pension bestowed upon him, or even that any was required of him.

Although injudicious living had played havoc with Heine's never robust health, he was still, within the first decade of his Parisian life, comely and even blithe of

[1] In 1837 Heine came to an arrangement with his publisher Campe, whereby, in consideration of the sum of 20,000 francs down, he made over the copyright of his works for eleven years.

aspect. There is extant a touched-up but fairly accurate depicture of him by Theóphile Gautier, in which the immortal "gentleman with the waistcoats" alludes to the poet as having the appearance of robust health, as being, indeed, nothing short of a German Apollo. Beardless, moustacheless, whiskerless, his face was "full and round, but of an elegant mould," and under his abundant blonde hair was "the marble tablet of his forehead," and blue eyes which sparkled with light and inspiration. Another decade or so, and the "German Apollo" was to shrink to a wan, shrivelled, and suffering creature.

So early as the second year of his stay in Paris, Heine commenced his celebrated essays upon the History of Religion and Philosophy in Germany, and upon the Romantic School. These in part, in the first instance, appeared in the *Europe Littéraire* and in the *Revue des Deux Mondes*, and were afterwards enlarged, translated, and published in book-form. He took pleasure in writing these valuable, witty, and able literary records, for he knew that they would not, like most of his other work composed in Paris, have to undergo remorseless mutilation at the hands of the official censors throughout Germany.

Even "The Romantic School," brilliant and interesting as it is, cannot be compared in value with any volume of Heine's verse. He was above all things the poet One of his flawless *Lieder* is worth many pages of his best prose; but apart from this there are two vital draw-backs to the permanent attraction of the latter—the ephemeral nature of the substantive value of much of it, and the more or less fragmentary treatment of even the most ambitious subjects. In a sense, indeed, the "German Religion and Philosophy" and "The Romantic School" are just as much fragments as the unfinished tale of "The Rabbi von Bacharach." In length they do not exceed some of those old Quarterly articles which De Quincey, and other giants of the pen, used to let loose upon the heads of our grandfathers; in vigorous concision and balanced judgment they are less weighty; and in scope they are far less complete. They are not sufficiently octopus-like. Their tentacles do not spread far enough in all directions equally, nor grasp sufficiently firmly that which is behind or all that lies collaterally. Yet they are compositions so full of knowledge, insight, understanding, frequent sympathy, and wit—and, withal, are written with a charm of style and a purity and directness of diction altogether unsurpassed in German literature, even by Goethe or Lessing—that at present the day of their oblivion is much more likely to be in the Greek Kalends than in any period within the prophetical ken of the most astute critic.

These "German" essays excited even at the time of their serial appearance much admiration. Readers wondered what manner of man this was who sang the sweetest songs in the Teuton tongue, whose tenderness and pathos were so subtle and whose virulence so extreme, and who wrote as a Parisian of the Parisians, as delicately as Gérard de Nerval, and with a polished grace scarcely inferior to that of Théophile Gautier. As has been well said of him, he would seem to be at once a grandson of Goethe and of Voltaire.

In his philosophical essay readers hailed with delight

a style that was lucid and exact, incisive and not intricate. The most abstract proposition became in his presentment easily intelligible, for where clarity of comprehension and ordinary methods of illustration failed to elucidate such proposition aright, he had recourse to sure and penetrative wit. Take, for instance, his account of Fichte's " Ego " and of his " objective " and " subjective ": "Fichte requires the mind to observe itself whilst in activity. Thought shall listen to itself while it is thinking, even while it is getting warmer and warmer, and at last becomes a thought. This reminds us of the ape who sits by the fireplace and cooks his own tail, asserting that the true science of cookery consists not only in objective cookery, but also in being subjectively conscious of being cooked."

This work is " a history "—a well-marshalled historical account, it might perhaps better be termed—of German religion and philosophy from Luther, through Kant, to Hegel ; and its leading motive may be defined as an *apologia* for Pantheism—not so much a later Spinozan as a St. Simonian Pantheism, akin indeed to that of the "God-intoxicated " Spinoza himself, the outcome of the inevitable disintegration at the bases of Christianity and Protestantism—of their structure and encumbrances, that is, not of their vital fundamental idea. Voltaire himself, he asserts, could injure only the perishable body of Christianity, not its unassailable soul, that inviolate and immortal idea. Heine had no narrow view of Protestantism, as, indeed, might have been expected of the man who wrote of the Bible as the most sacred book of humanity, and of the Virgin Mary as the fairest flower of poesy. Protestantism, in his view, is not merely the intellectual and spiritual protest of religious enthusiasts against effete dogmas ; it is the protest of light against darkness, of joy against gloom, of the flesh against phantasm, of life against death. Leo X. himself was a Protestant.

" As they protested at Wittemburg in Latin prose, so they protested at Rome in colour, in stone, and *ottave rime*. Or do not the powerful marble figures of Michael Angelo, the laughing faces of Giulio Romano's nymphs, and the intoxicated delight in life of Ludovico's verses, make a Protestant antithesis to the languishing melancholy of Catholicism? The painters of Italy engaged in far more effective polemics than did the Saxon theologians. The blooming flesh-tints upon the paintings of Titian are all Protestantism. The graces of his Venus are more real Theses than those which the German monk fixed on the church-door of Wittemburg."

This short extract will show at once the strength and weakness of Heine's method. He sympathises with the spirit, but not as spirit *with* spirit, rather as the flesh with its intangible partner in our mortal inheritance. The drift of his argument is just, but there is sophistication in the remark that the painters of Italy engaged in far more effective polemics than did the Saxon theologians. Titian's flesh-tints may be Protestantism ; but this method of theses-making can speedily be reduced to absurdity. The first Italian who took to the warm dram-drinking of the north instead of the thin mockery of Chianti of his native village would be a Protestant ; the genius who substituted the seductive waltz in place of the sedate minuet ; the individual who invented the umbrella as a shelter against the heaven-sent rain ; the gentleman who slew an organ-grinder as a practical

demonstration of his horror of the savagery of civilization—these, and the like, would also be Protestants.
There is none the less, of course, an obvious truth under-
lying the last three sentences of the passage quoted
above ; but the commonplace as to half-truths immediately suggests itself. It is but fair to add that Heine
immediately proceeds to do ample justice to Luther, " to
whom we owe the preservation of our noblest good, and
by whose merits we live to-day." The great Lutheran
hymn, " Ein' feste Burg ist unser Gott," he aptly terms
the Marseillaise of the Reformation. Ultimately he
discarded the pure universalistic theory of Spinoza as
completely as he did Christianity, but for the philosopher
himself and the spirit of his teaching he had ever the
greatest admiration. " In reading Spinoza," he says,
"there seizes us a feeling as when we behold nature in
vital repose. A forest of towering thoughts, whose green
summits are in wavelike motion whilst the immovable
trunks are rooted in the everlasting earth. There comes
a certain breeze from his writings which is inexplicable.
We feel, as it were, the light breath of the future." It
was his sympathy with Spinoza's pantheistic philosophy
that biassed him in the direction of that of Saint Simon,
then promulgated by Enfantin. In the Saint Simonian
religion of humanity he found much to attract him
besides the semblance of his own opinions. Enfantin, in
fact, became for a time his hero, and it was to him that
his " History of Religion and Philosophy " was dedicated
—as was but fitting, since it was at Enfantin's suggestion
that it was written. Shortly before his death, Heine with-
drew the dedication, for it had become an anachronism.

The "liberation war of humanity" had collapsed, so far, at any rate, as Enfantin and his fellow martyrs were concerned. These martyrs no longer bore a cross, unless it were, as Heine remarked, the cross of the Legion of Honour.

It is true that Heine himself fell away from the ranks, but can one read the long story of official and individual malice and wrong done to him—from the Governmental prohibition against not only what he *had* written, but against all he *might* write, to the ceaseless and slanderous rancour of Wolfgang Menzel and his associates—can one read this record and not realize how only too likely must failure be the end of all? "I am possessed with a very passion for peace," he writes, after a return of the chronic misery he suffered from official censorship and inimical misrepresentation. Alas! there was to be no peace. With the years—with the months rather—came added bitterness and disappointment, and therewith cynical laughter that laughed at itself and would fain have sobbed, were it not that sobs would have opened the flood-gates of tears.

The other portion of "Germany" is the most able of all Heine's critical writings. Entitled "The Romantic School," it is a searching examination, a sympathetic and yet unsparing account of the German poets of Romanticism. It is one of the best-known works of his in this country and in America, and so I need not dwell upon it here in detail. To begin to quote from such a composition is dangerous; one is led from flower to flower like an insatiable butterfly. Not only is it full of witty and shrewd remarks, but, particularly in the opening pages, it contains many fine epigrammatic dicta; for example, "Christianity, by inculcating hound-like humility and angelic patience, has proved the surest support of despotism;"—" Men cannot now be put off with promissory notes upon heaven; they now claim as their inalienable birthright the enjoyment of this earth ;"—" The very secret of Christianity, which at once attracts and repels us, is the deification of suffering." After a brief dissertation upon the poems and poets of the Middle Ages, and a comparison of them with those of Greece and Rome, and upon the allied arts of music and architecture, the author brings the reader to Lessing, to whom he alludes as the literary Arminius who freed the German stage from a foreign yoke. It is with no surprise we read that in all German literature Lessing is the author whom Heine most admires and loves ; and after Lessing, Herder. The history of literature he compares to a great *morgue*, wherein each of us searches for dead friends or relatives. When, amidst multitudes of vulgar corpses, Heine caught sight of Lessing or Herder, with their human face divine, his heart beat, nor could he pass by without a parting kiss upon the pale lips of the beloved dead. Goethe, the Schlegels, Tieck, Schiller, and all the minor lights of Romanticism, are duly discussed. In Book iii. there is a charming account of that fascinating collection of folk-songs, "The Boy's Wonder Horn" (or Magic Horn), the joint production of Clemens Brentano and Achim von Arnim, a work that Heine says he cannot praise too highly, as containing the very quintessence of the national genius, and as having exercised so important an influence on the lyric poets of the Romantic school. Everywhere in it there is a faint fragrance as of the German lindens, the favourite tree of the Germans, because the linden leaf is shaped like a heart—an observation Heine once heard made by a German poet, his favourite poet—himself! A few pages further on occur the famous passages about German and French ghosts: how a French ghost is almost inconceivable; how French ghosts, if they do exist, must be very good company; how, if there are Parisian ghosts, there must also be ghostly réunions, a ghosts' café, and even an "organ" called, say, *The Paris Ghost Review*. Finally, the writer is convinced that the ghosts of Paris must have a much merrier time of it than ever have living Germans.

The remainder of "The Romantic School" is occupied with Heine's contemporaries, men of "The Young Germany" school, like Laube and Gutzkow, and elders such as Fouqué and Uhland. In this section also the curious may delve for wise and witty sayings, and be well rewarded for their labour. How true this is: "At bottom all men are *doctrinaires*; they have always a doctrine at hand as an authority for all their likes and dislikes;" or this, "In the heart of a nation's writers there lies the image of a nation's future."

Among other prose writings which followed within the ensuing decade are the completed "Florentine Nights" (fragmentary in their nominal completion, be it noted); "The Suabian School," an indifferent satirical production; "Shakespeare's Maids and Matrons," a study of the heroines in the plays of the great dramatist; the fragmentary "Memoirs of Herr von Schnabelewopski," and the critical æsthetic papers collectively entitled "The Salon."

In the preface to the last named, written at Havre-de-Grâce, there is another of those fine passages about the sea, "with its drowned empires and forgotten lores, ever listening along all the coasts of the world with a thousand billowy ears," which come not infrequently and always with electric effect upon the readers of both his prose and verse. The essays in æsthetic criticism should be read for their witty and picturesque asides; but it is appropriate in any case to remark here that Heine's art criticism may be read by all, free as it is from technicalities and art jargon.

The Schnabelewopski Memoirs, though not in Heine's best form, and frequently too reckless in expression, contain some memorable and many characteristic passages. The hero and his six fellow-sojourners at "The Red Cow" of Leyden were a Rabelaisian company. The plenitude and variety of the daily dinner depended upon the ardour of the handsome Pole's amour with the fat hostess. When the roast was particularly bad they would argue concerning the existence of God. "The Lord, however, had always a majority. Only three of the seven were atheistically inclined, and even they would allow themselves to be convinced if they had good cheese for desert." "Herr Schnabelewopski" believes that the reason why the Jews seem to have been so scurvily treated by Jehovah is that they knew Him in His first crude deistic state, and daily remind Him in their synagogues of His former obscure and merely national rank! The Jews, he pertinently adds, have always been the Swiss Guards

of Deism. It was from a subsequent passage that Mr.
Mallock would seem to have derived the wittiest remark
in his "New Republic,"that where Mr. Saunders announces
the thrilling fact that the housemaid has with a sponge
inadvertently obliterated his newly written "Disproof of
God's existence": for Schnabelewopski narrates how
once, during his friend Simson's absence, the chamber-
maid removed his soiled linen to send it to "the wash," to
his intense chagrin, as with it went to the oblivion of the
bath-tub all his MS. "Evidences for the Immortality of
the Soul." It was this same little Simson who, in reply
to the atheistical Dricksen, remarked that he had once
at Frankfürt seen a clock that did not believe in a
clockmaker—it was made of pinchbeck, and kept time
wretchedly : an argument which might have signalized a
triumph had not Dricksen threatened he would show
that such a clock could at least strike. In this fantastic
fragment Heine's second self is also displayed, however.
One example must suffice.

"Our posterity will shudder when once they read what a ghostly
existence we have led, and how the human nature in us was divided,
and only the one half really lived. Our era—and it begins at the
Cross of Christ—will sometime be regarded as humanity's great
hypochondriacal period. . . . And yet what sweet dreams have we
not dreamed ! Our healthy descendants will scarcely be able to
comprehend it. From around us vanished all the splendours of the
universe, and we found them again in our inmost consciousness ; the
fragrance of the crushed rose and the sweetest songs of the affrighted
nightingale have fled for refuge into our souls."

Although not published till 1846, the famous—though
out of Germany little understood—satirical poem en-

titled "Atta Troll" was commenced in 1841, a time when the enmity in Germany against Heine was at fever heat—so great an *émeute*, he declares, that he could never have imagined Germany could have produced so many rotten apples as were then pitched at his head. This poem, or rather this versified polemic, is in unrhymed quatrains of a trochaic metre, and is of great length; it is partitioned into twenty-seven chapters, and occupies no less than one hundred and twelve pages in the "Collected Works." It is sub-titled "A Summer Night's Dream," though the final word seems curiously inapposite for a poem wherein the author is vivaciously alert. Its motive is the exposure and castigation of the political shams and evils of the day, and of the pretentious absurdities of the scribes known as the tendency poets, "artists who took freedom and the work of liberation as the subject of their verse, and were mostly limited, fettered spirits, Philistines, who wore pigtails under the red cap of liberty." Much of "Atta Troll" (the name is that of the bear who escapes to his native wilds after long captivity among men, and whose ruminations, grumbles, and advice to his bearlings constitute most of the poem) would probably be pointless to the ordinary reader of to-day. The allusions are generally remote and temporal, and even the humour is too essentially Teutonic to affect the blither fancy of less sedate races than the North Germans. It is impossible to give any idea of the poem by quotation, for the chapters are chains and the quatrains are links individually connected. It is suggestive to note Heine's own opinion of it, an opinion which betrays the act that, shrewd as the poet was, he misapprehended

the artistic value of that which after all was but the
passionate metrical expression of what should have been
written in prose. In a letter to his publisher, Campe, he
alluded to it as a politico-romantic poem calculated to
give a death blow to the prosaic, bombastic, tendency-
poetry. "You know," he adds, "that I am not in the
habit of boasting, but I am this time certain that I have
composed a work which will make more *furore* than the
most popular *brochure*, and will yet have a permanent
value as a work of classic poetry. . . . I wrote it in the
capricious dreamy fashion of the Romantic school in
which I passed my pleasantest years." True, no doubt,
that " By the eternal Gods, there was need then of some
defence of the inalienable right of the spirit:" but
polemical writing, valuable as it is, seldom consists with
artistic beauty. There is probably, however, not another
modern poet of any country, with the exception of Byron,
who could have so ably blent satire, criticism of life and
literature, extravaganza, and poetry, as Heine has done in
" Atta Troll ; " but to assert that it will have a permanent
value as a work of classic poetry is to claim too much.
It will long, perhaps always, have a value for the literary
student : it is already slipping away from the cognizance
of the ordinary German reading world. The literary
critic is at all times apt to consider as commonly
interesting that which is fascinating to himself, but it is
clear from the history of literature that argumentative
and polemical poetry reaches its perihelion either at
once or within the immediate period of its appearance ;
that, to vary the metaphor, when the commotion caused
by the stone-splash has in great part moderated, the gaze

of the crowd is attracted elsewhere, howsoever those who
admire the stone-thrower linger to watch the slowly sub-
siding ripples and widening circles upon the surface of
the water.

A year after the composition of "Atta Troll," Heine
suddenly made up his mind to journey to Hamburg to
see his old mother. His reverent love for the "old
woman at the Dammthor" is one of his finest traits; and
one of the most charming of the lyrics in the "Neue
Gedichte," called "Night Thoughts," (*Nachtgedanken*,
"Zeitgedichte, No. 24") is based upon this affection.

The visit was in many respects a sad one. Twelve
years had greatly aged the dignified and proud old
lady, and, moreover, she had suffered in the terrible fire
which in 1842 laid waste so great a part of Hamburg.
She was rejoiced, however, to see her beloved son once
more, and to hear all about his brilliant Paris life, about
Mathilde, and about the truth and falsehood of all she
heard and read about her Heinrich as an author. The
letters which Heine at this time wrote to his wife—his
"Treasure," his "Nonotte," his "Heart's Joy," or, as he
poetically calls her in the last poem of the "Neue
Gedichte," *schön wie der Morgen*, "beautiful as morning"
—are among the most charming ever written by a poet
to wife or mistress.

The visit lasted for some weeks, till well on in December, and seems to have been a pleasant enough episode
in its way, as now the celebrated author was a man to be
made much of, one that not even the great Salomon
could distinguish any longer as the fool of the family.

"Atta Troll" had been the floodgate to a new outburst

of poetry. After years of literary warfare, brilliant but desultory journalism, and the fine prose productions already alluded to, Heine's spiritual *ennui* gave way before a fierce lyrical impulse: that the epithet is not an exaggerated one will be admitted by all familiar with the New Poems and particularly with the daring satire of such poems as " The Emperor of China," or the " New Alexander," or the wild and despairful cynicism of outcries like " Verkehrte Welt " (Topsy-Turvydom).

In 1844 the " Neue Gedichte " were published, with the satirical " Deutschland"—the outcome of the poet's journey to Hamburg in the preceding year—appended thereto. The " Neue Gedichte " are partitioned into five main sections : " New Spring," with forty-four lyrics ; " Verschiedene " (" Dead Sea Fruit " would perhaps be the best English equivalent for this untranslatable word), with seventy-six, thus sub-sectioned—" Seraphine " (15), " Angélique " (9), " Diane " (3), " Hortense " (6), " Clarisse" (5), "Yolande and Marie " (4), " Emma " (6), " Tannhauser" (3), "Songs of Creation " (*Schöpfungslieder*) (7), "Frederika" (3), " Katherine " (9), " Abroad" (*In der Fremde*) (3), and " Tragedy" (3): thereafter into "Romances," twenty-four in number ; " Miscellaneous," consisting of ten pieces ; and twenty-four " Poems of the Times."

No wonder, with so many Seraphines, Angéliques, and Dianes, that the jealous little heart of Mathilde rebelled, and demanded of its lord whether he had the face to protest loyalty to his Nonotte again in the face of all these disgraceful love poems ! Heine laughingly assured her that poets must not always be taken seriously, and

that, moreover, he would repent and sing no love-songs
henceforth to any one save his "frisky Kitling." It must
be admitted that no wife could be expected to relish the
poem to Diane, commencing *Diese schönen Gliedermassen*,
or that to Hortense of "the sweet delicious laughter," or,
worse still, that to Katherine beginning *Ich liebe solche
weisse Glieder*, which reads like a German "episode" by
the author of the *Fleurs du Mal*.

The most poetical portion of this book is the "New
Spring," where the short *Lieder* are mainly lyrics of a
moment's yearning or a moment's sadness or joy: sweet,
irresponsible carols of song such as Heine wrote no more
in the bitterness of his later years. In the other sections
there is also much of the music of the lindens and the
nightingales, with the voice of the sea ever and anon,—
many a charming song and romantic ballad; but yet the
poet does not surpass his earlier poems, nor is there in
the collection anything supremely memorable. Although
much of it is hallowed of the light of love—of "shadowy
love and shadowy kisses"—there is a frequent coarseness
that is neither wit nor poetry, but simply dross amongst
the gold.

The "Wintermärchen" ("The Winter's Tale"), entitled
"Deutschland," is a poem of about the same length as
"Atta Troll," but written in rhymed quatrains. Notwithstanding its vigorous satire, it rewon many of the
author's forfeited friends and gained over a host of
admirers. Heine was here the German poet beyond
cavil. Below the banter, below the recklessness, the
beating of a wayward but generous heart could be heard.
Official and conservative Germany was furious, but the

mass of the nationalists in the best sense of the word hailed this stirring voice in the wilderness, and welcomed the return of the most redoubtable free lance among their exiled countrymen. Here we see the poet as the liberator, the wielder of that sword whose might, if not whose prowess, he undoubtedly somewhat over-estimated: and one cannot refrain at times from the wish that this "soldier in the liberation war of Humanity," as he called himself, could have died in the heat of the conflict, with his generous war-cry upon his lips.

"The Winter's Tale" is nominally an account of the author's journey from the German frontiers to Hamburg, and of what struck him as worthy of note in that city after his long absence. The most brilliant portions of it are those describing the writer's interview with the Emperor Barbarossa in the cavern of Kyffhausen, and his encounter and subsequent *tête-à-tête* with Hammonia, the goddess of the mercantile capital of North Germany. There is a good deal of farce mixed up with the satire, and a good deal of coarseness in the farce; but the wit is pungent and searching, and all the more so from the fact that its object was deserving of any quantity of forked lightning. As in "Atta Troll," there are, among the shining silver, not only several lodes of dross, but also streaks of virgin gold. It is curious to find the unadulterate ore in such company; for the beauty that leavens "Atta Troll" and "Germany" is of a kind alien to satiric comedy, presenting indeed, as it does, a combination only discernible to a like extent in Aristophanes. At the same time I must admit that I find myself unable to rank the literary quality of "Deutschland" so highly as do many critics.   It is interesting, it is valuable, it is witty, and it has occasional flashes of poetry ; but it is not a poem in the sense that a critic should accept. That it will long be readable is not a test of its poetic worth, any more than that a painting, such as " The Derby Day," is high art because its interest for most people will long endure.   From a literary point of view its real value is its Rabelaisian vigour, its Rabelaisian extravagance, combined with what may be called its pointedness.

It was with anything but a light heart that Heine returned to Paris.   True, he was glad to be again in his beloved New Jerusalem, to be with his vivacious Nonotte, to have the brilliant company which meant so much to him ; but his health had of late steadily declined, his nervous headaches had become more frequent, prolonged, and harassing, and his pecuniary affairs were more involved and precarious than he allowed himself to fully realize.

It was no half-imaginary surrender of health under which he suffered.   So far back as seven years prior to his Hamburg visit (that is, in 1837) he had complained of an intermittent but violent pain in the eyes.   For a time he thought it due to the inflammation of some local nerve, but ultimately he learned that blindness was imminent through a predisposition to atrophy of the optic nerve.   Under the treatment of a famous specialist, however, the infirmity was not only arrested, but ameliorated, and it is possible that the ill might not have proved irremediable had it not been for the disastrous news which, not long after his return to Paris, came to him from Hamburg.   Death had suddenly summoned the rich millionaire Salomon Heine ; but though his nephew was genuinely sorry for the rough and obstinate, but kindly, old banker, he could not but feel somewhat anxious as to what disposition concerning him would be found in Herr Salomon's will. That he would not be left unprovided for was certain ; but to what extent his crowning indebtedness would amount was a source of anxious speculation. A certain sum (about £190 per annum, with half to his wife in the event of her surviving him) had been definitely and solemnly promised, and upon this, at any rate, he might count. He was not kept long in suspense. Ere New Year's Day he learned that nothing save a small money present came to him by his uncle's will : but what was worse was a simultaneous announcement from his cousin, Karl Heine, the chief legatee, to the effect that he did not intend either to pay the legacy which his father had promised to Heinrich or to continue the annual allowance which the latter had enjoyed since his settlement in Paris.

Coming at the time it did, the shock was a fatal one. Much of the poet's misery and suffering may be attributed to the action of the mean-spirited hound who turned upon his friend and comrade of olden days—upon one, moreover, who had nursed him through an attack of cholera, at the risk of his own life, and at a time when every one with means fled from Hamburg as a city accursed. For the sake of adding a few more coins to his already excessive hoard, Karl Heine proved false to the bond of kinship and disloyal to the trust of a friend. It is unfortunate that men of his type generally flourish : to the cynically minded, their very existence is damnatory evidence as to the hollowness of the time-worn platitudes anent righteousness and welfare.

The injustice, the meanness, and the hypocrisy of his cousin Karl caused a serious relapse in Heine's health. All the skill of his physician availed not against the increase of a stealthy sort of creeping paralysis. The sight in the left eye dimmed till it became obscured, and the paralyzed eyelid fell over it like a cordless curtain shutting off a dark room. The other eyelid was also affected, although it was not till a little later that it also yielded to the disease. The poet could not at first credit the baseness of his cousin; but when he found that Karl was backed up by all the money-grubbing tribe of relatives, and that he was not even to have his "present" of cash down, unless he would engage never to write a word that could be offensive to the susceptibilities of any of his family, his wrath and indignation knew no bounds. Daily his excitement intensified, and it soon became evident to his friends that the very fervour of his emotions betrayed a morbid condition of health.

Heine was not the man to submit to base fraud in whatsoever legal guise it might present itself. He determined to fight for his promised inheritance with all his might, not so much for himself as on account of his wife who, if he should die ere long, he knew would be left penniless. Even if he had to contest the matter in the law courts he would not shrink from the dubious ordeal: he had his deceased uncle's letters and his friend Meyerbeer's evidence to substantiate his claims, and for ill or weal he girt himself together for the struggle. The one bright spot in the affair is the generous action of Meyerbeer, who not only freely testified in writing as to the justness of Heine's position, but himself offered to recoup the poet for the loss he had sustained.

It is unnecessary to dwell here upon this momentous but painful episode ; it must suffice to chronicle its final phase. Partly owing to the generous advocacy of the poet's friends, Ferdinand Lassalle and Varnhagen von Ense, partly to as near an approach to shame as a man like Karl Heine could experience, partly to the fear of the Hamburg connection that the injured man might take a terrible revenge in the Memoirs upon which he was reported to be engaged, and partly to fear of the threatened appeal to the law courts, the pension was ultimately paid. The final arrangement, however, grossly unjust and inadequate as it was, was not concluded till 1847, by which time the poet's health had become a wreck.

In the spring of 1846, the man whom Théophile Gautier had described as a "German Apollo" was a con-firmed invalid. Not only was one eye wholly closed, and the sight of the other dimmed (the lid of which, moreover, so drooped that Heine had to raise it with his finger whenever he wished to look at any one or inspect an object), but his lips had lost all sensitiveness and his heart, as he himself pathetically said, felt bound as by an iron frost. It became impossible for him to read long at a time—six minutes, indeed, he specifies as his limit : though he managed to write his letters and short poems or fragmentary pieces without secretarial aid. Ere long it became necessary for him to employ an amanuensis, though he never became reconciled to the performance of his literary work by dictation. The pen in hand was to him as the touching of an electric bell : the pen absent, the creative impulse halted and flagged for lack of its accustomed medium of transmission.

Even the high spirits of Mathilde gave way for a time under the complication of disasters that happened about this time. It is a sad picture that the poet draws in a letter to a friend, wherein he relates that not only had the palate also succumbed to paralysis—so that all he ate tasted like earth—but that the insensitiveness of his lips had become so pronounced that even kissing had no effect upon them. " I sit whole nights long silent by the side of the fire with my wife. ' *Quelle conversation allemande,*' she says, sometimes with a sigh."

In the autumns of the preceding years, Heine had always sought the neighbourhood of the sea, in the old quest for health and refreshment. He and his wife generally went to the coast either of Normandy or of Brittany, and those who may be familiar with his epistolary and journalistic writings will endorse the statement that a new and valuable series of "Travel Pictures" might be compiled therefrom. Once he went south, to Marseilles ; but the city jarred upon him unendurably. It was, he declared, but a French translation of Hamburg, and the latter he could not stand even in a translation.

But in the summer of this sad year of 1845, he had no heart for any distant journey. Towards the close of the winter there was a slight apparent improvement, and the poet thought not only of journeying to Berlin in order to consult a famous specialist, but of going to Hamburg so as to come to some personal arrangement with his cousin Karl. The second project came to nought : and as for the former, Heine was warned from an influential source that unless he wished to spend the remainder of his days in the prison at Spandau he should not set foot on Prussian soil. It was in vain that Humboldt used his personal influence with the king; his intercession simply, brought upon him a hint to attend to his own affairs.

Early in January (1846) Heine wrote to Varnhagen a letter of heart-broken weariness and indignation, but that he was not wholly without hope of recovery may be inferred from one or two remarks. " If the paralysis, which like an iron band presses my chest together, should decrease, my old energy will again bestir itself. . . . Yes, I am sick unto death, but my soul has not suffered mortal hurt. It is a drooping and an athirst, but not yet withered flower, which still has its roots firmly planted in the ground of Truth and Love." Ere the spring was past the malady had made further progress : the fingers had lost sensitiveness, and one foot had become so lame that Heine had to hobble along with a stick. In a brief while even this partial independence was to be withdrawn from him. In July he went to Barèges—having to be carried over the mountain roads in a litter owing to the pain caused by the movement of a coach. It was his last visit to the "free Nature" he loved so well, and the picturesque descriptions which he sent to the *Allgemeine Zeitung* show that his pen had lost nothing of its cunning though the fingers that guided it were feeble and slack.

At first the sunshine and hill air wrought favourably

upon his nerves, but ere long the inevitable relapse came, and he returned to Paris much worse than when he had gone. The mysterious pains had greatly increased, and it had become evident that somewhat more terrible than paralysis had taken possession of the enfeebled frame. But as the body died the mind more gloriously effloresced, like that fantastic flower of Borneo which displays its richest blooms as the stem rots slowly to the root. New ideas, fresh impulses, creative instincts arose within him: his mental horizon widened, the atmosphere became more rarefied, the perspectives more alluring and more vast.

Moreover, his courage gave not way: he braced himself not only resignedly, but heroically, for the inevitable conflict with destiny. That he would be driven from point to point and finally overcome he well knew; but he would not yield. "I shall perhaps while away a year or two of pitiful agony. Now, that is nothing to me; that is the business of the eternal gods. . . . Dying, indeed, is something to shudder at, but not death, if indeed death exist. Death is, perhaps, the last superstition."

In the autumn—on his return from Barèges he had taken apartments at No. 41, Faubourg Poissonnière—he did not expect to live longer than a year at most. In the will he made at this time he left everything to "my wife, Mathilde Crescence Heine, *née* Mirat, who, as true and loyal as she is beautiful, has cheered my existence." After full directions and messages he bids farewell to his "noble and high-hearted mother," and concludes: "Farewell, thou German fatherland, land of riddles and sorrows—farewell, ye kindly French people, whom I have loved so much."

It had long been one of Heine's leading motives, that of the reconciliation, the mutual understanding of and sympathy with each other, of France and Germany. To this end he had consciously laboured, and, as his name was at last of magic import in both countries, he hoped that even these last testamentary words might bring forth good results. It was about this time that he wrote to his friend Laube urging him to pay his promised visit soon, as otherwise—as he grimly puts it— he would find a very quiet man indeed. He added the advice that if Laube should not find him at " No. 41," he was to look for him at the Cemetery of Montmartre— not at that of Père-la-Chaise, which was too noisy to be pleasant !

When Laube did arrive, in the spring of 1847, there was no longer the least vestige of hope. The invalid himself saw through the well-meant consolations of the physicians, and clearly perceived nothing save a pitiable and slow martyrdom. He read all the medical treatises upon the subject he could procure, and was thus able to prognosticate every terrible symptom of his disease, which the doctors had found to be consumption of the spinal marrow : his studies, moreover, he declared would be useful to him hereafter, for he would be able to give lectures in heaven upon the incapacity of earthly doctors in the treatment of spinal complaints.

The best accounts of this sad period of Heine's life are the records by Alfred Meissner and Madame Stahr (Fanny Lewald).

The sufferings of the poet became terrible : the fire
of an undying fever scorched his veins, the frosts of a
living death cramped his muscles, "unborn agonies"
took possession of his racked nerves. With bent body,
half-blind, lame, without senses of smell or taste, with
hands unable to guide the pen save for a few roughly-
scrolled lines, with lips unable to respond to his wife's
kisses, with ears painfully alert to any discordant sound,
in straits of poverty, misunderstood, maligned, deceived,
and defrauded, his was indeed a pitiable case. Had it
not been for the sake of his wife and his old mother he
would have put an end to his great misery, but he was
of too heroic mould to entail suffering upon those who
loved him by voluntarily plucking the dark fruit that
grows so temptingly upon the boundary wall in the
garden of life.

But ere matters had reached this dire length in the
year 1848, Heine had passed through various vicissi-
tudes.   In January he had gone to a private hospital in
the Rue de l'Oursine, beyond the Jardin des Plantes,
and while here, he was still able to move about in tardy
invalid fashion.   One day in February he had driven to
his apartments in the Rue Poissonnière to dine with his
wife and the physician under whose general care he was.
Ere the dinner was over a strange echoing sound was
heard from the streets : it grew louder and louder, and
suddenly above the tumult rose the wild exultant strains
of the "Marseillaise." "Another revolution," exclaimed
Heine, without knowing to what extent his words were
true.   For the Revolution of 1848 had begun, and "the
poet among nations," as Mrs. Browning so aptly called

France, had entered upon a new and disastrous era. If he had been the Heine of ten years earlier he would have been eager and exultant : but, alas, he no longer cared for, because he no longer believed in, the baffled yet dogged ascent of man. It was all a wretched struggle, in which the brave and the good perished.

When it was time for him to return to the hospital, the carriage which he had ordered to come for him had not made its appearance. Ere long he learned that it had been upset to make a barricade : so the poet could smile grimly as he realized that he, the revolutionary exile, met with the same treatment as "un aristo'." It was not until after much delay and trouble that the invalid was conveyed back to the Rue de l'Oursine, and strange indeed must have been the thoughts of the lonely man as he drove through the interminable streets, and heard the excitable populace singing their favourite chant of revolution.

By April his jaws had become so stiffened that he could no longer dictate with ease, or without twinges of pain. He now became certain that he could not outlast the year, and the thought brought him infinite relief.

In May there was a brief improvement, and one day he went out for what he only too justly feared would be his last stroll in those Boulevards he loved so well. The most pathetic incident in his life occurred during "this last day of his life."[1]

"It was in May that Heine took his last promenade in the Boulevards. Masses of the populace rolled along the streets of

---

[1] In Meissner's words, as translated by Mr. Stigand.

Paris; driven about by their tribunes as by storms. The poet, half-blind, half-lame, dragged himself on his stick and endeavoured to extricate himself from the deafening uproar, and finally escaped into the Louvre close by. . . . Ere long he found himself in the room on the ground-floor in which the ancient gods and goddesses stand.

"Suddenly he stood before the ideal of Beauty, the smiling entrancing goddess, the miracle of an unknown master, the Venus of Milo, who in the course of centuries has lost her arms but not her witchery. Overcome, agitated, stricken through, almost terrified at her aspect, the sick man staggered back till he sank on a seat, and tears, hot and bitter, streamed down his cheeks."

It was but fitting that this last visit of Heine to the outer world should have been to the Goddess of Beauty, whose thrall he ever was and whose songs he had sung ever since the far-off days when, as a child, he had wandered by the banks of the Düssel, or had listened to the secrets of the birds in that favourite haunt of his among the green alleys of the Schlossgarten.

From that day forward the poet never left his bed save when, for change of position, his nurse lifted him from it as she would a child, and placed him in an arm-chair propped up with cushions.

Heine's death-in-life had begun : henceforth he was to know the bitterness of a mattress-grave. Yet from this *matrazzen-gruft*, as he himself called it, his voice was still to arise clear and strangely sweet and wild, as from the depths of the Mammoth Caverns thrills at times the song of a sightless bird.

CHAPTER VII.

I N the summer of 1848 the invalid was taken to Passy, but without beneficial result. In October Mathilde Heine took her husband back to Paris, where apartments were leased at No. 50, Rue d'Amsterdam. It was an unfortunate choice of rooms, for though the windows of the second-floor apartments looked upon the court instead of upon the traffic-noisy street, the sufferer could see from his chamber no green branch, could hear no bird-song, could feel no breath of keen air, and, save occasionally at noon, could feel no sunbeams playing upon his emaciated face or almost transparent hands. Moreover, the stairs were so steep that Heine could not easily be carried to and fro for the purpose of enjoyment of the open air ; and, as a final aggravation, there were in the opposite apartments two ladies, who spent hours daily in a frightful massacre of music.

The winter of 1848–49 was to prove the most terrible period of Heine's sufferings. In order to obtain the briefest intervals of rest, he had to take a great quantity of opium, but even the drug frequently failed to bring him surcease of pain. In Adolf Strodtmann's words, his blindness increased; his legs had become emaciated and soft, "like cotton wool," the sufferer declared; his back had become twisted; and in order to somewhat relieve the cramps in the spine it had to be cauterized. For a time it was the poet's wish to be taken to Germany, there to end his days quietly; but the problem of how to journey thither was insoluble, and ere long he realized that not only for this practical reason, but for his wife's sake he must await the inevitable end in Paris. Ere 1848 had passed away he was no longer able to lie upon an ordinary bed, but upon a heap of mattresses and pillows laid upon the floor; from this mattress-heap, this "mattress-grave," he looked out upon the world as a prisoner immured in a dungeon for life.

For the first year or two of this dreadful life, Heine was so much visited that the apartments in the Rue d'Amsterdam resembled rather the *salon* of some prosperous celebrity than the lodging of a poverty-stricken, disease-wasted, death-sick Jew. Even the aged Béranger once toiled up the steep stairs in order to greet a greater than himself; and from time to time Dumas the elder and Théophile Gautier cheered the sufferer by their visits: nor should special mention be omitted of the two friends who by their translations and essays did so much to make Heine's genius appreciated by the French public— Gérard de Nerval and Saint-René Taillendier. But at last, as was inevitable—since, as Heine himself remarked, he was so unconscionably long a-dying—the door-bell rang but rarely, and ultimately weeks would pass without any other than Mathilde to keep him company. True, "Nonotte" was pleasant company, even though she lavished more caresses upon her parrot than upon her Henri; or sat up all night to apply poultices to a cat which had scratched its ear, a sacrifice no human creature could have drawn forth. Once he even became anxious about his "good Mathilde," domesticated though he knew her to be. She had gone out one afternoon to take a drive, and had promised to be back by four o'clock; but half-past five, six, seven, eight struck, and there was no sign of her. Her husband wondered if an accident had befallen her; or if, wearied of her invalid, she had eloped with some lustier friend. "In my painful doubt I sent the sick-nurse to her chamber to see whether 'Cocotte,' the parrot, was still there. That set me at ease again, and I began to breathe more freely. Without 'Cocotte' the dear woman would never have fled from me!"

On another occasion, after a long period of loneliness, the invalid was visited by Berlioz, whom he had known in the happier days when he was wont to associate with Meyerbeer, and other famous musicians. "What!" exclaimed the sick poet, as the caller entered the darkened room, "somebody actually pays me a visit! Ah, but Berlioz was always so original!"

Early in 1849 a Hungarian physician, who had been the first to discover what the complaint of the poet really was, but whose opinions had been pooh-poohed, took Heine's case in hand. Under his care the invalid greatly improved. True, there was no hope of ultimate recovery; but Dr. Gruby was enabled to partially restore the obscured vision, to invigorate the upper part of the body to such an extent that his patient could sit up against his cushions, and make some use of his hands ánd arms, and even to reanimate the palate, so that once more Heine was able to enjoy his food. Later on, the poet was enabled to dictate to the Polish gentleman who acted as his secretary, to have books read to him, and even to give way to the creative impulse which had long lain dormant, not been annihilated, as he had feared.

Thus it was that after years of literary warfare, brilliant but desultory journalism, and prostration by insidious disease and disasters of another kind, the poetic spirit broke out afresh. Heine realized that he could never again write as in his " Nordsee " or " Heimkehr " poems, and that out of mockery comparatively little of durable poetic value could come; yet he felt that the well-spring within him was as vital as of yore, if more troubled at its source, and no longer ebullient with waters of crystal purity.

During those terrible years of suffering, 1850 and 1851, the genius of the poet reached its climacteric. It was then that he produced that wonderful series of poems collectively entitled " Romancero." Here every phase of Heine's genius is visible : here he is sombre, imagina- tive, tender, graceful, ironical, exquisitely delicate, and grossly cynical ; here, moreover, the variety and extent of his metrical skill must astonish and delight the critical reader.

The " Romancero " is partitioned into three books, respectively entitled " Histories," " Lamentations," and " Hebrew Melodies." Poems of the ballad nature pre- vail in " Histories," and of these the first two are Oriental pieces, " Rhampsenit " and " Der Weisse Elefant." " Rhampsenitus " is a humorous composition, founded upon an episode in Herodotus (bk. ii. c. 121), and

"The White Elephant" is an extravaganza from which Mr. Frank Stockton, the American novelist, would seem to have derived hints for one or two of his best-known tales. But a poem of a much higher order is the fine ballad, "The Field of Hastings," wherein is told how two monks, Asgod and Ailrik, seek, in her hermitage, the beautiful Edith the Swan-neck, once beloved of King Harold, so that she may help them to find the body of the king among the slain on the fatal field of Hastings; how all day long Edith passed to and fro amid the thousands of the dead, until at eve she came upon a corpse on whose bloody breast she flung herself, and whose pale lips she kissed, for it was that of the man whose love she had been in the days of old. Even finer, perhaps, is the well-known poem "Ferdusi," which recounts how Shah Mahomet repented him of his fraud upon the "Fount of Song," and sent great riches and tribute to Ferdusi where he dwelt afar off; but how, as the long caravan entered the city of Thūs amidst joyous shouts of "La Illa Il Allah," there simultaneously passed out at the Eastern Gate the funeral train of the dead poet. The veiled satire of such poems as "Charles I." and "Marie Antoinette" was naturally resented by official Germany, and still more so that people's song of "The Silesian Weavers," which, indeed, was suppressed at once by the censors. In "The Apollo God" there is an autobiographical undercurrent. The nun who in disguise traverses the Rhineland, and asks of every wayfarer if he has chanced to see Apollo, clad in a scarlet cloak and playing most sweetly upon a lyre, is probably meant to represent Poetry or the Ideal; the old man who informs her that "Apollo" was none other than a free-thinking, free-living German Jew, who lately was but a chorister in the Synagogue at Amsterdam, may be taken as Reality, or rather, Disillusion; and of course the shining Apollo of the nun, and the tawdry travelling Apollo of the pedlar, are the poet himself in his dual aspect. The romantic "Mohrenkönig" (The Moorish King), and that delicate phantasy, "The Asra," are welcome after the satirical "King Louis," "Our Marine," "The Two Knights," and other compositions of the kind. The pathetic ballad of "Geoffrey Rudèl," the Provençal poet who with Melisanda of Tripoli "drained the cup of wildest joy and deepest desolation," and the lengthy satirical but poetic piece called "Vitzliputzli," are among the most striking of these "Historien."

The most remarkable portion of the "Lamentations" is the short cycle of lyrical pieces grouped under the title "Lazarus." Of these, that "To the Angels" is a pathetic committal of his wife to the care of the mysterious powers of heaven—evidently written early in 1849, at the time when death seemed so imminent. Poems like "The Will" are unworthy of the poet's genius; but here as elsewhere the slow but sure disintegration of time will sift away all that is worthless. Heine will not be remembered for his banjo strains. But it is the third part of "Romancero," the "Hebrew Melodies," that contains some of Heine's finest poetical work. "The Princess Sabbath," though so fragmentary in effect, is full of a certain *bizarre* beauty; but the principal poem, one of the poet's longest and best productions, is "Jehuda Ben Halévy"—where, moreover, the Biblical influence is most strongly manifest. The sweet Jewish singer of the Middle Ages had always exercised a great fascination for Heine; and in this strange and picturesque poem he sings of him not merely with literary emotion, but with all the pain of the long "fifteen hundred years' tragedy," at his heart. The concluding piece, the wild medley called " Disputation," has been described as "the most Voltairean scene ever imagined by the sceptical demon of Heine's mind."

So aroused was Heine's literary activity by the partial improvement in his condition, that he not only wrote his " Romancero " poems, but employed his restless brain in many other ways. Among minor productions in verse should be mentioned the libretto for a ballet, entitled " Der Doktor Faust," which, in 1851, was sold to Mr. Lumley, then director of Her Majesty's Theatre in London, for the sum of £240, although it never appeared upon the English stage.[1] A much more important production, however, so far as literature is concerned, is the poetically conceived and ably written prose phantasy, entitled "The Gods in Exile," written in 1852-53, and first printed in the *Revue des Deux Mondes* (April, 1853). The idea was not a novel one with the author, for some sixteen or seventeen years earlier he had committed some portion of the subject-matter to paper. It is an attempt to focus some of the mediæval legends concerning the "last days" of the dethroned gods of ancient Greece and Rome,—

[1] Dr. Evans believes it, however, to have formed the basis of the ballet " Satanella," which Taglioni arranged for the Berlin stage some years ago. It is not to be confused with the discarded Faustpoem of his student-days.

that metamorphosis into demons, as he says, which the Greek and Roman gods underwent when Christianity achieved supreme control of the western world. The most striking episode in " The Gods in Exile" is the account of how Bacchus and his followers, in the guise of monks, cross a Tyrolese lake, and, on the further bank, meet a horde of Bacchantes and satyrs, and give way to wild revels and mad abandonment ; and how the terrified ferryman ultimately recognizes, in the superior of the convent to whom he goes for spiritual succour, none other than the metamorphosed wine-god himself.

But notwithstanding the comparative improvement in his condition, Heine still suffered torments intermittently, and as the weeks and months went past his body shrivelled, his hair became grey, and the frost of an unnatural old age rendered him pitiable of aspect. It was his one source of strength, at last, that the means of death at least lay ever within reach : "That I can reach out and take that opium, or clutch that dagger, alone gives me courage and enables me to endure."

" In many moments," he says again, with that characteristic cynicism which spared self as little as any other, "a doubt quivers through me whether man really is a two-legged god, as Hegel assured me five and twenty years ago. I am no more a Divine biped ; I am no more the high-priest of the Germans after Goethe—no more the great heathen No. 2—a Hellene of jovial life and portly person, laughing cheerfully down on dismal Nazarenes : only a poor death-sick Jew."

At the height of his illness the report was spread abroad in Germany that "the infidel mocker" had come

to see the error of his ways, and had taken refuge in
Christianity. That Heine did come to repent of much
in his life is true ; but as to his religious fervour—it was
of the kind immortalized in "when the devil was sick the
devil a saint would be,"—without hypocritical pretence,
however. Here, for example, is one of his confessions of
faith, made in his most desperate straits : " A religious
reaction has set in upon me for some time. God knows
whether the morphine or the poultices have anything to
do with it. I believe again in a personal God : to this
we come when we are sick, sick to death and broken
down. If the German people accept the King of Prussia
in their need, why should I not accept a personal God ?
When health is used up, money used up also, and sound
human senses used up, Christianity begins. . . . For the
sick man it is a very good religion."

Nevertheless a very real change resulted from his illness. It was no mawkish sentimentalism, no cowardly
hedging against the future, but a realization of the fact
that he had done much for which he had cause of bitter
regret. He would fain have been a truer soldier, fain
have followed closer his lost ideals, fain have been a Sir
Galahad. But he had failed, and there was an end of it.
Perhaps the curse of Israel was the blight that thwarted
his life. In the preface to the "Romancero," he makes
a statement which is none the less true because of its
cynical humour : " I have scratched many, bitten many,
and was no lamb ; but, believe me, those admired lambs
of meekness would bear themselves less piously if they
possessed the teeth and the claws of the tiger." Half in
earnest, half mockingly, as is his wont, he tells in this

preface the story of his latest "conversion." He returned
to God like the Prodigal Son, after having kept swine
with the Hegelians for some time. "Was it my wretchedness drove me back? Perhaps a less miserable reason.
A sort of heavenly home-sickness fell upon me and drove
me forth, amid forests and gorges, across the dizzy
mountain paths of dialectics. On my way I found the
god of the Pantheists (St. Simonism), but I could not
make use of him. This poor dreary being is inter-
penetrated with the world and grown into it, imprisoned
in it, as it were, and yawns at you will-less and impotent.
. . . The immortality of the soul, our permanence after
death, will then be given us into the bargain, like the
fine marrow-bone which the (Parisian) butcher, when he
is contented with his customers, throws gratis into the
basket. Such a fine marrow-bone is termed in French
la réjouissance, and the most excellent strengthening
broths are made therewith, which are also very soothing
for a poor pining sick man. That I did not reject such
a *réjouissance*, and rather took it to heart with comfort,
every feeling man must approve."

It is impossible to read Heine without being keenly
alert. One moment he will discuss in all seriousness the
supreme problem of immortality—the next he lets his
emotion escape, like some volatile essence, in a jest
about the inconvenience of ghosts. Even his friends
were constantly deceived. One day he assured Meissner
that if he could go out on crutches he would go straight
to church. Meissner was impressed, but somewhat in-
credulous : whereupon his companion reiterated that
most certainly he would go to church. "Where else

should óne go to—with crutches ? I' faith, if one could walk out without crutches, I should prefer to stroll along the lively Boulevards or to the Jardin Mabille."

Between 1852 and 1854 his most important writings were the " Letzte Gedichte " (the " Last Poems ") and the interesting prose autobiographical fragment known as the " Geständnisse," the " Confessions." The latter was intended to form a portion of the work on Germany, but was separately published, and in a French magazine. Eminently characteristic of the author, it should be read for its own sake as well as for its autobiographical value.

The "Confessions" begin with the well-known remark: " A witty Frenchman—a few years ago these words would have been a pleonasm—once dubbed me an unfrocked Romanticist." [1] Thereupon the author indites a kind of *apologia* of his literary position in connection with the Neo-Romantic movement. He admits that he has always been a Romanticist at heart, and that in a greater degree than he had himself realized : that after he had delivered many a broadside against Romanticism, he had in reality fought under its colours, and made good what he had destroyed. As he candidly says, he ought to have included in his account of the Romantic School a review of his own writings : for no countryman of his could with justice claim a more liberal space in the history of German Romanticism.

From Romanticism the writer of the "Confessions" passes to a statement of his intention to describe the philosophical and religious changes which had taken place in his mind since he had written his work on

---

[1] It was Nodier who alluded to Heine as *un romantique défroqué.*

Germany ; but—and how characteristic of Heine !—he thereupon breaks off in a dissertation upon women. After a parting shaft in the direction of Madame de Staël, the author becomes autobiographical, and recounts the story of his expatriation : but upon this witty narrative I have already drawn. The Hegel episode will also be remembered by the reader of the present volume. The passages concerning the author's views upon Israel and Hellas should be carefully perused by those who, on the one hand, consider that Heine had no reverence for the historic greatness of his race ; or, on the other, that he was so uncompromising a Hellene as to be unable to see anything but the highest spiritual development in Paganism. In a score of places, the "Voice of Israel," as an enthusiastic young Jewish poet recently apostrophised the author of the "Buch der Lieder," has borne earnest testimony to his profound admiration for, pride in, and sympathy with his people ; and that he was well aware of his own poetic indebtedness to the Israelite within him, to the long tragedy of his race since the crucifixion of the Aramean prophet, is undeniable.

A large portion of the later part of the "Geständnisse" is devoted to the refutation of "the silly and contradictory reports" which prevailed concerning the poet's religious change, and a sarcastic explanation of the true state of affairs. It may be summed up in the assertion that if Heine continued to adhere to the Protestant faith, it was simply because that faith did not at all inconvenience him.

Towards the conclusion he claims his due place in literature with a throb of pride that might be mistaken by enemies for arrogance. It is much to be a poet, he says, especially a great lyric poet : with no "sham modesty, the invention of worthless vagabonds," will he depreciate his poetic fame. None of his countrymen ever won the laurel at so early an age, and if Goethe could write, "the Chinese with trembling hand paints Werther and Lotte on porcelain," he could match this boast with "*my* poems have been translated into the Japanese language."

"But at this moment I am as indifferent to my Japanese fame as to my renown in Finland. Alas! fame, once sweet as sugared pineapple and flattery, has for a long time been nauseous to me ; it tastes as bitter to me now as wormwood. With Romeo, I can say, ' I am the fool of fortune.' The bowl stands filled before me, but I lack a spoon. What does it avail me that at banquets my health is pledged in choicest wines, and drunk from golden goblets, when I, myself, severed from all that makes life pleasant, may only wet my lips with an insipid potion ? What does it avail me that enthusiastic youths and maidens crown my marble bust with laurel wreaths, if meanwhile the shrivelled fingers of an aged nurse press a blister of Spanish flies behind the ears of my actual body ? Of what avail is it that all the roses of Shiraz so tenderly glow and bloom for me ? Alas! Shiraz is two thousand miles away from the Rue d'Amsterdam, where, in the dreary solitude of my sick-room, I have nothing to smell, unless it be the perfume of warmed napkins. Alas! the irony of God weighs heavily upon me! The Great Author of the Universe, the Aristophanes of Heaven, wished to show the petty, earthly, so-called German Aristophanes that his mightiest sarcasms are but feeble banter compared with His, and how immeasurably He excels me in humour and in colossal wit.

"Humbly do I acknowledge His superiority, . . . but here I venture to offer most submissively the suggestion that the sport which the Master has inflicted on the poor pupil is rather too long drawn out : it has already lasted over six years, and after a time becomes monotonous. Moreover, if I may take the liberty to say it, in my humble opinion the jest is not new."

The "Confessions" conclude with a comparison of the writer to a certain sweet-voiced leper of the Middle Ages, whose songs were the joy and delight of all, while the Minnesinger himself went to and fro like a living corpse, muffled from head to foot and with a hood over his face, and in his hand the Lazarus-Bell wherewith to warn all who might be in the neighbourhood of his approach. "Oh that old, familiar scorn, that cruel jest of God. . . . But there is nothing new under the sun. Perhaps *it* also is only an old warmed-up jest."

Readers of the "Geständnisse" will recollect that early therein the author alludes to the greater autobiographical detail of his "Memoirs." For many years past Heine had been slowly but steadily working at what he intended to be his *chef-d'œuvre*, the "romance of his life." Everything of his development, every important incident of his youth and manhood, his thoughts and opinions on all subjects, and not only about himself but about the celebrated men and women of all nations whom he had known, everything, in fact, that had made up *life* for him was to be included. It is known that so early as 1840 Heine had concluded the fourth volume of these "Memoirs," but unfortunately they are buried away from those who would fain read them. The poet's family disposed of them after his death, and they now abide innocuously in the archives of the Imperial Library at Vienna. That they should thus be held out as a bait to oblivion is from every point of view most reprehensible, even if they should be far more fragmentary and superficial—even if they should be the sheath of many unwhetted stilettos, if they should contain too much unspilt

venom—than could fairly be anticipated. Heine's own
words concerning them are explicit : " I know the future
belongs to me. Even if I die to-day I shall leave behind
me four volumes of autobiographical history which will
represent my thought and endeavour, and on account of
their historic matter, of their true exposition of the most
mysterious of transitive periods, will go down to posterity."

A wild cynicism, a savage irony, a humour that causes
tears rather than laughter, the wood-note-wild of passionate song and the shout of mockery, delicate pathos
and reckless abandonment, the sob of remembrance and
the cry of despair—these are the characteristics of the
" Last Poems." Most of them are quite untranslatable,
not only from a far from infrequent licence of expression,
but because they are so married to the original words
that divorce is impossible. A few have been presentably
rendered in English—" Body and Soul " (" Leib und
Seele ") by the late James Thomson; " Wie langsam krie-
chet sie dahin " (" How wearily it drags along ")—with
that bitter line, " I have two rooms : the one I die in
and the grave "—and " Ein Wetterstrahl, beleuchtend
plötzlich " (" A lightning flash, all suddenly ablaze ") by
the late Lord Houghton. It is suggestive that one of
these cries from the abyss relates to that long-lost love
of Heine's, the treachery or the malfortune of which had
stricken an undying heart-wound. Here, on his mattress-
grave, with his well-loved wife and the faithful friend
whom he called *La Mouche* (his Fly) his thoughts go
back to grimy Hamburg and to Amalie. Did space
permit I would quote Mr. Richard Garnett's admirable

rendering of " Du warst ein blondes Jungfraulein, so artig"
("Thou wert a blond-haired maid without a stain ").
"Für die Mouche" ("Die Passionsblume": "The
Passion-flower "), a poem of remarkable beauty, one of
Heine's finest, in my opinion, is noteworthy as having
been the last song of the tired singer, written only a
week or two before his death.   Yet it must not be
dismissed thus briefly.[1]   In an open carven tomb, amid
moonlit ruins of eld and a rout of fallen columns
and stone-wrought sphinxes, centaurs and other shapes
uncouth and mysterious, lies a dead man, with "pale,
long-suffering features."   Around the huge sarcophagus
"a wild and motley train " is sculptured : the laughing
gods of Olympus, Adam and Eve, Paris and Helen,
Hector before ruined Troy, the Hebrew prophets and
Bacchus and Silenus and Priapus, Esther and Judith,
Proserpine and Venus, Leda and Danae, Diana and
Hercules, Balaam's ass and John the Baptist, Peter with
the keys, and love-sick Jove, and the Child of the
Temple.   Then—

> " Quite suddenly it came into my head
> The dead man in the marble tomb was I."

Bending from his sarcophagus he sees a flower of rare
and extraordinary beauty, the Flower of the Passion—

> " Then, sorcery of dreams !   This flower of mine—
> This blossom from the heart of passion blown,
> Had changed into a woman's likeness, thine,
> Yes, thine, my best and dearest, thine, thine own."

---

[1] The only good translation I have met with is the admirable
rendering by Mrs. Emily Pfeiffer, from which I quote.

Nowhere more than in the lines following those just quoted is Heine's kinship with Shelley more manifest— the finest lines in what seems to me the loveliest of all the short poems of Heine's maturity—

> " We did not speak ; but ah, I could perceive
>   The inmost secret of your spirit clearly ;
> The spoken word is shameless, may deceive,
>   Love's pure unopened flower is silence merely.
>
> Voiceless communing ! Who could ever deem,
>   In tender converse which no ear might hear,
> That time could fly as in my happy dream
>   That summer night so full of joy and fear ? .
>
> What we then said, oh, ask it of me never !
>   Ask of the glow-worm what it says in shining ;
> Ask what the wavelet whispers to the river ;
>   Question the west wind of its soft repining.
>
> Ask the carbuncle of its fiery gleam ;
>   Ask what coy sweets the violet is betraying ;
> But ask not what beneath the moon's sad beam
>   The martyr's-flower and her dead are saying ! "

Then, in words almost identical with those of Baudelaire, he appeals to Death to let his soul know the last voluptuous bliss of sinking into stormless and painless silence. Suddenly harsh clamours and discordant noises environ the sarcophagus among the ruins. Even when Heine is in the very shadow of death, and is giving utterance to a deep and genuine emotion, his inevitable cynicism breaks the exquisite spell. The turmoil is due to the quarrelsome wrangling of the bas-reliefs upon the tomb !

> " Must lies still haunt the very stones, and can
>   These marble shadows fight for outworn glozes ?
> The startled shriek of the wild wood-god Pan,
>   Contending with anathemas of Moses ! "

It is the old battle, the poet exclaims, betwixt stern Reality and the Beautiful, the immemorial and eternal conflict between Barbarian and Hellene. And thus discordantly—yet with a choking sob at the end—does the poem conclude—

> " They shouted, raved, swore,—all the rest of it,
>   There was no end of tedious controversy ;
>   But Balaam's ass had still the best of it,
>   And brayed down gods and saints, and knew no mercy.
>
>   And at this vile ee-aw, which never ceas'd
>   This odious discord, truculent, defying,
>   In desperation at the stupid beast
>   I too cried out, and—woke myself with crying."

Among the Posthumous Poems [1]—though not necessarily of very late composition—there are two or three of great beauty, and one, " Bimini," that I should place first among all Heine's long poems. The two most noteworthy, the pathetic " Erinnerung " (" Remembrance ") and " Bimini," have been most ably rendered by Lord Lytton, the most Heinesque of all translators of the poet.

" Bimini " is the fabled island wherein springs eternal the Fountain of Youth, the same that in the early days of Spain's greatness was long vainly sought by Don Juan Ponce de Leon, the discoverer of Florida. It is written in those unrhymed and even nonassonantic irregular trochaic quatrains which Heine used so often, and always with such magical effect. It is beyond question one of the most distinctive of the poet's productions. None other than he could have written it : it is beyond even the

---

[1] " Letzte Gedichte und Gedanken von Heinrich Heine. Aus dem Nachlasse des Dichters." Hamburg : Hoffmann und Campe.

shadowy rivalry of the imitator. Were I not already at my limits of space I should quote the fifteen exquisite quatrains of Caca's lullaby: nothing more delicately fantastic was ever written by its author. In the fourth and concluding Part, Ponce de Leon, after weary wandering, at last reaches "Bimini," though not the isle of his search. A shadowy land it is :—

> " A still land, wherein so softly,
>   Under silent cypress shadows,
> Flows the streamlet whose good water
>   Likewise hath strange power to heal.
>
> Lethê, that good water's name is.
>   Drink thereof, and thou forgettest
> All thy suffering,—yea, forgotten
>   Thou and all thy suffering too.
>
> Good the water, good the land is !
>   Whoso once hath reached it, leaves it
> Nevermore.   For that land, truly
>   Is the real Bimini."

Fit stanzas these in their deep elegiac pathos to be chanted from the sick-bed of a dying poet. As Lord Lytton aptly remarks, this poem is Heine's epicedion.

CHAPTER VIII.

IN 1854 the scourge of cholera swept through Paris. So far as Heine was concerned, the plague might have entered the dark room in the Rue d'Amsterdam, and received a welcome; but for his wife's sake he agreed to a sudden move to what promised to be healthier quarters. Several of their friends had died of the epidemic, and the gentleman who acted as the poet's amanuensis had been seized by it. Mathilde became more and more anxious as she saw the signs of death increase along the whole extent of the street. Cholera she could understand, and dread: her husband's illness was a different matter, a terrible complaint that like rheumatic fever would pass away after it had expended its virulence. This inability to realise the import of Heine's infirmity, however, was by no means regretable so far as the poet was concerned. He never resented his beloved Nonotte's sanguine faith in his recovery; on the contrary, her invincible cheerfulness was an unmistakable factor in what went to enable Heine to maintain his long struggle against death. It made him feel not only more reconciled to what time still held in waiting for him, but rendered him less anxious for his wife's future. Of course he saw the weak side of this characteristic. When one day he was seized with dreadful spasms of coughing, he thought the end was at hand, but when the physician assured him that they would not hasten his death, he ironically panted out, " Do not tell my wife this : she has enough to bear already ! " None the less he valued greatly the sunny *insouciance* of Mathilde's nature. She, on her side, though she had nothing in common with her husband's intellectual life or spiritual experiences, entirely understood the man whom she so faithfully loved for over twenty years *as* a man. His satire fell heedlessly upon her ears : if too caustic it escaped her, if unmistakable she repaid it with a mirthful laugh. Once he expressed the most earnest wish that she might re-marry after his decease—for he was anxious that at least one man should lament his death ! " Have your jest, *mon ami*, but you know you cannot do without me," was Nonotte's sensible response.

Thus it came about that a bundle of mattresses was laid upon a litter, and a poor shrivelled " poet-corpse " upon it, and transferred to the Grande Rue, Batignolles. The change, however, was harmful. The rooms were dark and damp, and an inflammation of the throat warned Heine against continued residence.

Shortly afterwards Madame Heine found suitable and charming apartments at No. 3 in the Avenue Matignon. True, they were on the fifth floor, and had to be reached by an ascent of over an hundred steps ; but they were sunlit, well-ventilated, and had a balcony looking out upon the Champs Elysées. Here, in time, Heine was conveyed. On fine days he was laid on a mattress pile in the balcony, and through his half-veiled right eye could look once again on the joy and beauty of life. Even though this long-lost happiness came to him through an opera glass—for his dimmed sight could not perceive objects at a distance—it was almost too much for him. The first time he saw the green trees and the crowd of wayfarers he stared long and eagerly; but suddenly he laid down the glass with a sigh. He had seen a young vendor of pastries approach two ladies, by whose side leapt a pug-dog. *His whole heart had yearned with envy of the dog.*

It was prior to the departure from the Rue d'Amsterdam, however, that Heine commenced the Memoirs of his childhood and early life, to which reference was made early in the Introductory Note to the present volume. The composition, though as characteristic as anything that ever came from his pen, shows a falling-off in style : inevitable in the circumstances in which it was produced.

It was in the autumn of 1855 that his *schöner Todesengel*—the lovely Angel of Death of his last hours—came to him as though straight from heaven. Every one who knows Heine knows something of the *Mouche*—the *fine mouche*, the *chatte musquée*, the heart's delight, the soul's joy—who is so strangely and pathetically bound up with his latter days.

Even now no one seems to know the real personality of the lady who is familiar to literature as Camille Selden. She is still alive, but shuns more direct notoriety : and it is possible that the fair woman who shot a ray of happiness, and even hope, into the heart of the stricken poet, will never be further revealed to us than as the author of "The Last Days of Heinrich Heine." The utmost that has been discovered is to be found in Alfred Meissner's "Geschichte meines Lebens," where he alludes to "Camille Selden" as Elise de K——. Heine's niece, the Princess Della-Rocca, has written of her as an adorable creature, about twenty-two years of age (*i.e.*, in 1855), well-educated, and able to write and speak with equal ease in French, German, and English. What further we know of her is that she was of German origin, and that her late girlhood was spent in France; that she had been married at eighteen, and that her husband had taken her to London in order to get quit of her, and so far succeeded that he immured her in an asylum; that here she fell ill and became partially but temporally paralysed; and that finally, on her recovery, she was befriended by one of the doctors, who vindicated her sanity and procured her release.

One day in Paris she noted an advertisement in a journal. It had been inserted by Heine, who wished for a reader. She wrote and offered her services, not as a paid assistant, but as a friend, because of her great admiration for the poet.[1] Thenceforth she was the source of immeasurable comfort and happiness to her death-stricken friend.

But *La Mouche* is assured of immortality, whether her real name and the facts of her life ever become public or not. It can never be forgotten what she was to Heine,

[1] According to Strodtmann and other biographers. Her own account differs (*Vide* Introduction to her "Last Days of Heinrich Heine").

" The last flower of his mournful autumn," as he alludes
to her in one of his letters.   This friendship was indeed
a passion, a passion not of the body, but of the soul.
Even Heine, save for a single satirical outburst in one
of the poems he addressed to her (beginning " Words,
words "), never dreamt of it otherwise.   As he says in
one of the pathetic little notes he often sent to her, to
postpone a visit on account of unendurable agony, he
loved her with the tenderness of a dying man.

The " Last Days " have been adequately rendered into
English by a friendly translator, and the slim volume is
easily procurable.   No student of Heine should fail to
read it : and I shall not dwell, therefore, upon its fascinating story.[1]   How " Camille Selden " first met the
" pitiless banterer," how she charmed him by her manner, her voice, her native fluency in German, and, above
all, by her electric sympathy and intellectual insight :
how she loved and admired and bore with and ministered
to the sweetest singer of his time : and how within four
months a new life bloomed for each—all will be found
in these scanty pages, whose publication a few years ago
sent a thrill throughout Europe and the West.

Lest any reader, however, should infer that this late
love of Heine's is significant of indifference to his wife,
it may be as well to reiterate that to the last day of his
life he loved Mathilde better than any woman whom he
had ever known.   She was the queen of women to him :
it was not her fault that she was but a loving woman,
unconscious of " soul," and, though alertly intelligent,

---

[1] "The Last Days of Heinrich Heine." By Camille Selden.
Translated by Clare Brune.   Remington and Co., 1884.

unintellectual. Heine realized this, and his love never wavered. His letters to her, during his revisits to Germany, are charming by their almost youthful fervour of affection. This loyalty in the "butterfly poet," as Menzel scornfully alluded to him, in "that blackguard," as the most anti-poetic of all men of genius, Carlyle, called him, is one of his most characteristic traits. The two persons who had best reasons to be aware of it were his wife and his mother.

It is to Meissner that we owe a record which should suffice to wipe out the memory of all Heine's coarsenesses and banalities. One day this good friend entered and found the poet dictating a letter to his mother. "What!" he asked, "does the old lady who dwells by the *Dammthor* still live?" "Truly: though old, and sick, and feeble, still beats the warm mother-heart for me." "And do you often write to her?" "Regularly every month." Whereupon exclaimed Meissner, how unhappy the old lady must be at her son's condition. "At my condition? Oh, I should explain that we hold peculiar relations. My mother believes me to be as well and sound as when I last saw her. She is aged and reads no newspapers, and the few old friends whom she sees are in like condition. I write to her often, as well as I can in a cheerful humour, and tell her of my wife and how happy I am. If she notices that only the signature is mine, the explanation is that I have pains in the eyes which will soon pass off. And thus she is happy. For the rest, that a son should be as sick and wretched as I am, no mother would believe." In addition to these precautions, Heine had warned all his Hamburg relatives and acquaintances against the disillusioning of the "dear old lady."

Is there anything more pathetic in the history of literature? I doubt it.

To revert for a moment to Camille Selden : perhaps the only thing to object to in her " Reminiscences " is her absolute obliviousness to Mathilde's existence. There could have been nothing in common between the two women : but that the *naturkind*, the child of nature, as her husband spoke of her, was in some respects the nobler-natured may be inferred from the absence of resentment wherewith she saw her place taken by another, and from the apparently scornful reticence which characterizes " The Last Days."

But from the summer of 1855 onward, a stealthy weakness grew upon the poet's enfeebled constitution. His sufferings increased. Spasms, coughs, and frightful vomitings wrecked his already agonized frame. Often, often he prayed to be delivered from "this cancer of life. Yet, at intervals, ill and wretched as he was, he clung to life with the profound instinct of nature. " I never saw," declared a friend who visited him late in the autumn, " I never saw a man bear such horrible pain and misery in so perfectly unaffected a manner. He neither paraded his anguish nor tried to conceal it, or to put on any stoical airs."

But amid all his sufferings Heine's indomitable spirit rose triumphant. His irony, his wit, remained with him to the last. When Adolf Stahr re-visited him after a long absence, he apologized for his continued existence, but assured his guest that when he next came he would find no dying poet : a prolongation of the joke would be too tedious for his friends.

The first day of the new year was one of distressing suffering. The poet could see. no one, not even his "Lotus-Flower," as he often called *la mouche*. But he managed to send her a line with his best new-year wishes, having signed it—in bitter mockery of his own degradation from the pride of manhood—"Nebuchadnezzar II.," and, as by an afterthought, "Formerly atheist to his Prussian Majesty, now worshipper of the Lotus Flower."

Towards the end of January, Théophile Gautier paid his friend what proved a last visit. The French poet was shocked by the appearance of his *confrère*, but hardly anticipated a speedy end. A deathly pallor had usurped the wonted marble paleness. The hands were those of a dead man miraculously simulative of life. Yet the keen flame of wit flickered about those dying lips ; and with an elfish enjoyment of his own sallies Heine would raise the paralyzed lid of his seeing eye to note the effect of some keen shaft upon his auditor. In the recovery from a worse chest attack than usual, he was asked by his doctor if he could manage to whistle. "Pouvez vous siffler " (Can you whistle—or hiss, as the word also means)? "Hélas non ! " gasped the poet, "pas même les pièces de Monsieur Scribe ! "

On another occasion he was found by Berlioz prostrate with *ennui* after a visit from a pedantic German professor, who left as the musician entered. "I am afraid you will find me very stupid, my dear fellow," exclaimed Heine, "but the fact is I have just been *exchanging thoughts* with Dr. ——."

One day early in February—after a period of terrible agony, when "his brain was full of madness, and his heart of sorrow"—Camille Selden entered his room and saw him covering large sheets of paper with feverish haste, "with a pencil that assumed the sharpness of a murderous weapon." "I heard a cruel laugh, the laugh of satiated revenge. I looked at Henri : 'I have them,' he cried, 'dead or living they shall not escape. The tiger's claws shall survive the tiger.'" Heine was alluding to some additional matter he had just composed for his "Memoirs." The box containing these he once pointed out to Meissner with the remark : "Look you ! There are my memoirs. Therein I have been collecting for many years past a series of portraits and frightful *silhouettes*. Many know of this box and tremble. In this chest is shut up one of my best, but by no means the last, of my triumphs."

Yet from this sardonic humour this strange being passed to the extreme of tenderness. A little poem about his wife, composed at this time, might have been written by the author of " The Songs of Innocence."

February opened cold and wet, and the feeble flame of the poet's life languished. The two latest notes he addressed to his Lotus-Flower echo his depth of weariness. "Deepest Sorrow, thy name is Heinrich Heine," he exclaims in one of them. On the evening of Friday, the 15th of February, a sudden access of emotion made his "beloved Mouche" break into sobs. "We remained silent, but he placed his hand on my head and seemed to bless me. Thus passed our last interview." "As I was on the threshold I heard him call out in his vibrating, spasmodic tones, 'Come to-morrow; do not fail.'" Alas, she went not on the morrow, upon the evening of which there was no longer any invalid poet to whom to minister.

A frightful and incessant sickness had completely prostrated the sufferer. It became evident that death was imminent. By the night of the 16th, he himself knew that the end was at hand. "Am I about to die?" he asked of his physician, whom he saw steadfastly regarding him. "It is well."

Ere midnight an anxious friend called to inquire as to his state, and to bid farewell. With officious zeal he asked if the dying man had made his peace with God "Do not trouble yourself," replied the poet, with a wan smile, "*Dieu me pardonnera; c'est son métier.*"

These were the last words uttered by Heinrich Heine His untamable irony illumined even the shadow of death.

At four o'clock on the morning of the 17th he awoke from the sleep into which he had fallen, muttered something, and again slept, but did not awaken any more. And in this calm fashion it was that he came into his inalienable inheritance, that he, too, like Ponce de Leon, discovered Bimini.[1]

[1] Readers of Camille Selden's "Last Days of Heine," will recollect a strange episode in connection with the poet's death. Heine died somewhere between five and eight o'clock on the morning of the 17th. Madame Selden's words are as follows: "I awoke in a singular manner. Towards eight o'clock I heard a noise in my room, a kind of fluttering like that produced by moths. I opened my eyes but closed them again, *for a black form was writhing like a gigantic insect in the dawn, and sought some way of escape.*" Madame

When the friend, whose advent was always so welcome, entered the death-chamber she was not appalled by the visible signs of death, but by the inscrutable silence. There was nothing human in that cold corpse, nothing which recalled the man who had loved, hated, and suffered. Nought to look upon but an ancient mask, over which the final calm had cast a frost of haughty indifference. She had foreseen all save this sudden silence, all save this limitless calm.

On the forenoon of the 20th a few friends, including Théophile Gautier, Alexandre Dumas, Mignet, Alexandre Weill, and Paul de Saint-Victor, followed the dead poet to his grave in Montmartre. The coffin was so large and heavy for the wasted child-frame within, that Gautier was reminded of the lines in the " Lyrisches Intermezzo," where there is an allusion to the gigantic coffin that shall one day convey the singer to his rest, gigantic because of the vast love and the vast sorrow that shall therein be buried along with the insensate body.

The memorial stone in Montmartre bears the simple inscription, " Henri Heine." No longer had the poet cause to yearn over that " melodious grave of the enchanter Merlin, which is in the forest of Broceliand in Brittany, under high oaks whose tops shine like green flames to heaven."

*   *   *   *   *

Some seven years before Heine's death his unfortunate friend Gérard de Nerval wrote of him as follows : " It is

Selden hurriedly dressed soon afterwards, and when she reached the Avenue Matignon heard that Heine had passed away just before dawn.

no vain antithetical by-play to say of Heine that he is
at once cruel and tender, *naïf* and perfidious, sceptical
and credulous, lyrical and prosaic, a sentimentalist and
a mocker at sentiment, impassioned and reserved,
spirituel et pittoresque, an ancient and a moderner,
moyen-âge et révolutionnaire." This extraordinary com-
plexity, this many-sidedness, has been at once the fascination and the stumbling-block of critical students,
German, French, and English. In their extremity they
have variously compared him to Aristophanes, Rabelais,
Cervantes, Burns, Sterne, Jean Paul Richter, Swift,
Voltaire, Byron, Shelley, Béranger, Villon, and Catullus.
The very variety of these comparisons is significant.
What manner of man is this who has something in
common with the great masters of irony of all time—
than whom Catullus never sang more poignantly, or
Burns or Béranger with a freer lilt, a wilder music? It
is perhaps inevitable to attempt to classify even the
most absolutely unique phenomenon, howsoever that
attempt may be foredoomed to failure: but never did
a more hopeless subject present itself to the literary
scientist than the extraordinary genius represented by
the words "Heinrich Heine." Though therein it is easy
to trace that wide relationship which critics have been
pleased to designate, it is impossible to find the immediate kin of this poet. He was born in some happy Vale
of Tempe that we know not of, among Parnassus-grass
engirt with thickets of oleander, citron, and pomegranate:
but who were his parents? Perhaps some passionate
Oriental, and a dreaming blue-eyed maiden from the
forests beyond the Danube, who at times would sing her

magic faerie-lore and at times chant of the slaying sword
and the skull-borne mead of the tribesmen.   Or was he
but a dream of fallen Judæa, caught up by the mocking
breath of the Earth-Spirit and blown beyond Jordan and
waste Babylon to the hills of Greece?   What strange
noviciate was his: on what heights did he watch the
gods and behold the beauty of the world, in what
desolate places consort with unclean animals and evil
spirits?   Do what we will we cannot affiliate, we cannot
classify Heine.   When we would apprehend it, his genius
is as volatile as his wit—a subtle essence that can be
condensed in a few lines of perfect song, or that, like the
vapours of the Arabian wizard, can expand into cloudy
mists.   Of only one thing can we be sure : that he is
of our time, of our century.   He is so absolutely and
essentially modern that he is often antique.   Yet never is
he other than Heinrich Heine : Jew or Hellene, *Bursch*
or *Parisien*, a soldier in the van or an idler on ungranted
furlough, wild mocker or sweet singer, his idiosyncrasy
is dominant.   There never has been any other such as
he : and another Heine can hardly appear again.   As
Théophile Gautier wrote of the poet after his death,
what long and slow combinations will it cost nature
before she can reproduce such a head !   There are
flowers which bloom much more rarely than the aloe
—human flowers which unfold their fadeless petals but
once, it may be, in the whole slow growth of
humanity :

It is a poet of our own country, and of our own time,
who has uttered the best definition of Heine that has
yet been said.

> "The spirit of the world
> Beholding the absurdity of men—
> Their vaunts, their feats—let a sardonic smile
> For one short moment wander o'er his lips.
> *That smile was Heine !* "

In these words Matthew Arnold is more incisively interpretative than even in his able, though occasionally inaccurate and inadequate essay on the poet, upon whom he justly says that incomparably the greatest portion of Goethe's mantle fell—whom, still more aptly, he calls the Paladin of the modern spirit.

But it is not among his superficial complexities, it is among more fundamental bases that we must seek for the prime factors in Heine's genius. Yet these complexities, how puzzling they are ! How one is tempted to enlarge upon Gérard de Nerval's *cliquetis d'antithèses.* An Israelite and yet not a Jew ; one of the " bodyguard of Jehovah," and yet a deserter and a mocker ; a Christian, and an infidel ; a free-liver, and yet loyal to his wife and reverent of his mother ; a Romanticist, and the chief antagonist of Romanticism ; a true poet, and a born journalist ; an historian without method, a philosopher without real philosophy ; the most tender of German poets, and the most savagely cynical ; a German, yet the bitterest scourge of Germans, and, though without a drop of French blood, a Frenchman of the French ; an intense admirer of Shakespeare and the poets of England, and a hater of the nation and of everything English ; a cynic who laughed at sentiment and generosity, whose tears would rise at the sight of something beautiful, and whose purse, and brain, and courtesy were at the service even

of strangers and the unworthy; impatient and irritable
in health, of heroic endurance in ills more terrible than
ever fell to the lot of poet before; laughing at hope and
scorning resignation, yet nobly resigned and cherishing,
as it were, the living soul of a dead negation.

First and foremost Heine was a Jew, and born in an
enslaved country, and half a century too soon. To be a
German Jew even so comparatively lately as fifty or sixty
years ago—what a fate for a poet! Worse still, to have
inherited the pride of Israel, to scorn the workers of her
ignominy, to realize the frightful accumulation of her wrong,
her untold misery, her long despair, her undying hope!
And yet again worse to have sold one's soul for a mess
of pottage. If ever an act for which ethically there is no
excuse, but which the charitable must greatly palliate,
wrought its own revenge, it was Heine's apostasy. He
hearkened to Mephistopheles, and in cold blood signed
the agreement whereby he, a Jew, renounced Judaism,
he, an Israelite, became a Christian. Even in these days,
when God seems to have withdrawn at least a solar system further away, a man cannot barter his spiritual
birthright with immunity—or rather they may who have
no care but to eat, drink, and be merry; though the poet,
the man of genius, dare not sin without being haunted
for ever by the flaming sword even at the gates of earthly
Edens.

It is because of Heine's "intense modernism," of his
saturation with modern ideas, that he is so pre-eminently
the exponent of the yearning spirit of our century, that
he is of such various appeal. He saw what many better
and perhaps wiser men than himself failed to perceive:

the deep undertone of his time was clearly audible to
him. He has given voice to our inarticulate resentment
against we know not what; he has been our advocate
against a blind tyranny of nature ; he has given expression
to our unexpressed pain. A new note, an intensely
modern note, vibrates in the nervous prose of his
sentences and in the magic of his verse. For the first
time a strange voice is heard laughing at the sanctities
of four thousand years ; not a mere mockery, the ripple
of which has passed over the sea of humanity from all
time, but the laugh of the modern man who has reached
the summit, or what he believes to be the summit, of
human life, and does not see even the most ordinary
Pisgah beyond, much less a Promised Land. It is true
that in a sense this is but a phase that Heine represents ;
yet even if the phase do not prove recurrent in similar
or novel guise, he must always remain as the typical
exponent of one of the most spiritually troublous periods
in the history of man.

As for his song-motive, I should say it was primarily
his *Lebenslust*, his delight in life : that love so intensely
human that it almost necessarily involved the ignoring
of the divine. Rainbow-hued as is his genius, he himself was a creature of earth. It was enough to live.
Upon his mattress-grave he envied even the pug-dog
which ran to and fro beneath in the Champs Elysées ;
it was alive and sound—what happiness, what magical
fortune ! He would cling to life, even though it were
by a rotten beam, he declared once in his extremity.
And the poet of life he unquestionably is. There is a
pulse in everything he writes : his is no galvanised

existence. No parlour-passions lead him into the quicksands of oblivion. The sun shines, a fair girl laughs, the
lightning flashes, the sea frets and fumes and déstroys,
the woman wounds—loves, hates, enmities, despairs, all
the passions of mind and body—all these we have,
intensely human, but never the rapture of the mystic, the
ecstasy of the visionary. His sight is keener than an
eagle's, but spiritual horizons are for the most part beyond
his ken. Better still to say that he sees all the stars in
heaven, but pays no heed to those which the eye of
scientific faith perceives thronging in depths beyond.
He loves and is loved, and the sun shines, then all is
well ; love evanishes and *ennui* comes, and 'tis an east
wind, then ho for poison that will rankle and stilettos of
speech that, like Sefchen's sword, will thirst for blood.
At his best Heine is a creature of controlled impulse ; at
his worst he is a creature of impulse uncontrolled.
Through extremes he gained the golden mean of art ;
here is his *apologia*. By himself he must be judged, nor
could the justest arbiter materially interfere with the
poise of the scales set by Heine himself.

As a prose writer Heine is unsurpassed by any German
—even by Goethe—for lucidity, ease of movement, and
admirable concision. He can be as classical as Winckel-
mann, as chaste as Lessing, as clear-cut as Goethe, as
"lucidly nebulous" as Novalis or the worthy Jean Paul :
and over and above all he can be blithe and debonair as
no German scribe before or since. Never had any
stream so many back-waters, so many little rushy coves,
but all are as crystal-clear as the central current. He
who would hunt for muddy shallows will find them if he

be diligent, but then these rarities belong to trampled ground where one would expect miriness. In the higher phases of style, however, Heine falls below Goethe. His inconsistencies, his vagrant fancy, his endless divergencies, his ambuscades for the unwary reader, have a charm all their own—a charm somewhat palling, almost common-place now—but these are not the characteristics of a great style. Yet he will be read as a master of German prose long after his compositions have been relegated to the upper shelves.

His position towards religion concerns little those who have come after him. The points of vantage shift so constantly that a dead man's instructions are as likely to be provocative of boredom as of material help. Funda-mentally he was a rationalist ; Reason, he declared, had been the *passion malheureuse* of his life. If he missed much that is good, he saw clearly what was infeasible, absurd, or evil. He hated priestcraft, whether Christian or Judaic ; a paid clergy seemed to him a spiritual anomaly. But if clergy there must be, then let them be out-and-out exemplars of their faith ; rather the fierce hell-threatening priest than "the molly-coddle homœopa-thic soul-doctor who pours the thousandth part of a pint of reason into a gallon of morals, and sends people to sleep with it on Sundays." And it is because he was a friend of Religion, and a friend of the Church, that he "loathed that abortion called State-Religion, that monster born of the intrigue between temporal and spiritual power." For notwithstanding all his repudiations and blasphemies Heine believed in a Supreme Power : *what* he knew not and does not try to explain. His sole *credo* is the very characteristic, " I may not be over partial to anthropomorphism, but I believe in the Glory of God."

Towards politics his position was that of an unconcerned seer, so just, so incisive was his vision. Many will recall his memorable phrase: " There are no nations in Europe now ; there are only two factions. One is called Aristocracy : it thinks itself privileged by birth, and monopolizes all the glories of the commonalty. The other faction is called Democracy ; it vindicates the rights of man, and in the name of Reason demands the destruction of the privileges of birth."

Emancipation ! This was Heine's synonym for *Vorwärts :* his slogan in all his brilliant though desultory assaults. Emancipation of all oppressed peoples and races, emancipation of the whole world, and especially, first, of Europe, " that is now old enough to be its own master, and is breaking away from the iron leading-strings once held by the privileged aristocracy."

It is true what a brilliant English essayist of his own race has said of him, that his writings will be remembered by the wise, and that they " tell of a man whose life was filled with rapturous love for humanity, of a man angry until death with the shallow forms and conventionalities possessed no longer of any spiritual import." True ; and yet, after all, it is to Heine the poet that we turn when we wish to see the rainbow-hues of immortality. Here his radical fault of fragmentariness, of incompleteness, is less obvious, if at all. There is, of course, a formal fragmentariness in art which, however, is not essentially distinct from completeness—as exemplified, for instance, in the best of Heine's verse. But his prose work : how

often, nay, how almost invariably, its fragmentariness is
its present bane as it must prove its ultimate loss. All
his life he was a beginner. His beginnings are always
brilliant and often splendid : yet they are only com-
mencements. What magnificent essays his "Religion
and Philosophy in Germany" and his "Romantic
School" are ! how inadequate, how merely introductory
they are as histories ! This is Heine's weakest point, his
most fatal flaw.

But in poetry where is his equal as a lyric voice? One
is inclined to alter Browning's lines, and cry—

> " O lyric voice, half demon and half bird,
> And all a wonder and a wild desire ! "

Unfortunately, in his poetry as in his prose, Heine is
far from infrequently not only needlessly blasphemous,
but recklessly coarse and even occasionally obscene. It
is impossible not to note this canker ; the wisest plan is
to regret the flaw in the exquisite flower, and then to cut
it away as it were, to overlook it. Something of the
same excuse that is made for Rabelais must be made for
Heine ; for the rest, his banalities are nothing more nor
less than the strains of an ugly warp of vulgarity which
intertwined with his essential refinement—the mud, let
us say, in which his golden feet too often voluntarily
slipped. I certainly agree with Lord Lytton that this
obscenity is an even greater defect of genius than of art.
Yet too much has been made of this defect of Heine's
by friends as well as by foes. There is a place in the
economy of nature even for what is foul ; and as never
was man more *ein Naturkind*, a child of nature, than

Heine, he may be forgiven the display of some inherited traits.

Mr. Matthew Arnold has expended some felicitous phrases upon the poet whom, after all, he did not wholly understand ; but nowhere has he proved himself so incisive as the critic just alluded to when the latter states that Heine's poetic life was the outcome of the intuitive and continuous contemplation of suffering from a poetical point of view. His lyric crown was indeed a crown of thorns. It was Heine's destiny, concludes Lord Lytton, in his admirable critique upon the poet's posthumous publications, it was his destiny to become the permanent representative of the pain which is born of contrast. One great and everlasting form of human suffering found in him its appropriate poet.

Goethe thought that the one thing lacking in his lyric rival was love, but though the Jupiter Tonans of Weimar —as the younger poet called him—gauged correctly so far as he went, he did not penetrate deeply into Heine's real as distinct from his assumed nature. Matthew Arnold perhaps comes nearer to the truth when he declares that the fundamental weakness lay not in incapacity of love, but in lack of moral balance. An American critic thinks that we must rather look to a physiological cause. From early boyhood the poet's nervous system was morbid, or at least with constant tendencies to an abnormal condition ; and throughout his life his brain must have been more or less strenuously affected by cerebral excitement. No doubt each is right to a certain extent. The poet himself would have scoffed at the physiological as well as at the moral

diagnosis. Probably the real weakness was that Heine
was too much in love with life; he became its slave,
worshipped as a slave, grovelled as a slave, and met with
the slave's heritage of mockery and contumely. To win
life's secret one must barter many resignations for a few
veiled favours. After all, his own indication is best :
" In my cradle lay my line of march marked out for my
whole life."

And yet this *enfant terrible* of poetry, as his *Mouche*
rebelliously calls him, was the most Hellenically sensuous
as well as the most Biblically or Hebraicly ascetic of
singers. His imagination roams everywhere, but from
choice in the sunswept southlands, and, above all, in the
East. Spain, Italy, Greece—what inspirations he found
from these: but it was to "mystic Ind," with its vast
lotus-covered rivers and its gorgeous past and brooding
present, to the extreme Orient, to Persia in particular,
that his heart yearned. "O Firdusi !" he exclaims
somewhere, "O Firdusi! O Ischami ! O Saadi! How
miserable is your brother ! How do I long after the
roses of Schiraz !"

East and west, north and south : how marvellous the
range of this poet—Hellene, Oriental, dreaming and
imaginative German, sceptical Frenchman. What a
strange medley his poems seem when one's memory
surveys them in one illuminating flash. "Strange
dreams," writes his dearest friend, "where raillery cloaks
tenderness ; roseate clouds, where fair angel-heads
appear between baneful demon-faces ; transparent fogs,
illumed by an imaginary sun ; shifting landscapes full of
contrasts ; sometimes a cloister-garden, and close beside

it the blue waters of a Greek river; sometimes Gothic ruins, and close by the Indian cactus, displaying its blood-red purple blossoms."

It is vain, however, to attempt any exposition of the magic of Heine's verse. As he says in his last poem, "Die Passionsblume : " question the glowworm as to whence comes its brightness, or bid the wave explain its murmuring: ask the west wind the meaning of its moanings and plaints, or seek the purport of the perfume in the rose or of the fire in the carbuncle.

Heine must always hold his place as a poet : his poems have become as deeply imbedded in the heart of the German nation as are the groves of coral in Indian seas. The author of the "Buch der Lieder" may not be to Germany what Burns is to Scotland : but he is certainly far more to his country than Béranger—the third in the trio of the greatest of modern song-poets—ever was to France.

Heine passed as a drifting cloud : but his songs remain like stars in the heaven of poetry. "*Und so ist der blaue Himmel grösser als jedes Gewölk darin, und daurerhafter dazu,*" as says Jean Paul Richter : "The blue heaven is greater than any cloud that passeth over it."

Two thousand years ago—I read somewhere recently—there might have been seen at Laurium a certain yellow flower, which must have flourished in the golden age of Greece, and have faded for a while with the greatness of her people. "For when the piles of rubbish and scoriæ were removed," says the narrator, "and the fresh air and sunlight played upon the soil below, we are told the seeds, long buried, revived, and a little flower, unknown to the botanists or this century, sprang forth, and blossoms and lives as the Flower of Laurium."

One can well imagine that if, two thousand years hence, the German tongue were to have developed into a practically alien language, some curious philologist of a poetic turn might one day welcome with delight, after laborious research among the *débris* of a vanished literature, certain long buried yet fragrant blooms. These he would assuredly lovingly gather and transplant, so that a new cycle of humanity might rejoice in the "Laurium Flowers" of Heinrich Heine. For it is of the nature of the Flowers of Laurium that they are imperishable.

THE END.

INDEX.

BIBLIOGRAPHY.

BY

JOHN P. ANDERSON

(British Museum).

I. WORKS.

Heinrich Heine's Sämmtliche Werke. 6 Bde. Philadelphia, 1857-59, 8vo.

Heinrich Heine's Sämmtliche Werke. [Edited by A. Strodtmann.] 21 Bde. Hamburg, Wien [printed], 1861-66, 8vo.

Heinrich Heine's Sämmtliche Werke. (Neue vermehrte Ausgabe.) 18 Bde. Hamburg, Leipzig [printed], 1873-74, 8vo.

Sämmtliche Werke. Neue Ausgabe. (Biographie von G. Karpeles.) 12 Bde. Hamburg, 1884, 8vo.

Heinrich Heine's Werke. Illustrirte Pracht-Ausgabe. Herausgegeben von H. Laube. Wien [1884, etc.], 4to.

Heinrich Heine's Sämmtliche Werke. Bibliothek-Ausgabe. 13 Bde. Hamburg, Leipzig [printed], 1885, 8vo.

Heinrich Heine's Sämmtliche Werke, mit Biographie von J. Reuper nebst Einleitungen und dem Porträt des Dichters. Halle a. S. [188⁵, etc.], 8vo.

Heinrich Heine's gesammelte Werke. Herausgegeben von G. Karpeles. (Biographische Einleitung von C. A. Buchheim.) Berlin, Leipzig [printed], 1857, etc., 8vo.

Vermischte Schriften. 3 Bde. Hamburg, 1854, 8vo.

Poetische Werke. Hamburg, 1857, 8vo.

Heinrich Heine's Sämmtliche Gedichte. 2 Bde. Amsterdam, 1869, 8vo.

Dichtungen. 2 Thle. Amsterdam, 1861, 8vo.

Dichtungen. Ausgewählt und erläutert von K. Hessel. Mit einem bisher unbekannten Bildnis des Dichters, aus dem Jahre 1828, einer Biographie desselben und einem Verzeichnis der Compositionen Heinescher Lieder. Bonn, 1887, 8vo.

The Poems of Heine complete; translated in the original metres [from the German]. With a sketch of Heine's life. By E. A. Bowring. London, 1858, 8vo.

——Another edition. (*Bohn's Standard Library.*) London, 1861, 8vo.

II. SINGLE WORKS.

Atta Troll. Ein Sommernachtstraum. Hamburg, 1847, 8vo.

——Atta Troll and other poems. Translated into English by T. S. Egan. London, 1876, 8vo.

Briefe . . . herausgegeben von F. Steinmann. 2 Thle. Amsterdam, 1861, 16mo.

Briefe von H. Heine an seinen Freund M. Moser. Leipzig, 1862, 8vo.

Aus dem Nachlass Varnhagen's von Ense. Briefe von Stägemann, Metternich, Heine und Bettina von Arnim, etc. [Edited by L. Assing.] Leipzig, 1865, 8vo.

Buch der Lieder. Hamburg, 1827, 8vo.

——H. Heine's Book of Songs. A Translation [from the German] by J. E. Wallis. London, 1856, 8vo.

——Heine's Book of Songs. Translated by C. G. Leland. Philadelphia, 1864, 16mo.

——Third edition. New York, 1863, 8vo.

——The Book of Songs. Translated from the German by Stratheir. London, 1882, 8vo.

——Heine's Book of Songs. Compiled from the translations by Sir Theodore Martin and E. A. Bowring. New York, 1884, 16mo.

——A Romance in Song. Heine's Lyrical Interlude. Translated by F. Johnson. Illustrated. Boston [1884], 8vo.

Der Doktor Faust. Ein Tanzpoem, nebst kuriosen Berichten über Teufel, Hexen, und Dichtkunst. Hamburg, 1851, 8vo.

Französische Zustände. Hamburg, 1833, 12mo.

Gedichte. Berlin, 1822, 8vo.

Letzte Gedichte und Gedanken. Aus dem Nachlasse des Dichters. Hamburg, 1869, 8vo.

Neue Gedichte. Hamburg, 1844, 8vo.

Heinrich Heine's Memoiren und neugesammelte Gedichte, Prosa und Briefe. Mit Einleitung herausgegeben von E. Engel. Hamburg, Leipzig [printed 1884, 8vo.

Supplementband to "H. Heine's Sämmtliche Werke."

——The Memoirs of Heinrich Heine, and some newly-discovered fragments of his writings. With an introductory essay by T. W. Evans. London, 1884, 8vo.

Heinrich Heine's politisches Glaubensbekenntniss oder : Epistel an Deutschland. Geschrieben und gedruckt, 1832, neu an's Licht gezogen, 1848. Leipzig [1848], 8vo.

H. Heine über L. Börne. Hamburg, 1840, 8vo.

——Ludwig Borne : recollections of a revolutionist. Abridged and translated by T. S. Egan. London, 1881, 8vo.

Reisebilder. 4 Thle. Hamburg, 1826-34, 8vo.

——Heine's Pictures of Travel. Translated by C. G. Leland. Fourth edition. Philadelphia, 1863, 12mo.

——Fifth edition. New York, 1866, 8vo.

——Die Harzreise. Hamburg, 1853, 16mo.

——German Classics, edited with English notes, etc., by C. A. Buchheim. Vol. viii. Heine's Harzreise, etc. (*Clarendon Press Series.*) Oxford, 1886, 8vo.

——A Trip to the Brocken. Translated by R. McLintock. London, 1881, 8vo.

——Ideas. "Buch Le Grand" of the Reisebilder of Heinrich Heine, 1826. London, 1884, 8vo.

Romanzero. Hamburg, 1851, 8vo. This forms Bd. iii. of Heine's "Gedichte."

Der Salon. 4 Bde. Hamburg, 1834-40, 8vo.

Shakespeare's Maedchen und Frauen, mit Erlaeuterungen von Heinrich Heine. [With plates.] Paris [printed], Leipzig, 1839, 4to.

Tragödien, nebst einem lyrischen Intermezzo. Berlin, 1823, 8vo.
  Contains the "William Ratcliff," "Intermezzo," and "Almansor."

Zur Geschichte der neueren schönen Literatur in Deutschland. Paris [printed], Leipzig, 1833, 12mo.
  Appeared originally in the "Europe Littéraire" in 1833. Reprinted under the title of "Romantische Schule," and in French it forms part iv. of "De l'Allemagne."

——Die Romantische Schule. Hamburg, 1836, 12mo.

——The Romantic School. Translated by S. L. Fleishman. New York, 1882, 8vo.

——De l'Allemagne. 2 vols. Paris, 1835, 8vo.
  These vols. form vol. v.-vi. of the French edition of Heine's works published in 1834-5.

——Letters auxiliary to the history of modern polite literature in Germany. Translated by G. W. Haven. Boston, 1836, 8vo.

Zur Geschichte der Religion und Philosophie in Deutschland. Hamburg, 1835, 8vo.

——Religion and Philosophy in Germany : a fragment. Translated by John Snodgrass. (*English and Foreign Philosophical Library*, vol. 18.) London, 1882, 8vo.
  The original of this translation was first published in the *Revue des Deux Mondes* in 1834. In the French version (1835) of Heine's works it appears as the first part of the two volumes "De l'Allemagne."

III. SELECTIONS.

Metrical Translations from the German of Goethe, Schiller, Uhland, Heine, and others, by a German lady. Hamburg, 1852, 8vo.

Selections from the Poetry of Heinrich Heine, translated by J. Ackerlos [*pseud*, *i.e.*, John Stores Smith]. London, 1854, 8vo.

Poems. Translated by Julian Fane. Privately printed. Vienna, 1854, 8vo.

Poems from the German. By Richard Garnett. London, 1862, 8vo.
   Contains seven poems from Heine.

Leisure Hour Series. Scintillations from the prose works of Heinrich Heine. I. Florentine Nights. II. Excerpts. Translated from the German by S. A. Stern. New York, Newburgh [printed], 1873, 8vo.

Prose Miscellanies from Heinrich Heine. Translated by S. L. Fleishman. Philadelphia, 1876, 8vo.

Selections from the poetical works of Heinrich Heine. Translated into English. London, 1878, 8vo.

Poems and Ballads. Done into English verse by Theodore Martin, etc. Edinburgh and London, 1878, 8vo.

Wit, Wisdom, and Pathos, from the prose of Heinrich Heine, with a few pieces from the "Book of Songs." Selected and translated by J. Snodgrass. London, 1879, 8vo.
——Second edition. Paisley, 1888, 8vo.

English Fragments from the German of Heinrich Heine. Translated by S. Norris. Edinburgh, 1880, 8vo.

The City of Dreadful Night, and other Poems. By James Thomson. London, 1880, 8vo.
   Translations from Heine, pp. 165-184.

Poems and Ballads. Translated by E. Lazarus. To which is prefixed a biographical sketch of Heine. New York, 1881, 8vo.

Translations from Heine and other verses, by Ernest Radford. Cambridge, 1882, 8vo.

Heine. Selections from the Reisebilder and other prose works. Edited by C. Colbeck. (*Macmillan's Series of Foreign School Classics.*) London, 1883, 8vo.

German Classics, edited with English notes, etc., by C. A. Buchheim. Vol. vii. Heine's Prosa, being selections from his prose works. (*Clarendon Press Series.*) Oxford, 1884, 8vo.

Representative German Poems, ballad and lyrical. Original texts with English versions by various translators. Edited by K. Knortz. New York, 1885, 8vo.
   Heinrich Heine, pp. 229-257.

Poems and Translations. By Bessie Craigmyle. Aberdeen, 1886, 16mo.
   Contains sixteen translations from Heine.

The Prose Writings of Heinrich Heine. Edited, with an introduction, by Havelock Ellis. (*The Camelot Series.*) London, 1887, 8vo.

Poems, selected by Kate Freiligrath Kroeker. (*Canterbury Poets.*) London, 1887, 16mo.

Travel Pictures, including the Tour in the Harz, Norderney, and Book of Ideas, together with the Romantic School. Translated by Francis Storr. With map and appendices. (*Bohn's Standard Library.*) London, 1887, 8vo.

Songs and Lyrics, by H. Heine and other German poets. Done into English verse by J. Geikie. Edinburgh, 1887, 8vo.

IV. MISCELLANEOUS.

Kahldorf über den Adel in Briefen an den Grafen M. von Moltke. Herausgegeben von H. Heine. Nürnberg, 1831, 8vo.

Der sinnreiche Junker Don Quixote von La Mancha von M. Cervantes de Saavedra. Mit einer Einleitung von Heinrich Heine. 2 Bde. Stuttgart, 1837, 8vo.

Sittengemälde aus dem elsässischen Volksleben. Novellen von A. Weill. Mit einem Vorwort von Heinrich Heine. 2 Bde. Stuttgart, 1847, 8vo.

V. APPENDIX.

BIOGRAPHY, CRITICISM, ETC.

Arnold, Matthew.—Essays in Criticism. Third edition. London, 1875, 8vo.
Heinrich Heine, pp. 181-224.

Boden, August.—H. Heine über L. Börne. Zur Charakteristik Heine's. Mainz, 1841, 8vo.

Born, Stephan.—Heinrich Heine. (Oeffentliche Vorträge, Bd. 3.) Basel, 1875, 8vo.

Börne, Ludwig.—Ludwig Börne's Urtheil über H. Heine, etc. Frankfurt-am-Main, 1840, 8vo.

Braun, Heinrich. — Heine'sche Lieder im Bilde. Silhouetten von H. Braun. [With the text.] Berlin [1874], fol.

Buchanan, Robert.—A look round Literature. London, 1887, 8vo.
Heine in a court suit, pp. 210-217.

Bussy, Rosa.—Lose Blätter aus Heine's Buch der Lieder in Farbendruck nach Original-Aquarellen von R. B. [6 plates.] Berlin, 1866, 4to.

Ducros, Louis.—Henri Heine et son temps, etc. Paris, 1886, 8vo.

Eliot, George.—Essays and Leaves from a Note-book. London, 1884, 8vo.
German Wit: Heinrich Heine (from the *Westminster Review*, 1856), pp. 79-144.

Gaedcke, Hugo.—Aus Heinrich Heine's Dichterwerkstatt. Eine Studie. Hamburg, 1875, 8vo.

Gautier, Théophile.—Portraits et Souvenirs Littéraires. Paris, 1875, 8vo.
Henri Heine, pp. 105-123.

Gostwick, Joseph.—German Poets. A series of memoirs and translations. London [1875], 4to.
Heine, pp. 245-265.

——German Culture and Christianity, etc. London, 1882, 8vo.
H. Heine, pp. 360-364.

Gottschall, Rudolf.—Porträts und Studien. Leipzig, 1870, 8vo.
Heinrich Heine nach neuen Quellen, Bd. 1, pp. 185-264.

Hedge, Frederick Henry.—Hours with German Classics. Boston, 1886, 8vo.
Heinrich Heine, pp. 502-523.

Heine, Heinrich. — Heinrich Heine. [Biographical and critical notice, with selections from his works.] Cassel, 1853, 16mo.
Forms Bd. 12 of *Moderne Klassiker.*

——Joyas Prusianas. Intermedio, Regreso y Nueva Primavera, poemas líricos de E. Heine. Interpretacion española precedida de un estudio biográfico del poeta por M. M. Fernandez y G. [onzalez ?] Madrid, 1873, 8vo.

Heine, Heinrich.—L'Atta Troll, tradotto da G. Chiarini, con prefazione di G. Carducci e note di K. Hillebrand. Bologua, 1878, 8vo.

——Poemas y fantasias. Traducción en verso castellano de J. J. Herrero. Con un prólogo de D. M. Menéudez y Pelayo. Madrid, 1883, 8vo.

——Il Canzoniere. Traduzione di B. Zendrini, procedeto dalla introduzione alla terza edizione e seguito dal saggio critico, Heiue e suoi interpreti. Quarta edizione. 2 vols. Milano, 1884, 8vo.

——Poesias de Heine. Libro de los Cantares. Traducción en verso, precedida de un prólogo por T. Llorente, etc. Barceloua, 1885, 8vo.

——Poesie complete. Traduzione del Conte G. C. Secco-Suardo, con cenni biografici. 2 vols. Torino, 1886, 8vo.

——Il Libro dei Canti, tradotto da C. Varese, con prefazione di Paolo Lioy. Firenze, 1886, 8vo.

Heine, Maximilian.—Erinnerung-en an Heinrich Heiue und seine Familie. Von seinem Bruder Maximilian Heine. Berlin, 1868, 8vo.

Houghton, Lord.—Monographs, personal and social. London, 1873, 8vo.
The Last Days of Heinrich Heine, pp. 293-339.

Hüffer, Hermann.—Aus dem Leben Heinrich Heine's. Berlin, 1878, 8vo.

Japp, Alexander Hay.—German Life and Literature, etc. London [1880], 8vo.
Numerous references to Heine.

Jeske-Choinski, Teodor.—Henryk Heine, portret literacki. Kra-ków, 1885, 8vo.

Karpeles, Gustav. — Heinrich Heine uud das Judentbum. Breslau, 1868, 8vo.

——Heinrich Heine.—Biograph-ische Skizzen. Berlin [1870], 8vo.

——Heinrich Heine's Biographie. Hamburg, 1885, 8vo.

——Heinrich Heine und seine Zeitgenossen. Berlin, 1888, 8vo.

Lewald, August.—Aquarelle aus dem Leben. Manuheim, 1836, 8vo.
Heine, Th. ii., pp. 89-139.

Magnus, Lady.—Jewish Portraits. London, 1888, 8vo.
Heinrich Heine, pp. 45-81 ; appeared originally in *Macmillan's Magazine* for 1883.

Martini, Felice.—Heine e Zen-drini, ghiribizzo critico. Milano, 1879, 8vo

Meissner, Alfred. — Heinrich Heine. Erinnerungen. Ham-burg, 1856, 8vo.

Meyr, Melchior. — Ueber die poetischen Richtungen unserer Zeit. Erlangen, 1838, 8vo.
Ueber des Buch der Lieder, pp. 51-58.

Mirecourt, E. de [*i.e.,* C. J. Jacquot].—Les Contemporains. Pt. 70. Henri Heine. Paris, 1856, 12mo.

——Histoire Contemporaine. Henri Heine. No. 120. Paris, 1871, 12mo.

Proelss, Robert.—Heinrich Heine. Seine Lebensgang und seine Schriften, etc. Stuttgart, 1886, 8vo.

Robert-Tornow, Walter.—Goethe in Heine's Werken, etc. Berlin, 1883, 8vo.

Rocca, Maria della, *Princess.*— Ricordi della vita intima di Enrico Heine. Firenze, 1880, 8vo.

——Souvenirs de la vie intime de Henri Heine, recueillis par sa nièce Princesse Della-Rocca née Embden-Heine. Paris, 1881, 8vo.

——Errico Heine. Ricordi, note e rettifiche, etc. Roma, 1882, 8vo.

——Skizzen über Heinrich Heine, etc. Wien, 1882, 8vo.

Saint-Réné Taillandier. — Ecrivains et Poëtes Modernes. Paris, 1861, 8vo.
Henri Héine, pp. 89-153.

——Histoire de la Jeune Allemagne. Paris, 1848, 8vo.
Henri Heine, pp. 90-133, 388-393.

Schanz, Giulio.—Enrico Heine in Italia, coll'aggiunta di alcuni documenti letterari, etc. Dresden, 1868, 8vo.

Schärt, Hermann. — Heinrich Heine und sein Vaterland. Czernowitz [1879], 8vo.

Scheible, J.—Heinrich Heine, der Unsterbliche. Eine Mahnung aus dem Jenseits, etc. (*Kleiner Wunder-Schauplatz*, Th. 12.) Stuttgart, 1857, 16mo.

Schiff, Hermann. — Heinrich Heine und der Neuisraelitismus. Hamburg, 1866, 8vo.

Schmidt, Julian.—Bilder aus dem Geistigen Leben unserer Zeit. 2 Bd. Leipzig, 1870-71, 8vo.
Heinrich Heine, Bd. 2, pp. 283-350.

Schmidt-Weissenfels, E.—Ueber Heinrich Heine, etc. Berlin, 1857, 8vo.

Schwenk, Konrad.—Literiarsche Charakteristiken und Kritiken. Frankfurt am Main, 1847, 8vo.
H. Heine's Buch der Lieder, pp. 341-349.

Selden, Camille.—Les derniers jours de Henri Heine. Paris, 1884, 8vo.

——The last days of Heinrich Heine. Translated by Clare Brune. London, 1884, 8vo.

Sintenis, F.— H. Heine. Ein Vortrag. Dorpat, 1877, 8vo.

Steinmann, Friedrich.—H. Heine. Denkwürdigkeiten und Erlebnisse aus meinem Zusammenleben mit ihm. Prag, 1857, 8vo.

——Der Froschmäusekrieg wider H. Heine's Dichtungen. Amsterdam, 1861, 8vo.

Stephani, Max. Jos. — Heinrich Heine und ein Blick auf unsre Zeit. Halle, 1834, 8vo.

Stigand, William. — The Life, Work, and Opinions of Heinrich Heine. 2 vols. London, 1875, 8vo.

Strodtmann, Adolf. — Heinrich Heine's Wirken und Streben, etc. Hamburg, 1857, 8vo.

——H. Heine's Leben und Werke. 2 Bde. Berlin, 1867-69, 8vo.

——Zweite Auflage. 2 Bde. Berlin, 1873-4, 8vo.

Weill, Alexandre.—Souvenirs intimes de Henri Heine. Paris, 1883, 8vo.

Weiss, John.—Life and Correspondence of Theodore Parker. 2 vols. London, 1863, 8vo.
Vol. ii. contains translations from Heine.

Z, X, Y. — Die Recensenten-Hölle oder oberflächliche Kritik und Heine'sche Tiefe. Rendsburg, 1856, 8vo.

Zett, Alfred von. — Im Karste. Nach H. Heine's "Harzreise." Pola, 1881, 8vo.

Zianitzka, K. Th. — Heinrich Heine der Liederdichter. Ein romantisches Lebensbild. 6 Th. Leipzig, 1864, 16mo.

15

viii BIBLIOGRAPHY.

Songs, etc, Set to Music.

Three Songs from H. Heine's *Reisebilder*. [*British Vocal Album*, No. 26-28.] By Sir G. A. Macfarren, 1845, etc.

Sechs Lieder von Heine. By M. Wielhorski, 1852.

Six Songs from the German of Heine. By A. L. Eigher, 1860.

Twelve Lieder von H. Heine. By H. Hertz, 1867.

Sechs Lieder von H. Heine. By R. Franz, 1867.

Zwei Balladen von H. Heine. By M. Weyermann, 1869.

Liebestraum. Ein Cyclus von sechs Gesangen. By A. Klughardt, 1870.

Almansor. Fragment aus H. Heine's gleichnamiger Tragödie. Concert-Arie für Bariton mit Orchester. Begleitung. By C. Reineke, 1874.

Sechs Gesänge. [Nos. 1, 3, and 5 written by Heine.] By S. Warteresiewicz, 1874.

Sechs Lieder. [Nos. 1-3 written by Heine.] By A. Urspruch, 1875.

Six Songs of Heine. By C. V. Stanford, 1876 and 1878.

Liebeslieder (nach Texten von Heine). By A. Urspruch, 1876.

Three Lyrics from Heine's Book of Songs. By M. G. Carmichael, 1876 and 1878.

Gesänge. Zwölf Dichtungen von Heine. By P. Geisler, 1876.

Sechs Lieder. (Gedichte by H. Heine.) By L. Gruenberger, 1877.

Gesänge. Zehn Dichtungen von Heine. By P. Geisler, 1877.

Sechs Lieder, etc. [Nos. 1-3 written by Heine.] By M. Roeder, 1878.

Lieder, etc. Heft 1. By A. Fuchs [Nos. 1-4, 6 written by Heine], 1878.

Zwei Lieder von H. Heine. By M. V. White, 1878 and 1882.

Blumen von H. Heine. By F. Vanderstucken, 1879.

Sechs Gesänge. Op. 28. [Nos. 4, 6 written by Heine.] By G. Hasse, 1879.

Vier Lieder, etc. [Nos. 1, 2 written by Heine.] By A. von Sigmond, 1880.

Sechs Lieder. Op. 60. [Nos. 3, 6 written by Heine.] By F. Siebmann, 1880.

Sechs Lieder, etc. [Nos. 1, 2 written by Heine.] By. R. Philip, 1880.

Sechs Lieder. Op. 20. [Nos. 2, 4, 5 written by Heine.] By L. Hartmann, 1880.

Romanze, etc. [Nos. 1, 2, 5-8 written by Heine.] By B. Junck, 1880.

Drei Lieder. [Nos. 2, 3 written by Heine.] By H. Schaeffer, 1881.

Three Songs. [Nos. 1, 2 written by Heine.] By U. K. Hartree, 1881.

Sechs Lieder. Op. 85. [Nos. 1, 2 written by Heine.] By J. Brahms, 1882.

Fünf Lieder. Op. 7. [Nos. 3, 4 written by Heine.] By A. Becker, 1882.

Trois Lieder sur des poésies de H. Heine. By G. de Kervéguen, 1882.

Sechs Liebeslieder von Heine. By A. Hervey, 1883.

Drei Lieder für drei Frauenstimmen. Op. 32. [Nos. 1, 2 written by Heine.] By A. Klughardt, 1884.

Ratcliff. Gesangescene. By. A. Fuchs, 1884.

"Ah! sure if the little flowers." (From the German of H. Heine.) 1876.

"Alla mia dormente." By B. Junck, 1884.

"All in the lovely month of May." By A. Foote, 1874.

"Allnächtlich im Traume seh 'ich dich." By S. Warteresiewicz. (*Sechs Gesänge*, Op. 6, No. 1), 1886.

"Am einsamen Strande da plätschert die Fluth." — *Die Nixen.* By F. W. Kuecken, 1876.

"Am fernen Horizonte." By W. Claussen (*Fünf Lieder*, Op. 3, No. 4), 1875 ?

"Am Fenster stand die Mutter." By O. Ludolffs, 1873.

"Am Kreuzweg ward begraben." By B. Hopffer (*Zwölf Lieder* Op. 9, No. 4), 1870 ; E. Meyer-Helmund (*Vier Lieder*, Op. 11, No. 2), 1885.

"Am Leuchtende Sommermorgen." By F. Siebmann (6 *Lieder*, Op. 47, No. 3), 1864.

"An die blaue Himmelsdecke." By F. Gumbert ; L. Hartmann (*Sechs Lieder*, Op. 22, No. 2), 1882. E. Rudersdorff, 1860.

"An die bretterne Schiffswand." By H. Reimann (*Vier Lieder*, Op. 4, No. 2), 1881.

"Andre beten zur Madonne." By L. E. Bach, 1884.

"Anfangs wollt' ich fast verzagen." By R. Schumann (*Mélodies*, No. 8), 1867.

"Auf die schlafende Zuleima." By R. Kruckow (*Drei Lieder*, No. 1), 1874.

"Aus alten Mährchen." By T. Seifart, 1858.

"Aus meinen Thränen spriessen." By R. F. Ellicott, 1881 ; R. Schumann (*Dichterliebe*, No. 2), 1861.

"The baby wept." — *Fleeting Sorrow.* By E. J. Danvers, 1876.

"La belle étoile tombe." By J. Merkens, 1886.

"Berg' und Burgen schau'n herunter. By R. Schumann (*Mélodies*, No. 7), 1867.

"Die blauen Frühlingsaugen." By R. F. Ellicott, 1881 ; J. Pauls (*Lieder*, Op. 12, No. 6), 1886 ; F. Ries (*Vier Lieder*, Op. 25, No. 3), 1876 ; A. Rubinstein (*Songs and Duets*, No. 8), 1869 ; A. Rubinstein, 1878 ; O. Tiehsen (*Sieben Gedichte*, Op. 6, No. 3), 1860 ? ; R. Wüerst (*Vier Zweistimmige Lieder*, No. 2), 1874.

"Buch der Lieder." By R. Schumann (*Dichterliebe*), 1861.

"Das ist ein Brausen und Heulen." By C. Krill (*Fünf Lieder*, No. 2), 1874.

"Das ist ein Flöten und Geigen." By L. Ehlert (*Fünf Lieder*, No. 4), 1860 ?

"Das ist ein schlechtes Wetter." By P. Viardot-Garcia, 1870.

"Dass du mich liebst das wusst' ich." By L. Heidingsfeld (*Zwei Lieder*, Op. 10, No. 1), 1879 ; A. Horn, 1874 ; O. Tiefenbach, 1884.

"Deh ! non giurare e bacia solamente." By H. M. Costa, 1881.

"Dein Angesicht so lieb und schön." By E. Degele (*Drei Gesänge*, Op. 12, No. 2), 1873 ; G. Hasse (*Sechs Gesänge*, Op. 27, No. 4), 1877 ; C. Ritter (*Zwölf Lieder*, Op. 4, No. 8), 1857.

"Du bist gestorben und weisst es nicht." By A. Horn, 1875.

"Du bist wie eine Blume." By A. Amadei (*Sechs Gesänge*, Op. 9, No. 4), 1885; A. Bungert *Junge Lieder*, Op. 3, No. 2), 1872; M. Halbmayr (*Zwei Lieder*, No. 2), 1880; G. Henschel (*Vier Lieder*, Op. 37, No. 3), 1885; H. Reimann (*Vier Lieder*, No. 4), 1881; A. Rubinstein (*Songs and Duets*, No. 3), 1869; A. Rubinstein, 1876 and 1881; G. Sgambati (*Canti*, No. 3),1885; C. Voss, 1852; E. von Waldeck, 1881; F. Warnbe (*Drei Lieder*, Op. 22), 1884; H. Wichmann (*Sechs Lieder*, Op. 3, No. 3), 1845 ?; A. Winterberger (12 *Gesänge*, Op. 12, No. 2), 1865.

"Du hast Diamanten und Perlen." By G. Hoelzel, 1853.

"Du liebst mich nicht." By E. A. Macdowell (*Drei Lieder*, Op. 11, No. 2), 1885; T. Nehfeld (*Drei Lieder*, Op. 18, No. 2), 1885.

"Du schönes Fischermädchen." By C. Eckert, 1852; W. Fink (*Vier Lieder*, Op. 4, No. 4), 1865; G. Hasse (*Vier Gesänge*, Op. 9, No. 4), 1874; G. Meyerbeer, 1848; W. S. Rockstro (*Lyra Anglo-Germanica*, No. 14), 1853; F. Schubert, 1850.

"Thou beauteous fishermaiden." By B. Tours, 1868.

"Entflich mit mir und sei mein Weib." By H. Ehrlich, 1880; C. V. Stanford, 1882.

"Es fällt ein Stern herunter." By W. Claussen (*Fünf Lieder*, Op. 3, No. 5), 1875 ? A. Klughardt (*Vier Lieder*, Op. 41, No. 2), 1884.

"Es fasst mich wieder der alte Muth." By M. J. Beer (*Sechs Lieder*, No. 3), 1876.

"Es hat die warme Frühlingsnacht." By J. Weiss (*Vier Lieder*, Op. 3, No. 1), 1885.

"Es schauen die Blumen." By J. Brahms (*Vier Lieder*, Op. 96, No. 3), 1886; H. Krigar (*Sechs Lieder*, No. 6), 1873.

"Es treibt dich fort von Ort zu Ort." By O. De La Cinna, 1859; R. Schumann, (*Mélodies*, No. 2), 1867; J. Weiss (*Vier Lieder*, Op. 3, No. 2), 1885.

"Es war als hätt' der Himmel." By W. Sturm (*Vier Gesänge*, Op. 16, No. 2), 1876.

"Es war ein alter König." By F. P. Frontini, 1883; A. Heitsch (*Sechs Lieder*, Op. 5, No. 5), 1884; G. Henschel (*Vier Lieder*, Op. 37, No. 1), 1885; A. Hoffmann (*Zehn Gesänge*, Op. 5, No. 4), 1884; F. W. Kuecken (*Duette*, Op. 105, No. 1), 1877; A Lucae (*Vier Lieder*, No. 2), 1882; E. Meyer - Helmund (*Vier Lieder*, Op. 3, No. 2), 1886; F. Ries (*Vier Lieder*, Op. 25, No. 1), 1876; M. Zenger (*Fünf Lieder*, No. 2), 1877.

"Es war einmal ein König." By B. Ramann (*Drei Lieder*, Op. 23, No. 1), 1872.

"Ferne flammenhelle Sterne." By C. G. Reissiger (*Ernste Lieder*, Op. 96, No. 1), 1850 ?

"Ein Fichtenbaum steht einsam." By K. Heubner (*Fünf Lieder*, Op. 4, No. 4), 1885; F. Hiller (*10 Gesänge*, Op. 90, No. 9), 1863; A. Jensen (*Drei Zweistimmige Lieder*, No. 2), 1883; C. Ritter (*Zwölf Lieder*, Op. 4, No. 11), 1857; H. Roesel (*Drei Duette*, Op. 25, No. 2), 1884; A. Rubinstein, 1886; F. Von

Woyrsch (*4 Lieder*, Op. 2, No. 1), 1884.

"Fioriva il tiglio." By P. Guarini, 1880.

"Frühlingsmythus." By F. Von Holstein, 1880.

"Gekommen ist der Maie." By R. Schwahn (*Drei Lieder*, Op. 3, No. 2), 1874 ; O. Tiehsen (*Sieben Gedichte*, Op. 6, No. 2), 1860 ?

"Das gelbe Laub erzittert." By O. De La Cinna, 1859 ; V. E. Nessler (*Vier Lieder*, Op. 23, No. 3), 1870.

"Già il sol dal monte." By E. Aromatari, 1883.

"Der Herbstwind rüttelt die Bäume." By Mendelssohn (*Three German Songs*, Op. 34, No. 3), 1845.

"Herr Peter und Bender sassen beim Wein." By R. Emmerich, 1873.

"Herzens Stimmen." — Translated from the German of Heine. By A. Hervey, 1884.

"Herz, mein Herz, sei nicht beklommen." By W. Claussen (*Fünf Lieder*, Op. 3, No. 3), 1875 ? B. Hopffer (*Zwölf Lieder*, Op. 6, No. 3), 1870.

"Ho pianto tanto in sogno." By A. Rotoli, 1882.

"Hör' ich das Liedchen erklingen." By M. Ernemann (*Sechs Lieder*, Op. 13, No. 1), 1850 ? C. Fink (*Fünf Lieder*, Op. 3, No. 5), 1857 ; J. Kiel (*Liederkreis*, No. 8), 1874.

"Ja du bist elend und ich grolle nicht." By H. Erler, 1872.

"Ich geh! nicht allein, mein feines Lieb." By J. Schaeffer (*Funf Lieder*, No. 1), 1874.

"Ich grolle nicht." By R.

Schumann (*Dichterliebe*, No. 7), 1861.

"Ich hab dich geliebt." By E. Rentsch (2 *Lieder*, No. 2), 1878.

"Ich hab' im Traum geweinet." By F. d'Alquen, 1877 ; St. C. Baddeley (*Sechs Lieder*, No. 6), 1883 ; E. Lassen (*Sechs Lieder*, Op. 48, No. 2), 1873 ; W. Schulthes, 1856 ; R. Schumann (*Dichterliebe*, No. 13), 1861.

"Ich halte ihr die Augen Zu." By F. W. Kuecken, 1850.

"Ich hatte einst ein schönes Vaterland." By E. Hermes (*Vier Mannerquartette*, No. 1), 1881.

"Ich hatte einst schones Traum." By F. Gumbert (*Drei Lieder*).

"Ich lieb' eine Blume." By A. Levinsohn (*Drei Lieder*, Op. 2, No. 2), 1886.

"Ich stand gelehnet an den Mast." By R. Franz (*Sechs Gesänge*, Op. 48, No. 3), 1878 ; H. Hartung (*Sechs Lieder*, No. 3), 1877.

"Ich stand in dunklen Träumen." By G. Jensen (*Drei Lieder*, Op. 21, No. 3), 1885 ; M. M. Lindner, 1878.

"Ich wandelte unter den Bäumen." By R. Schumann (*Mélodies*, No. 3), 1867.

"Ich weiss nicht, was soll es bedeuten." By C. L. Fischer. 1885 ; J. Mathieux (*Sechs Lieder*, No. 4), 1840 ? F. Silcher, 1858.

"Ich will meine Seele tauchen." By G. Hasse (*Acht Lieder*, Op. 26, No. 7), 1877 ; A. Kleffel (*Lenz und Liebe*, No. 5), 1869 ; C. Ritter (*Zwölf Lieder*, Op. 4, No. 7), 1857 ; M. Roeder (*Zwei*

Lieder, No. 2), 1884; R. Schumann (*Dichterliebe*, No. 5), 1861.

"Ich wollt' meine Schmerzen ergössen." By A. Fesca (*Six German Songs*, Op. 32, No. 5), 1850.

"Im Mondenglanze ruht das Meer." By S. Ochs (*Drei Gedichte*, Op. 7, No. 2), 1885.

"Im Rhein, im heiligen Strome." By R. Schumann (*Dichterliebe*, No. 6), 1861.

"Im Schloss zu Düsseldorf am Rhein." By C. Reinecke, 1875.

"Im Walde wandl' ich." By E. W. B., 1867; L. E. Bach, 1884.

"Im wunderschönen Monat Mai." By F. W. Kuechen, 1851; R. Schumann (*Dichterliebe*, No. 1), 1861; H. G. Richter (*Fünf Lieder*, No. 3), 1875.

"In deinen Augen hab' ich's gelesen." By A. Klughardt (*Drei Lieder*, Op. 39, No. 2), 1883.

"In dem Mondenschein im Walde." By Mendelssohn (*Sechs Lieder*, Op. 19, No. 4), 1849.

"In dem Traum siehst du." By R. Franz (*Sechs Gesänge*, Op. 41, No. 2), 1867.

"In dem Walde spriesst und grünt es." By A. Levinsohn (*Drei Lieder*, Op. 2, No. 3), 1886.

"In meiner Erinn'rung blühen Bilder." By C. Ritter (*Zwölf Lieder*, Op. 4, No. 1), 1857.

"In mein gar zu dunkles Leben." By F. von Kerstorf (12 *Deutsche Lieder*, No. 9), 1874.

"Ein Jüngling liebt ein Mädchen." By C. Grossmann (*Sechs Lieder*, Op. 1, No. 6), 1870.

"Kind, es wäre dein Verderben." By G. Henschel *Vier Lieder*, Op. 37, No. 4), 1885.

"Das Leben ist der schwüle Tag." By L. Heidingsfeld *Zwei Lieder*, Op. 4, No. 1), 1878.

"Lehn' deine Wang." By A. Bungeért, 1884; E. Sjögren (*An Eine*, Op. 16, No. 5), 1886.

"Leise zieht durch mein Gemuth." By M. Ernemann (*Vier Lieder*, Op. 26, No. 1), 1875?; R. Franz (*Sechs Gesänge*, Op. 41, No. 1), 1867; N. W. Gade (*Eight duettinos*, Op. 9, No. 1), 1849; F. J. van der Heijden (*Fünf Lieder*, No. 4), 1883; C. Isenmann (*Fünf Mannerchöre*, Op. 66, No. 4), 1884; T. H. MacDermott, 1880; Mendelssohn (*Sechs (Lieder*, Op. 19, No. 3), 1849; F. Reichel (*Fünf Gesänge*, No. 4), 1878; H. Von Sahr (*Acht Gesänge*, No. 4), 1877; F. Siebmann (*Sechs Zweistimmige Lieder*, Op. 54, No. 1), 1872; W. Sturm (*Sechs Lieder*, Op. 19, No. 3), 1877.

"Lieb' Liebchen leg's Händchen auf's Herze mein." By J. Gauby (*Zwei Lieder*, Op. 14, No. 2), 1882; F. Ries (*Sechs Lieder*, Op. 8, No. 4), 1869.

"Lieb' Liebchen, lieb' Liebchen." By C. A. F. Eckert (*Sechs Lieder*, Op. 28, No. 5), 1872; R. Schumann (*Mélodies*, No. 4), 1867.

"Die Lotosblume ängstigt sich." By R. Schumann, 1865; F. von Woyrsch (4 *Lieder*, Op. 2, No. 2), 1884.

" Mädchen mit dem rothen Mündchen." By F. Kuelz (*Drei Lieder*, Op. 43, No. 3), 1884 ; O. Ludolfs, 1885 ; E. Meyer-Helmund (*Drei Lieder*, Op. 25, No. 2), 1886 ; F. Ries (*Sechs Lieder*, Op. 6, No. 1), 1869 ; F. Ries (16 *Mélodies*, No. 1), 1869 ; M. Zenger (6 *Lieder*, No. 3), 1864.

" Maiden mine " [Mädchen mit dem rothen Mündchen]. By Sir W. E. Bennett, 1875 ; H. A. Harding, 1877.

" Mag da draussen Schnee sich thürmen." By W. S. Rockstro (*Lyra Anglo-Germanica*, No. 11a.), 1853.

" Maggio è tornato." By B. Junck, 1884.

" Maria, Maria ich liebe dich." By F. von Suppé, 1884.

"Das Meer erglanzte weit hinaus." By F. Schubert, 1857.

"Das Meer hat seine Perlen." By M. W. Balfe, 1862 ; C. E. Pinsuti, 1865 ; O. Tiehsen, 1846 ; M. V. White, 1880.

" Mein Knecht steh' auf und sattle schnell." By E. Meyer-Helmund (*Drei Lieder*, Op. 29, No. 1), 1886 ; M. Stange (*Drei Gesänge*, No. 1), 1881.

" Mein Liebchen, wir sassen beisammen." By J. Brahms (*Vier Lieder*, Op. 96, No. 4), 1886 ; L. Franz (*Drei Lieder*, No. 3), 1885 ; E. Lassen (*Sechs Lieder*, Op. 48, No. 1), 1873 ; Edward MacDowell (*Drei Lieder*, Op. 11, No. 1), 1885 ; F. Siebmann (6 *Lieder*, Op. 47, No. 4), 1864.

" Mein süsses Lieb, wenn du im Grab." By M. Renner (*Vier Gesänge*, No. 3), 1883.

" Mir träumte von einem Königskind." By A. Deprosse (*Sechs Lieder*, Op. 33, No. 5), 1875 ; A. Kleffel (*Sechs Gesänge*, No. 5), 1873.

" Mit deinen blauen Augen." By C. Ritter (*Zwölf Lieder*, Op. 4, No. 5), 1857.

" Mit Myrten und Rosen." By R. Schumann (*Mélodies*, No. 9), 1867.

" Mit schwarzen Segeln segelt mein Schiff." By M. J. Beer *Sturm und Stille*, No. 3), 1877 ; A. Rotoli, 1885.

" Der Mond ist aufgegangen." By E. Naumann (6 *Lieder*, Op. 29, No. 5), 1866 ; F. Siebmann (6 *Lieder*, Op. 47, No. 2), 1864.

" Morgens steh ich auf." By R. Schumann (*Mélodies*, No. 1), 1867.

" Mutter zum Bienelein." By R. Franz (*Sechs Gesänge*, Op. 41, No. 5), 1867 ; M. Zenger (*Fünf Duette*, No. 3), 1877.

" Nacht liegt auf den fremden Wegen. By W. A. Aiken, 1880 ; A. J. Becher (*Acht Gedichte*, No. 3), 1840 ! W. Claussen (*Fünf Lieder*, Op. 3, No. 2), 1875 ; H. Krigar, (*Sechs Lieder*, No. 2), 1873.

" Die Nachtigall sie sang so süss." By F. von Suppé, 1884.

" Nel mio giardin s'asconde umil." By A. Tessarin, 1876.

" Nun leg' dein liebes Kopfchen." By C. Riccius (*Vier Lieder*, Op. 20, No. 2), 1884.

" L'onda scintilla e corre via Giuliva." By A. Vanbianchi, 1886.

" Oben wo die Sterne glühn." By Edward Macdowell (*Drei Lieder*, Op. 11, No. 3), 1885.

"Ein Reiter durch das Bergthal zieht." By A. Winterburger, 1875.

"Die Rose, die Lilie." By R. Schumann (*Dichterliebe*, No. 3), 1861 ; M. Zenger (*Sechs Chorgesänge*, Op. 24, No. 5), 1877.

"Sag'mir, wer einst die Uhren erfund." By P. Umlauff (*Fünf Lieder*, Op. 26, No. 5), 1886.

"Die schlanke Wasserlilie." By R. Franz (*Zehn Gesänge*, Op. 51, No. 7), 1879 ; F. von Woyrsch (*4 Lieder*, Op. 2, No. 3), 1884.

"Die schönen Augen der Frühlingsnacht." By R. Franz (*Zehn Lieder*, Op. 51, No. 5), 1879.

"Ein schöner Stern geht auf in meiner Nacht." By F. von Holstein (*Sechs Lieder*, Op. 42, No. 5), 1880.

"Schöne Wiege meiner Leiden." By J. P. Goldberg, 1873 ; R. Schumann (*Mélodies*, No. 5), 1867.

"Schon wieder bin ich fortgerissen." By H. Hofmann (*Liedercyclus*, Op. 27, No. 3), 1875.

"Der See hat seine Perlen." By R. Franz, 1863.

"The sea hath its pearls ;" poetry by H. W. Longfellow (from H. Heine). By L. Caracciolo, 1885.

"Sie haben mich gequälet." By E. A. G. Bell, 1861.

"Sie liebten sich beide." By C. Grossmann (*Sechs Lieder*, Op. 1, No. 2), 1870.

"Sterne mit den goldnen Füsschen." By G. Hasse (*Vier Gesänge*, Op. 13, No. 2), 1874; A. Reichardt, 1861.

"Ein Stern ging auf vor meinem trüben Blick." By C. Davidoff (*Lieder*, Op. 25, No. 4), 1883.

"Still ist die Nacht." By J. H. Franz (*Drei Lieder*, Op. 17, No. 1), 1869.

"Still versteckt der Mond sich draussen." By F. Draeseke, 1882.

"Täglich ging die wunderschöne." By R. Emmerich (*Sechs Gesänge*, Op. 41, No. 1), 1874 ; A. Rubenstein, 1880.

"Der Tod, das ist die kühle Nacht." By A. Amadei (*Fünf Gesänge*, Op. 8, No. 3), 1885 ; J. Brahms (*Vier Lieder*, Op. 96, No. 1), 1886 ; G. Hasse (*Sechs Gesänge*, Op. 32, No. 1), 1881; F. Lew (*Drei Lieder*, No. 2), 1885; C. J. Schmidt (*Drei Nachtstücke*, No. 3), 1879.

"To-night she will dance." By A. W. Batson, 1876.

"Tragodie." F. Hiller (*Drei Lieder*), 1874.

"Über die Berge steigt schon die Sonne." By G. Hasse (*Vier Gesänge*, Op. 13, No. 3), 1874.

"Un di t'abbandona." By A. Vanbianchi, 1886.

"Und wüssten's die Blumen." By C. Kammerlander (*4 Lieder*, No. 4), 1865 ; M. Moszkowski (*Drei Lieder*, Op. 13, No. 2), 1877 ; A. Reichardt, 1859 ; M. Roeder (*Fünf Gesänge*, Op. 3, No. 3), 1873 ; R. Schumann (*Dichterliebe*, No. 8), 1861 ; M. Zenger (*6 Lieder*, No. 2), 1864.

"Vaghe stelle del ciel." By G. Ruta, 1884.

"Vergiftet sind meine Lieder." By F. Mannstaedt (*2 Lieder*, No. 1), 1871 ; V. E. Nessler (*Vier Lieder*, Op. 23, No. 2,) 1870.

"Verrieth mein blasses Angesicht." By H. Hofmann (*Fünf Lieder*, Op. 26, No. 3), 1875.

"Vor dem Dome steh'n zwei Männer." By F. Draeseke,1882.

"Warte, warte, wilder Schiffmann." By R. Schumann (*Mélodies*, No. 6), 1867.

"Warum sind denn die Rosen so blass." By A. P. Lighthill, 1864 ; C. A. Ranken, 1881.

"Was will die einsame Thräne." By H. Bellermann, 1877 ; C. G. Reissiger (*Ernste Lieder*, Op. 96, No. 8), 1850 ; J. Roch, 1877 ; O. Wangemann (*Fünf Lieder*, Op. 30, No. 5), 1884.

"Die Wellen blinken und fliessen dahin." By J. Brahms (*Lieder, etc.*, Op. 71, No. 1), 1876, etc. ; F. von Gumbert, 1855.

"Wenn du gute Augen hast." By C. Ritter (*Zwölf Lieder*, Op. 4, No. 6), 1857.

"Wenn ich auf dem Lager liege." By A. Bungert (*Junge Lieder*, Op. 2, No. 3), 1872 ; W. Claussen (*Fünf Lieder*, Op. 3, No. 1), 1875 ; R. Kruckow (*Drei Lieder*, No. 2), 1874 ; Mendelssohn, 1851 ; F. Reichel (*Vier Terzetten*, Op. 6, No. 3), 1874 ; M. Zenger, (6 *Lieder*, No. 4), 1864.

"Wenn ich in deine Augen seh !" By F. Nehfeld (*Drei Lieder*, Op. 18, No. 1), 1885 ; R. Schumann (*Dichterliebe*, No. 4), 1861.

"Wenn zwei von einander scheiden." By R. Franz (*Sechs Gesänge*, Op. 48, No. 1), 1878 ; G. Henschel (*Vier Lieder*, Op. 37, No. 2), 1885.

"We sat by the fisher's dwelling." [Wir sassen am Fischerhause.] By W. Bell, 1877 and 1879.

"Wie des Mondes Abbild zittert." By S. Ochs, 1883 ; H. Petri (*Lieder*, Op. 6, No. 4), 1884.

"Wir wollen jetzt Frieden machen." By S. Ochs, 1883.

"Wohl durch der Wälder einödige Pracht." By H. Krigar (*Sechs Lieder*, No. 3), 1873.

MAGAZINE ARTICLES.

Heine, Heinrich. Revue Universelle, by E. Quinet, tom 6, 1834, pp. 219-229.—Revue des Deux Mondes, by E. Quinet, February 1834, pp. 353-369.—Fraser's Magazine, vol. 26, 1842, pp. 733-736 ; vol. 74, 1866, pp. 588-607. — Revue des Deux Mondes, by D. Stern, 1 Dec. 1844, pp. 844-862.—Revue des Deux Mondes, by Saint-Réné Taillandier, Jan. 1845, pp. 297-332.—North American Review, by W. H. Hurlbut, vol. 69, 1849, pp. 216 249.—Sharpe's London Magazine, vol. 1, N.S., 1852, pp. 291-298, 362-369.—Revue des Deux Mondes, by Saint-Réné Taillandier (with portrait after C. Gleyre), April 1852, pp. 5-36.—Revue Contemporaine, by L. Ratisbonne, tom 19, 1855, pp. 643-669.—Putnam's Monthly Magazine, vol. 6, 1855, pp. 475-481 Dublin University Magazine, vol. 54, 1859, pp. 590-598.—Cornhill Magazine, vol. 7, 1863, pp. 247-251 ; same article, Littell's Living Age, vol. 79, pp. 51-62.—Cornhill Magazine, by Matthew Arnold, vol. 8, 1863, pp. 233-249.—Fortnightly Review, by J. D. Lester, vol. 6, N.S., 1869, pp. 287-303 ; same article, Littell's Living Age, vol. 103, pp. 180-190.—Glasgow University Album, 1869, pp. 78-95.—Every Satur-

Heine, Heinrich.
day, vol. 8, 1869, p. 417, etc.
—Englishwoman's Domestic
Magazine, vol. 11 N.S., 1871,
pp. 17-21, 83-87.—Lippincott's
Magazine, by Kate Hillard,
vol. 10, 1872, pp. 187-194 ;
same article, Victoria Magazine,
vol. 22, 1873, pp. 501-515.—
Theological Review, by C.
Beard, vol. 13, 1876, pp. 174-
201.—Blackwood's Edinburgh
Magazine, vol. 122, 1877, pp.
74-90.—Appleton's Journal of
Literature, by J. H. Browne,
vol. 2 N.S., 1877, pp. 23-31.
—Western, by J. K. Hosmer,
vol. 4, 1878, p. 667, etc.—
Contemporary Review, by
Charles Grant, vol. 38, 1880,
pp. 372-395. — Lippincott's
Magazine, by A. Parker, vol.
26, 1880, pp. 604-612.—British
Quarterly Review, by A. H.
Japp, vol. 74, 1881, pp. 265-
298.—Macmillan's Magazine,
by Lady Magnus, vol. 47, 1883,
pp. 59-66 ; afterwards reprinted
in *Jewish Portraits,* 1888.—
Revue des Deux Mondes, by
Emile Montégut, tom. 63,
1884, pp. 241-277. — Westminster Review, April 1888,
pp. 426-441.
——*And his Interpreters.* Nuova
Antologia, by B. Zendrini, vol.
27, 1874, pp. 793-821 ; vol. 28,
pp. 5-26.
——*And his Works.* National
Quarterly Review, vol. 13, 1866,
p. 56, etc.
——*Atta Troll.* Revue des Deux
Mondes, by Saint-Réné Taillandier, 1 Nov. 1843, pp. 462-465.
——*Deutschland.* Nuova Antologia, by G. Chiarini, vol. 20,
1880, pp. 401-428.

Heine, Heinrich.
——*Grave of.* Every Saturday,
vol. 16, 1873, p. 128, etc.
——*Last Days of.* New Monthly
Magazine, vol. 117, 1859, pp.
363-370.—Southern Magazine,
by J. A. Harrison, vol. 15,
1874, p. 246.
——*Last Poems and Thoughts.*
Fortnightly Review, by the Hon.
R. Lytton, vol. 7 N.S., 1870, pp.
257-277.
——*Last Years of.* Putnam's
Monthly Magazine, vol. 8,
1856, pp. 517-526.
——*Life and Works of.* Temple
Bar, by E. B. Shuldham, vol.
29, 1870, pp. 210-227.—Fraser's
Magazine, by H. G. Hewlett,
vol. 14 N.S., 1876, pp. 600-
623.—London Quarterly Review,
vol. 58, 1882, pp. 411-438.
——*Lytton on.* Every Saturday,
vol. 9, 1870, pp. 211, etc.
——*Memoirs.* Nuova Antologia,
by G. Chiarini, vol. 45, 1884,
pp. 201-218.
——*on Religion and Politics.*
Fortnightly Review, by L. A.
Montefiore, vol. 22 N.S., 1877,
pp. 325-339.
——*Poems of.* Revue des Deux
Mondes, by Gérard de Nerval,
15 July, 1848, pp. 224-243, and
15 Sept. 1848, pp. 914-930.—
North British Review, vol. 32,
1860, pp. 389-415.
——*Prose Works of.* Southern
Magazine, by E. Spenser, vol.
13, 1873, p. 506, etc.
——*Translations from.* Blackwood's Edinburgh Magazine,
by Theodore Martin, vol. 121,
1877, pp. 504, 505 ; vol. 122,
pp. 501-505, 628-633 ; vol. 123,
pp. 89-96, 221-224, 426-433,
599-602.

Heine, Heinrich.
——*Visit to London.* National Review, by Thomas Pryde, Dec. 1887, pp. 542-548.
——*Wit and Writings of.* Westminster Review, vol. 9, N.S., 1856, pp. 1-33 ; same article, Eclectic Magazine, vol. 37, pp. 316-328, and Littell's Living Age, vol. 48, pp. 513-531.

Heine, Heinrich.
——*Works and Times of.* Tait's Edinburgh Magazine, vol. 18, 2nd Series, 1851, pp. 618-622, 679-683 ; same article, Eclectic Magazine, vol. 26, pp. 481-491.
——*Writings of.* Edinburgh Review, vol. 104, 1856, pp. 192-209.

VI. CHRONOLOGICAL LIST OF WORKS.

www.ingramcontent.com/pod-product-compliance
Lightning Source LLC
Chambersburg PA
CBHW030101030726
47498CB00007B/2209